CHRISTMAS
Wolf Surprise

TERRY
SPEAR

sourcebooks
casablanca

Published by Sourcebooks Casablanca, an imprint of Sourcebooks
P.O. Box 4410, Naperville, Illinois 60567-4410
(630) 961-3900
sourcebooks.com

Printed and bound in Canada.
MBP 10 9 8 7 6 5 4 3 2 1

Thanks so much to Darla Taylor, whom I hope to see in San Antonio when I can get to that part of Texas, for beta reading my books, for sending me flower seeds to make my garden pretty, and for being my good friend!

CHAPTER 1

CHRISTMAS DAY WAS A LITTLE OVER A WEEK AWAY, AND red wolf shifters Maverick Wilding and his older twin brother, Josh, were setting up their reindeer exhibit at a shopping mall in Astoria, Oregon, when they saw a competing Oregon reindeer ranch staff arrive to set up its own display with four sexy female elves and Santa.

Maverick and Josh frowned at the lines of kids waiting to see the Calypso Reindeer Ranch Santa, some of the dads appearing more interested in Santa's elves.

"Hell," Josh said. "I can't believe they keep showing up at the same locations we are."

"To piggyback on our business," Maverick said, motioning to the kids and parents, excited to see the reindeer calves he and Josh had brought. But this was the third damn time the Calypso Ranch personnel had arrived at one of the locations they'd booked with local businesses and tried to steal the show out from under them. "They're watching our schedule that's posted on all the social media sites, and since we scheduled these a year in advance and wanted the most media coverage for the buck, they're using our promotions to bring our customers to their camp. They must have signed up at the locations we scheduled right after we did." Maverick wished they could somehow stop the trend from continuing.

"We're not resorting to using sexy elves to boost our sales," Josh said.

Maverick chuckled. "Hardly. Bringing the reindeer calves this time has really changed the dynamics. The kids—and most of the adults—want to see the calves."

"Yeah, they're not here to see sexy elves."

"Exactly." Even so, Maverick wanted to turn into his wolf and chase off the other reindeer ranch hands. When they signed contracts for next year, Maverick and Josh would ensure that the place hosting them signed a clause that stated they would be the only ones providing a reindeer exhibit at that time in that place. But for now, they couldn't do much about the situation through the rest of the holiday season.

Then a dark-haired, middle-aged man and woman came up to speak with them, smiling, then frowning. They looked vaguely familiar to Maverick, but he couldn't place them. Not with all the people they saw over the years at these exhibits.

"Hey, you own the reindeer, don't you?" the man asked.

"Yeah," Maverick said, shaking his hand. "I'm Maverick Wilding of Wilding Reindeer Ranch, and this is my twin brother, Josh."

"Andy and April Reynolds. We are the radio show hosts for Wild Times Radio Show. You probably don't remember us, but we were here last year to see your reindeer. We've been here before that, but we might not have spoken." The man smiled. "We love the calves. So what's the deal with those people?" He motioned to the Calypso Ranch exhibit.

"Usurpers, using our promo to promote their own ranch," Maverick said, not about to water down how he was feeling. Over the years, they'd had no problems with either of the other two reindeer ranches in Oregon, so the Calypso Ranch's actions had been a real surprise to them this year.

"Well, that's not right." April sounded as annoyed as Maverick felt.

"Yeah, we agree. They're using our schedule to hop on the reindeer sleigh, and there's nothing in our contracts that says we can stop them," Josh said.

"We'll help you out there," April said.

Maverick smiled, figuring there wasn't anything the couple could do, but he was glad to hear he and his brother had fans who loved their reindeer.

"Seriously, Andy and I can talk about it on our show," April said.

Hell yeah! Maverick shared a smile with his brother. Josh was grinning from ear to ear.

"We wanted to tell you that while we were hiking in the Fort Stevens State Park near here, we saw a reindeer," April said. "We worried it might be one of yours since you were going to be here, and we wanted to see you. We didn't realize the other reindeer ranch would be here too. They weren't here the last two years when we came to see you."

"No, we're not missing any." But Maverick hoped the other ranch hadn't lost one either.

"We'll check with them, then," April said.

"Okay, uh, thanks for alerting us. Let us know what they say, and if he's not one of theirs, we'll search for the one you spied in the state park after we're done here." Maverick wasn't sure about it, figuring that the couple were mistaken and had seen a mule deer or a wapiti, another kind of deer that roamed the state park. But if by chance it was a tame reindeer, they had to find and capture him. They'd provide for it until they learned to whom he belonged.

"Thanks. We knew you could be trusted to take care of him," April said. "Come on, Andy. Let's go talk to the others, then."

"Thanks for coming to see us," Josh said.

"You bet. We love the spirit of Christmas and everything to do with Christmas, including seeing your reindeer. Coming to visit them has become an annual tradition for us."

"Well, we sure appreciate it," Maverick said.

"Our pleasure." Then Andy took April's hand and headed over to the other reindeer ranch's setup.

They heard April say to the Calypso staff, "Are you missing a reindeer?"

"No," one of the Calypso Ranch hands abruptly said.

"Okay, well, we saw one in the state park."

"You're wrong," the ranch hand said. "Unless the Wildings misplaced one of their own." He cast Josh and Maverick a conceited smile.

"Why are you attempting to steal the show here? We've been here to see the Wildings' reindeer in the past and couldn't believe you would try to rob their spotlight," Andy said.

With their enhanced wolf hearing, Josh and Maverick were enjoying the show.

"Is that what they said?" the ranch hand asked, glancing in the Wildings' direction, as if he planned to straighten them out for saying so.

"They didn't have to. We've been here before to see their reindeer, and you weren't here. Don't worry. We'll let the public know." April shook her head, she and Andy left, and the ranch hand stared after them as they headed back to the Wildings' corrals.

"That's what we need. Fan support to spread the word," Maverick said privately to Josh.

Josh laughed. "Yeah. That was great."

When the couple reached them, April said, "Okay, we'll be sharing this on our show tonight. They said they're not missing a reindeer though."

"We'll both be looking for him," Maverick promised.

"I told you they would," she said to Andy. "Let us know if you find him. We'll share that with our viewers."

"Sure thing," Maverick said. He and his brother shook their hands, and then they left.

"What do you think?" Josh asked.

Maverick was certain it wasn't a reindeer. "It's probably just a deer, but we have to check into it, just to be sure. A reindeer wouldn't normally be living on his own in the park."

"I agree."

After the show ended, the Wildings packed up their reindeer and took them to a wolf-run cattle ranch near the park. They always had gear in the truck on these trips in case they got stranded in bad weather, so they parked at the trailhead and began their hike, smelling for reindeer scents on the way.

"We'll set up the tent and then shift. We'll be able to cover a lot more territory that way," Maverick said.

They finally reached the spot that was perfect to set up

the tent, and Josh said, "We'll start off together, but we'll probably need to split up to search more of the area, not to mention traveling as two wolves could get more attention than we bargained for."

"Yeah." That's all they would need—for someone to see them as wolves, forget spotting reindeer in the snowy woods in Oregon.

———

Gina Hutton, her brother, Weston, and two of his friends, Bromley and Patterson, were off on another Bigfoot hunting adventure, this time at Fort Stevens State Park, Oregon. Not that she really believed in the legendary creature, but she'd been hiking and camping with her brother since she was little, and she loved the time they spent together when they weren't working. Now he was searching for elusive werewolves too, courtesy of his friends who had gone hunting in Maine for Bigfoot. They had claimed they had seen a woman shift into a white wolf, and then everything had twisted into some kind of a horror flick. Their friends, who were from Millinocket, Maine—calling themselves the Dark Angels, she'd later learned—had killed a couple of men they had sworn were werewolves after that. A wolf protecting his owner killed one of the Dark Angel hunters, and another of the hunters had gone to jail for murdering the men he believed were werewolves. The third Dark Angel hunter had just vanished—presumed dead.

Gina and her brother had felt bad about what had

occurred. They hadn't been able to learn what had happened to the third hunter either. At least her brother and his friends had said there was no way *they* would have killed the supposed werewolves themselves. But what if they had felt they were defending themselves?

Before they were able to leave for Maine on that hunting trip, she, her brother, Bromley, and Patterson had come down with a bad case of the flu and had stayed behind in Portland, Oregon, their home. She was glad they hadn't been with the others in Maine because of what had gone down. They could have been caught up in the same crazy showdown if they'd been with the others. Though she had hoped if they had gone, they would have been able to stop the other hunters from hurting anyone in the first place.

Her brother and his friends were still open to the possibility that a werewolf, not a real wolf as had been the case, had killed the one hunter and that the men they'd murdered had actually been werewolves. It didn't matter that all the forensic evidence in the case pointed to the dead men having been fully human, no wolf DNA whatsoever. She did wonder if the coroner had really checked for that though.

Still, Weston believed the Arctic werewolf had killed two of his friends, and now he was even more than determined to find werewolves too. He reasoned that if werewolves lived in Maine, they could live anywhere. Gina had always assumed—if werewolves were real—they would be gray wolves, not Arctic wolves.

Bromley and Patterson, who believed the same as

Weston, were setting up the campsite with him while Gina went to get some water from the nearby lake. The sun would be setting in an hour, and she wanted to get some pictures of the starry, full moon night later. She walked out on the ice for some distance, saw where the ice looked thinner, and began to chip away at it with an ice pick to make a hole. The guys always sent her because she was lighter than they were.

Suddenly, she saw what looked like a reddish German shepherd running across the frozen lake straight for her. She scrambled backward away from the ice she was trying to break through.

Just as the dog was upon her, woofing, the ice cracked and gave way, and he fell into the lake. She screamed. Her heart practically seized, her leg breaking through the ice, and she nearly fell in as well but managed to scuttle away from the edge, only getting one of her legs wet.

"Ohmigod, no, no, no! Weston!" she screamed. She laid on her belly, reaching into the frigid water, trying to get hold of the dog so she could pull him out of the lake. But he was too heavy, thrashing about, trying to get out on his own, not trusting her to help him out in time.

"Weston!"

She knew the dog would exhaust himself before long, succumb to the cold, and drown if she didn't rescue him soon enough. As a zoologist, Gina loved animals, and one of her conditions for going on the hunt with her brother and his friends was that if they ever found what they were looking for, they wouldn't harm the werewolf or Bigfoot.

"Weston!"

"Gina, what's wrong?" Weston shouted and came out of the woods and onto the shore, carrying some wood for the fire. He immediately dropped the firewood.

"The dog was trying to warn me about the ice, and he fell through. We have to get him out." She would never forgive herself if the dog drowned after trying to warn her of the danger.

"I'll get some rope." Weston ran off.

Gina reached into the lake again, trying to keep the dog's head above water, when the ice cracked more underneath her, and the dog snapped at her in warning to get back, snagging his tooth on her hand. He cut the skin, and it stung like crazy. She hoped he'd had his rabies vaccination. She quickly moved back away from the widened hole in the ice, praying her brother would hurry with the rope.

Then she saw all three men running toward the lake with ropes and a tarp.

"The ice is cracking more," she called out.

"Come back to shore," Weston said as Patterson tied the rope around his waist and then her brother walked more slowly across the ice to reach her and the dog, the second rope over his shoulder and the rolled-up tarp under his arm.

On solid ground, Patterson and Bromley were holding the other end of the rope in case Weston fell through the ice.

She was afraid they were going to think the mission of rescuing the dog was too risky. She didn't want to leave him, though she was at a loss as to how to rescue him. She just didn't have the strength to lift him out of the frigid water.

"I'm going to get the dog, but if you fall in, you won't have a safety line. Return to shore, Gina." Weston dropped to his belly as he got closer to her, gingerly making his way out on the ice, sliding, and she slowly backed away toward shore, thinking belatedly that she hadn't gotten the water to use to cook their meal, the water bag still hanging from her neck.

She was nearly to the shore when her brother reached the dog. He laid the rope and tarp down, and then he reached into the water to try to pull the dog out, the ice cracking more.

"Hold on, pooch," her brother said. "I'll get you out." Then Weston tried again, and he had the dog partway out, his large paws scrambling for purchase, but then he slipped from her brother's grasp. "Damn!"

Gina's heart raced, and she wanted to help the dog too. Maybe the two of them could do it together.

"You can do it, Weston," Patterson shouted. "Use all those muscles you've been working on."

"Yeah, unless you need Patterson to help you," Bromley volunteered.

She noted Bromley didn't volunteer himself.

"No, we can't have too much more weight over here." Weston grabbed the rope. "Stay where you are. If you come out here, your weight will likely put us all in the lake."

Hers might too.

Weston quickly made a lasso. He leaned into the water with the lasso, pulled it over the dog's head and around his front legs and body, and secured him. "Okay, come on, boy. You can do it. Jump up when I pull, and we'll get you out of there."

This time Weston got some traction, and the dog's front paws dug into the edge of the ice. Weston pulled hard, and he and the sopping-wet dog fell back onto the ice, safe for the moment. Feeling a modicum of relief, Gina and their friends cheered. But then they heard the ice cracking.

The dog just laid on the tarp, his chest heaving, but he was too cold and exhausted to move even his head. Carefully, Weston wrapped the dog in the tarp and then started inching his way back to the shore on his butt, the ice cracking even more.

"Hurry, Weston!" Gina shouted, though she knew he had to be careful too. She didn't trust the lake ice to hold the dog's and her brother's weight with the way it was breaking up.

The other men held the rope still so they could pull Weston out in case he fell through. Then there was an even louder cracking sound. Gina's heart took a dive as the ice broke away and Weston slid into the lake with the dog in his arms.

"Weston! No!" Gina was pulling at the rope now too and hoping her brother didn't lose the dog as they tried to extract both of them from the frigid water.

"Hold on, Weston," Patterson shouted, pulling on the rope with all his strength. "We've got you."

"Don't lose the dog," Gina said, or all of this would be for nothing.

They all kept pulling Weston, breaking up the ice more until he came to solid ice and they managed to extract him. Thankfully, Weston was still holding tight to the poor dog.

She was so relieved. He loved animals as much as she did, so she hadn't really thought he'd let go of him if he could help it. The guys hurried to wrap Weston and the dog in the tarp and get them to the shore.

"We've got the fire going. Let's get the two of them warmed up," Patterson said.

To Gina, Patterson looked like a Bigfoot character himself, six seven, black hair and dark-brown eyes, huge feet and giant hands. She'd seen him bathing in the lake on one of these treks in the summer last year, and he was hairy too. She'd always thought if anyone saw him in the woods, they might have thought *he* was Bigfoot.

He helped Weston back to camp, and Bromley—who was six feet tall like her brother but blond and blue-eyed, whereas her brother had dark-brown hair and eyes like her—carried the dog to the campsite.

While the others were taking care of Weston, she tied the end of the rope to a tree on the lake's shore and then to herself, carefully making her way back out to where she could fetch the water for their supper. At least she didn't have to go out very far this time because of Weston falling through the ice closer to shore. She finally got the water and headed back in, trying not to break any more of the ice on the way back.

At their campsite, Bromley and Patterson had helped strip her brother out of his wet things, dressed him in dry clothes, and then wrapped him in an emergency reflective blanket. Weston huddled next to the fire. The dog was lying on the tarp beside him, but he needed one of her blankets. Neither of the other guys was offering theirs. Weston would need all of his own blankets to keep warm after what he'd been through. She secured one of her blankets from her tent, brought it out, and covered the dog with it. He watched her, his beautiful brown eyes appearing grateful, but he was still too weak to even lift his head.

"We need to return to the vehicles and have Weston and the dog seen to." She figured the guys wouldn't want to return home this early, not when they'd only been out here for two days of their five-day trip. But she was concerned about her brother's health. And the dog's. "You guys can continue on."

"I'll be fine. We've hardly even begun our search for Bigfoot and the werewolves. If I went home and Patterson and Bromley found one of these creatures, I would never forgive myself," Weston said. "Can you make me your hot chili and some hot cocoa so I'll warm right up?" But he was shivering hard, and she wanted him warmed up even more before he considered staying that long. "I'll be fine by morning," Weston said.

If not, she was going to insist they go home.

The dog closed his eyes and appeared to be sleeping. She put some water in a bowl for him for when he had the energy to drink it. She intended to keep him warm in her tent tonight. Pulling the blanket back, she felt around his neck for a collar, but he wasn't wearing one. He looked up at her, and she swore he smiled.

As Gina made the cocoa and chili with the water she'd gathered, she wondered if the dog had been off chasing rabbits or something and had gotten lost. Maybe his owner was out here camping somewhere too. She didn't think he was a wild dog. His coat was nice and shiny, not matted, and he smelled of a nice spicy-smelling shampoo.

"Not to change the subject, but I still say we ought to check out Maine and see if we can locate the Arctic werewolf our friends said they saw," Bromley said.

Weston drank some more of his cocoa. "I checked."

"For our missing friend. Not for the werewolf," Bromley said. "And since that's the only verified sighting we know about, why not check it out?"

Verified, *as if*! Their friends hadn't taken any pictures of the verified werewolf shifting or anything.

"And how safe would that be if a werewolf killed two of the men?" Gina asked, not believing it, but if she was going to play along with the story, that was the first thing she thought of. "Besides, the lone werewolf might not have been a loner at all but part of a big pack."

"That's what I keep saying," Patterson said. "That it's not just one but a whole pack. Our friends didn't stand a chance. And neither would Weston if he'd run into them."

She shouldn't have added to the tale, but she couldn't help herself. "You never know—Sarge might have been bitten and turned into one of their kind."

The guys all agreed.

They ate their chili and drank their hot cocoa. "You did a great job on dinner," Weston said.

"Thanks. It was nice and hot for a cold night." Gina loved how everyone took turns making the meals on these trips. Everyone made great meals.

When they were ready to retire for the night, she made

CHRISTMAS WOLF SURPRISE 15

sure her brother had enough blankets and was sufficiently warm in his sleeping bag in his tent. "Are you going to be all right?"

"Yeah, Gina, I'm fine."

"Thanks for saving the dog." She gave her brother a hug.

"I wasn't going to let him drown."

"I know." But if he couldn't have held onto him, that would have been another story. "Good night, Weston."

"'Night, Sis."

Then she left his tent and asked Patterson, "Can you move Shep into my tent and lay him next to my sleeping bag?"

"Shep?"

"The dog. I think he's a German shepherd."

Patterson shook his head and lifted the dog, carried him into her tent, and laid him next to her sleeping bag. Then she covered Shep with a new dry blanket. She hoped *she* didn't get cold tonight.

"Thanks, Patterson."

"You're welcome," he said, leaving her tent.

Zipping her tent door closed, she realized her hand was stinging where Shep had cut her with his teeth, and she rummaged through her bag to find her liquid skin bandage and applied it. *Stinging, ack!*

Then she curled up in her sleeping bag. She was thinking about caring for Shep on their hike and realized they didn't have any dog food for him, but she had some extra protein bars and beef jerky in case of an emergency that she could feed him. Reaching over to him, she ran her hand over his head. She would take good care of him if they couldn't find his owner while they were hiking in the woods. Sighing, she hoped he wouldn't run off either, but if he did, they really couldn't do anything about it. In the event he might want to run off and join his family, she wasn't going to put him on a rope leash.

His ears twitched, and for now, he seemed perfectly content to lie there next to her.

She sighed. "Thank you for warning me about the ice. You saved my life." Then she remembered her apartment had just given notice that renters couldn't have new pets at the complex. People who had rented prior to the policy change could keep their pets there until they moved on. She chewed on her lip. She'd pretend she'd always had him and hope none of her neighbors would tell on her to management.

CHAPTER 2

WHEN MAVERICK WILDING HAD GONE RUNNING AS A red wolf with his twin brother, Josh, he had seen the woman trying to fetch water in her water bag for a campfire meal, he suspected, having smelled the smoke from the campfire. It was good that Maverick and his brother had split up to cover more territory while looking for any sign of a reindeer in the area.

But as far out on the lake as the woman had walked and then seeing her trying to break a hole in the ice, he knew it was too dangerous. With his sensitive wolf hearing, he'd heard the ice cracking in a way that meant danger, and he'd raced to warn her, to chase her back away from the peril in the event she didn't heed the warning. He sure hadn't expected to fall into the lake himself, and he was still chiding himself for the mistake that could have killed him.

He was grateful that the woman's brother, Weston, had rescued him. Maverick's fur coat had kept him warm and helped stave off the initial shock of the cold, but the longer he'd been in the water, the worse he had felt, and the more he had realized his struggles to pull himself out of the lake had been in vain.

Now the woman, Gina, was petting him in her tent, and he was finally feeling better, warmer. She'd put that awful-smelling antiseptic on her hand, and he wondered if she'd cut her hand on the jagged ice. He'd smelled her blood and hoped the cut wasn't too bad. He glanced at her, enjoying the warmth from her body, her blanket helping dry his fur coat as well. He breathed in her scent—woodsy, sweet, and human. She was a pretty brunette, her hair tangled about her shoulders, her dark-brown eyes closed now.

He had to get out of there as soon as possible so he could meet up with his brother before Josh worried something bad had happened to him.

"I don't know. Do we push on and keep searching for Bigfoot, or do we turn back like Gina said?" Bromley asked the other man still at the campfire as they put out the fire.

"I think we should wait and see how Weston is feeling in the morning," Patterson said.

"They will never stop hunting for Bigfoot and werewolves, even if it kills them," Gina whispered to Maverick. "As if any of that were real, of course, just between you and me. But I do worry about them encountering bears or a wild boar or even a cougar—much more likely and more dangerous than Bigfoot or werewolves."

Werewolves. The last time Maverick's red wolf pack had heard about Bigfoot and werewolf hunters, their pack leader, Leidolf Wildhaven, had gotten involved, learning that the hunters had actually witnessed an Arctic wolf shifting in Maine. Those same men then killed two of the werewolves from the pack that they'd discovered, injecting them with silver nitrite, though that would kill any human, part wolf or not. One of the werewolf killers, who had all called themselves the Dark Angels, was dead. One had been convicted of the crime of killing the two men, who he swore at his trial were werewolves. And Leidolf had actually bitten the third man and turned him into one of their kind to get him to reveal the location of the other werewolf killers. Sarge was now working for him and Leidolf's mate, Cassie, at the pack ranch as their accountant. Sgt. Elijah Wilkinson had formerly been a finance NCO in the army, but everyone called him Sarge.

Maverick would have to warn the rest of the pack not to strip and shift out in the open where these men were located. He was afraid Josh would track his scent here and worry that these people had hurt him. What if Weston and his buddies thought Josh was a werewolf too?

Maverick shouldn't have gone out on the lake, though he shouldn't have fallen in as a wolf. Then again, if he hadn't warned Gina, she might have fallen through the ice and died.

He kept watching her for now. She wasn't speaking any further to him. He listened to her heartbeat slowing during deep sleep, and her eyelids were heavily closed. And he thought about the cut on her hand. He smelled her again, but she was all human, though he did have a slight concern he had cut her with his teeth and she hadn't injured her hand on the ice.

He listened as the two men said their good-nights, walked to their tents through the snow, and unzipped and zipped their tents.

When Maverick was certain Gina and the others were sound asleep, he shifted and unzipped her tent. He listened for any indication anyone was still awake, but it was quiet out there. He stepped out of her tent, zipped it up, shifted into his wolf, and ran like the wind.

Maverick hadn't gone very far from the campsite when he ran into his twin brother, Josh, thankfully. Maverick figured Josh had given up trying to track the reindeer down to search for him instead. His brother looked understandably relieved to see him, nuzzled him in greeting, and smelled all the human scents on him.

Yes, a woman's feminine scent was all over Maverick's head where she'd petted him, which he had to admit had felt really nice after the ordeal he'd gone through. And three men's scents were on him because they had carried him. Josh would wonder what the hell had happened to him. Unless he had tracked Maverick's scent to the lake, saw the broken ice, and put two and two together. Yeah, knowing his retired police detective brother—who was also a wolf—that's what he'd done and come to his rescue. Luckily, the Bigfoot hunters had thought Maverick was just a dog.

He and Josh ran back through the snowy woods to their campsite, and Maverick knew his older twin by five minutes would question him as to what in the world had happened.

Inside the tent, they shifted, and Josh hurried to dress. "Okay, spill." At the same time, he was looking Maverick over, checking him for injuries as Maverick quickly dressed.

"I spied a woman who was trying to break through the

ice to get some water, and I ran toward her to warn her the ice was too thin there. I heard it cracking. I knew I was light enough to cross it, but then I fell through the lake ice."

Josh's dark eyes widened. "Hell, Maverick."

"They rescued me. When everyone was sleeping, I managed to slip out of the woman's tent and tore off. She called me Shep, thinking I was a German shepherd." Maverick couldn't quit thinking about the beautiful brunette with her dark-brown, sultry eyes and how she had loved him—as a dog. If she had known he was a wolf, he figured it would have been a whole other story. "She planned to keep me."

Smiling a little, Josh shook his head.

"Hey, you know if our roles had been reversed and you had seen the woman putting herself in danger, you would have been there for her."

"Yeah, you know it. But you're all right, correct?"

"Yes, even Gina's brother, Weston—"

Josh arched a dark brow as they began packing up their tent.

"They were all talking, okay? Her brother went through the ice when he was carrying me, so he'd risked his life for me. But we need to warn Leidolf that the men are looking for Bigfoot and—"

"None of us have ever seen him, so no problem."

"Not just Bigfoot, werewolves too. And get this— apparently they knew the men hunting back in Maine whom Leidolf and other wolves had to deal with."

Josh paused and frowned at him. "What about Sarge?"

"Yeah, him too, since he was one of the men out there.

They were friends of theirs." Maverick got on his phone and told Leidolf what he'd heard.

"At least the hunters are located about two hours out from the pack's ranch and an hour and a half from your reindeer ranch," Leidolf said. "What are you doing up there right now? Christmas is your busiest season."

"We had a reindeer gig up here, and then a couple who came to see the reindeer said they saw one running through the forest while they were on a hike. Reindeer don't normally live here, so we put our own reindeer to bed at a neighboring ranch and headed out to search for one that might be in the woods in the state park. We did check with the other two reindeer ranches in Oregon to make sure they hadn't lost any. Neither of them had. And you know we can cover a lot more territory running as wolves. We didn't smell any reindeer scents. It was probably just a deer."

"Okay, then that's good. I'll talk to Sarge about the situation so he knows what to say if these people ever come to our neck of the woods and run into him," Leidolf said. "And I'll see you all tomorrow for the Santa and reindeer show at the pack Christmas party."

"Sounds good," Maverick said, but now that he had connected with Josh and let him know he was all right and squared things away with Leidolf, he had another plan in mind.

Josh and Maverick finished packing up, grabbed their backpacks, and started hiking to their vehicle so Josh could drive back to the wolf-run cattle ranch where the reindeer had bedded down for the night.

"If these men know the ones Leidolf and the other wolves

took care of in Maine, they probably wonder what happened to Sarge," Josh said.

"Right. I hope they never run into Sarge. I'm not sure how good of an actor he is. Leidolf said he'd talk to him about making up a story just in case. If they do meet up with him, they'll question him about the others, about the Arctic wolf shifting in front of them and ask if he saw it too. It could be a real mess."

"What I wonder about is why Sarge never told Leidolf or any of the rest of us in the pack that he had more friends out there who had heard about the werewolves and were trying to hunt them down." Josh adjusted his backpack. "I wonder if there's anything else he hasn't told us about."

"I don't know. He seemed to be getting along with the pack members well enough."

Josh got a call, pulled out his phone, and smiled. His mate, Brooke, was calling, and he answered. "Yeah, honey, we're headed back to the ranch for the night. No sign of any reindeer out here. The show was a success, and we'll see you in the morning. Love you too."

When they arrived at their pickup truck, Maverick said, "I'm going back to their campsite."

"What?"

"I can't quit thinking about it, but when the woman tried to pull me out of the water, I thought she cut herself on the ice."

Josh's eyes widened. "Hell, you didn't bite her, did you?"

"I don't know... I was thrashing around, trying to get out of the water before I lost all my strength to do so. But I smelled her blood when she applied some liquid skin bandage to her hand. And...well, I don't want to leave things to chance. Especially when she can shift, if I turned her, since it's the full-moon phase."

"Aww, damn, Maverick."

"I know. She was in her own tent, so it didn't appear she had a significant other, but he might have stayed home. The one guy was her brother, so she has family. I just have to know if she's one of us or not." Which meant he had to get close enough to her to smell her scent. She had smelled like she was only human earlier, but if he'd bitten her, it could take a while for the change to occur, and then she would smell like a wolf. "You need to take the reindeer home. We have the show to do with the pack. The ranch hands can assist you."

"No turning into your wolf," Josh warned him.

"No. I'll set up camp with just the small tent, and when they're on the hike tomorrow, I'll track them and see if I can smell her scent—just to make sure she's still human. But if she has a wolf scent now, I'll have to deal with this." And hope that she didn't shift around her brother and friends, which could be a disaster. "I'll keep watch for the reindeer too."

"You're not going to interact with the campers."

"No, not unless I have to. If she's not one of us, it will be no big deal. If she is, then I'll have to come up with a plan." Maverick had been looking forward to a nice hot shower at the guest house at the ranch. He wished he had a she-wolf in his life, but he was glad Josh had retired as a police detective, and when he wasn't helping Brooke with her antiques shop, he was assisting Maverick with the reindeer ranch like he used to do when he had time off from police work.

"You won't change into your wolf?" Josh asked again.

"No. I'll be strictly human." Maverick knew his brother didn't want to let him do this on his own, but they had to move the reindeer back to their ranch. "I'll keep in touch with you the whole time. I've got the satellite phone and my cell phone with me."

Josh began helping his brother repack, giving him the extra food supplies, water, and another camping blanket.

"I can turn wolf if I need to get warm."

Josh frowned at him. "You assured me you wouldn't shift."

"Only in my tent, if I'm cold. Otherwise, no, I won't shift."

"What are you going to do if you learn she's one of us?"

"I told you, Brother, I'll have to wing it. If she's a wolf like us and I try to talk to her, she'll probably recognize my scent as Shep, the German shepherd. I could see things really getting out of hand. It would be hard enough trying to explain all this to someone who's alone, but when she's got a brother and a couple of friends who are werewolf hunters with her? So, yeah, I really don't know. I'll just have to figure it out as I go. Though she might think I'm Shep's owner and that's why I smell like him."

"If that's the case, maybe you can get to know her better, tell her your brother took Shep home with the reindeer, thank them for saving him if they mention it."

"Okay, that sounds good." Josh was always a great sounding board for Maverick. He gave Josh a hug. "I'll keep in touch. I'm off to set up camp. Early in the morning, before they take off, I'll try to learn what I can about her."

"All right. Be careful."

"I will be." But all Maverick could think of was what he was going to do about having turned Gina if he had. They had to watch out for newly turned wolves. A newly turned wolf had to sever ties with family and friends. They had to be among their new kind. Did she work? Have other family? A boyfriend? Lots of other friends? It could be a real nightmare.

Maverick returned to the place he and Josh had set up their campsite, erected the one-man tent, and got some sleep before he began the next phase of his new mission, which he knew was going to be fraught with missteps and could be deadly, given what Weston's other friends had done back in Maine to the werewolves they found there.

———

Gina woke to hearing something scratching around her tent. A raccoon, she thought, and instantly she saw that Shep was no longer sleeping beside her. She glanced at the tent zipper, thinking she'd forgotten to zip it up last night, but she hadn't. It was still zipped. How had he managed to leave her tent?

Maybe he'd woofed without waking her to let everyone know he had to relieve himself, and one of the guys had let him out. But why hadn't Shep returned? Maybe he had left to find his real family. She felt disappointed, saddened even that he was gone. Then again, maybe that was the sound she had heard—not a raccoon but Shep.

She yanked on her boots and parka. Pulling the zipper to the tent flap up, she peered into the dark and saw a raccoon digging around the camp. A flashlight should scare him off. Once she grabbed hers and shined it in his eyes, he took off, and she didn't see any sign of the dog. She sighed and glanced at her watch. It was only two in the morning, and the moon was peeking out from behind a cloud. Stars were sprinkled across the dark night, and she realized that with all the excitement, she'd forgotten to take pictures of the night sky. But she was so tired, she just turned off her flashlight, looked again at the campsite, making sure the furry little raccoon hadn't come back, and then zipped up her tent.

She removed her parka and boots, curled up in her sleeping bag, and stared at the place where the dog had slept. She frowned. The tent should have been totally black as dark as it was out. In fact, when she had first seen the raccoon, she hadn't even had the flashlight in her hand. She crawled out of her sleeping bag and unzipped her tent, peering out into the night. She could see the other tents, the trees, the ring of stones for the fire, as if the light from the campfire and the lanterns was still lighting the way. Glancing at her watch again, she figured it wasn't working right—again—and it had to be nearly dawn.

It was a dive watch, but maybe when she reached into the frigid lake to try to save the dog, the cold water had affected it. She noticed that the cut on her hand was completely gone. Weird. She zipped her tent back up, returned to her sleeping bag, closed her eyes, and fell back to sleep no matter what time of night—or early morning—it was.

Until she felt at some point that she was burning up with a fever. She unzipped her sleeping bag and laid on top of it. But she was still so hot, and she knew she had to remove her clothes at once to cool down the fever racing through every bit of her. She yanked off her sweatshirt followed by her socks and sweatpants. Then suddenly, she was standing on her sleeping bag, feeling perfectly fine, her temperature stabilized—comfortable, not cold or hot. She curled up on her sleeping bag and started dreaming of being a dog, running through the woods, smelling the pines and fir trees around her, the campfire, the chili and cocoa they'd had.

Then sometime later, she felt the heat fill her whole body, the fever renewed. She was panting, hot, then suddenly chilled to the bone, tugging her sleeping bag around her, trying to get warm.

Something snapped, as if someone had broken a stick close to her ear, finally waking her. She sat up in her sleeping bag. Ohmigod, when had she pulled off her clothes? She glanced at her watch. Five. So it was working to an extent. Then she got out of her sleeping bag, searched through her backpack, and grabbed a change of clean clothes. *Cold, cold, cold.* She hurriedly dressed, pulled on her boots and parka, and then headed outside with her flashlight. But she hadn't even turned it on, and she could see everything. Her watch was playing tricks on her.

She took care of business and then returned to the campsite and began building a campfire.

Patterson emerged from the tent armed with a flashlight

and lantern. "Hell, what are you doing up so early? And why are you building a campfire in the dark?"

"It's not that dark out. I can see perfectly fine. My watch isn't working. What time is it?"

"It's twenty minutes past five. And it's dark as can be out here. What does your watch say?"

"The same thing." So she guessed her watch *was* working okay, but she couldn't understand how he thought it was dark out.

Patterson left the lit lantern for her and took off to do his business, focusing the flashlight on the path he was taking, even though she realized she had seen just fine on the path without a light.

Her brother emerged from his tent with his flashlight on, frowning at her. "Why are you up so early?"

"How are you feeling after falling into the lake? Are you okay?"

"Yeah, but I could have slept for another couple of hours." He ran his hand through his disheveled hair. "We never get up this early."

"I'll have the fire going and the coffee ready in no time." She just couldn't wake up enough to get a move on though, like she was moving in slow motion, as if she'd barely had enough sleep last night.

He grumbled under his breath, "You could have done that at seven." Then he took off through the woods.

At least her brother seemed to be fine this morning after the chilling lake accident. She was glad for that, though he could be a grouch before his first cup of coffee, especially if he had to get up earlier than he normally did. That was the thing about his job as a software engineer—he worked from home and had flexible hours. So did she as a freelance zoologist and she didn't have any assignments right now, which was why she was on the hike with her brother and his friends.

Bromley was the only one still sleeping in his tent. She swore he could sleep through anything.

She finally finished making the fire and sniffed the air. More snow was coming. Then she started the water for the coffee, and Patterson came back from his trek through the forest carrying more wood for the fire. Finally, Bromley unzipped his tent, grunted, and headed into the woods.

Her brother returned, and she said, "Okay, so who let Shep out of my tent?"

"Not me. Once I was cozy in my sleeping bag after being so chilled from the dip in the lake, I didn't leave my tent until you saw me this morning," Weston said.

"Me either," Patterson said.

Bromley was just coming back from the woods. "What did I miss? And why is everyone up so damn early?"

"Who let the dog out of my tent?" Gina got a cup of coffee, and the men followed suit.

"Not me. I slept soundly until I smelled the coffee brewing." Bromley began to make the eggs and bacon for breakfast. He grumbled about making breakfast in the dark.

She sighed. "Okay, someone let him out, unless the dog was extremely talented and could unzip the tent by himself and left."

The men all smiled at her.

"You walk in your sleep when you're overly tired," Weston said. "You must have done it yourself and don't even remember it."

Maybe she had. Only rarely did she recall when she walked in her sleep. Her parents or her brother had witnessed the times she had and told her about it, or she wouldn't have known about the other cases. But she was kind of scared to think she might sleepwalk in the forest in the middle of the night while they were on a campout and lose her way or come upon a predator. Talk about a rude awakening.

"The dog probably needed to pee, you let him out, and then you zipped the tent back up. You fell fast asleep, and he took off to find his owner," Patterson said.

She hoped that's what had happened and that he had found his way home.

CHAPTER 3

MAVERICK HAD TRAVELED IN THE DARK EARLY TO REACH Gina's campsite and saw her making the campfire before dawn. It hadn't been a good sign. As a human, she would have to have had a lantern or flashlight to aid her. She didn't even seem to notice that she was working in the dark without light.

He had wanted to approach her in the worst way, to smell if she had her own unique wolf scent that would verify she was one of their kind—and that he had made her that way. He was sorry for that. But if he had approached, he figured she would have screamed at the sight of him emerging from the dark woods. Then Patterson had left his tent, so Maverick had stayed put, silently watching them. Patterson was a giant of a man, and Maverick thought they didn't need to look any further for Bigfoot.

What else could Maverick have done but secretly observe them? He didn't know if they were armed with weapons. They could have seen him as a threat, coming out of the dark to greet them.

When Patterson had left the camp, Weston had come out of his tent. Maverick had moved away from their camp, still shrouded in darkness except for the campfire Gina had started and Patterson's lamp. After a short while, everyone had gathered around the campfire to have breakfast.

"I can't believe we're up so early. It will be dark for another hour and a half," Bromley had said, serving up the breakfast.

Maverick had had a granola bar on the hike back to their camp. The eggs, bacon, and coffee had smelled really good to him.

He'd noticed Gina had been asking about the time, unable to figure out why it was so light out, and he suspected she was a wolf now. Then she had been asking if any of the men had let Shep out of the tent, and luckily her brother had come up with a legitimate reason—she was a sleepwalker and had let him out herself. Not that it was a really good thing. What if she could shift into a wolf in her sleep and then sleepwalk? Maverick had never known anyone who sleepwalked, so he was unsure what that would mean.

After breakfast, Gina and her friends packed up and then continued their search for Bigfoot and werewolves, but what she saw had her detouring from the rest of the party—Shep's paw prints in the snow and the smell of his scent.

"Where's Gina?" Weston called from some distance away.

"Over here." She was surprised her brother wasn't with her, looked around, and saw that she was on her own. But she kept moving, wanting to find Shep in the worst way. She wasn't going to find Bigfoot or werewolves, but if she located Shep, she could put him on a short rope and take him home with her at the end of this trip. So much for letting him run on his own. She was too worried about him.

From farther away, Weston called out, "Gina!"

"Over here!" She wasn't giving up her pursuit of Shep. If she discovered the dog was with his owner at a campsite, she'd feel a whole lot better about it.

Patterson and Bromley called out, "Gina!"

But their combined voices were such a distance away, she realized they had no idea where she was. *Damn it.* Why couldn't they hear her when she could hear them perfectly well? She was shouting as loudly as she could. She didn't want to stop tracking Shep.

She sighed and then started running through the woods to where the men were, and after several minutes, she finally found them.

"There you are," Weston said, relieved but annoyed too.

"I thought you'd come to me when I called out to you, but you sounded like you were getting farther and farther away," she said.

"We couldn't find you at all. We didn't hear you respond or anything," Weston said, frowning at her, worried.

"I heard you, and I was calling out in response. Come on. I found Shep's paw prints in the snow. I want to learn where he's gone to. If he found his family, I want to know it. Otherwise, I'm taking him home with me," she said.

Weston shook his head.

"Hey, I always come with you on these hikes, and I love to do it, but this time I have something I really want to track and for a good reason. So are you coming or not?" Gina was not giving up her pursuit of Shep no matter what. Though she would prefer her brother and their friends to stay with her, for safety concerns. She could imagine getting lost, and then who would save her?

"Maybe the dog is tracking werewolves or Bigfoot," Patterson said. "Let's go."

She really did like Patterson. Not in a boyfriend way, but he always stuck up for her when she needed her brother to see things her way.

"Well, that way is as good as any other," Weston said, and Bromley agreed.

Then they headed back the way she'd come, though they didn't seem to have any clue where she was going. She knew exactly how to get there. She could smell her scent all the way back to the path she'd been on while tracking Shep. And she'd left her own footprints in the snow.

When she reached Shep's tracks, she smelled his scent again. "This way."

"You know those paw prints look like a wolf's," Weston said, studying them more closely.

"They're Shep's tracks." She could smell him.

"You're right, Weston," Bromley said. "Those are wolf tracks. Look at the spread and gait. And look, over here, there are more wolf tracks. Two joined up together, right here."

She smelled a second—well, dog, she thought. Shep and another. Then she frowned. "Do you think Shep was a wolf?" Ohmigod, she had slept with a wolf?

"Hell, maybe," Weston said. "Here I rescued a wolf in the lake."

"I carried him across the ice," Bromley said.

"And I carried him into Gina's tent last night," Patterson said.

"It was getting dark last night, and who would have thought the dog was a wolf?" Bromley said.

"Or these could be wolf prints and not Shep's," Weston said.

No, she smelled Shep's scent in the vicinity, no other canine, clear as day. "I think you might be right and Shep isn't a German shepherd after all but a wolf." Shivers ran up her spine at the thought that she could have been petting a wild wolf that might have bitten her. She glanced at her hand where Shep had cut it with his tooth. The bloody cut truly was completely healed.

"Hell, here we've been thinking we're going to find Bigfoot or werewolves and Gina finds a wolf in the lake and sleeps with it even," Bromley said. "And now she's the one who is tracking him and finds there are two of them. Suddenly, she's one hell of a tracker."

"Ha ha," she said. "I was just looking for a dog." But still, she worried now that he was a wolf. And there were two of them. She didn't want her brother or their friends to shoot at them if they were afraid the wolves would attack them.

They continued to follow the wolf tracks, while Gina remained in the lead. She was going slower now, even though she could smell their scents and didn't even need to see their paw prints in the snow any longer.

The tracks finally led them to a campsite, the gear all gone, and so were the wolf tracks.

"Okay, so what just happened?" Weston said, looking around the campsite.

"We found our *werewolves*. Look, the tracks end there right where a tent had been, and all we find now are hiking boot prints," Patterson said. "Two men-sized boots. No more wolves. They are werewolves."

Gina smiled. She'd never figured she would find "were-wolves" for the men to follow. They would now believe she was a super werewolf sleuth. She began tracking the men's boot prints, but something bothered her about them. Not only was she tracking the men's footprints, but she could smell Shep's scent and his buddy's too. Only there were no canine prints anywhere to be found.

Which meant...what? Were the men carrying the dogs? Wolves? No way were they werewolves. That was just too unreal. And if they were wolves, the men wouldn't be carry-ing them. Nor would they be carrying a couple of big dogs either, she didn't think.

They finally found the end of the men's tracks and the place where a vehicle had been parked at a trailhead.

"They got away," Weston said. "The werewolves got away."

"You know what this means?" Patterson asked. "The werewolves aren't just in Maine."

Bromley agreed.

Gina wanted to shake her head, but she didn't know what to think about any of this.

"Okay, is everyone ready to go on a new adventure?" Weston asked.

———

It had been a quarter to eight when the sun rose and Gina and everyone had grabbed their backpacks, leaving their campsite intact and heading out on the search for Bigfoot and werewolves. She had been in such a rush to track Maverick's wolf prints in the snow, she had become separated from the others. He had been observing her, trying to get downwind of her so he could smell her scent, but he couldn't. He had also been just watching out for her in case she became truly lost or she ran into a cougar or bear and was in trouble. But she had been like a bloodhound, following Maverick's tracks until her brother and the other men began calling out to her. They had been a long way from her location.

"I'm here," she had called out. "I found Shep's tracks."

Though Maverick and Gina had heard the men, they hadn't heard her, which most likely meant she now had enhanced wolf hearing. But he had to be sure. He still had been afraid to approach her, to scare a woman to pieces who was alone in the woods. He hadn't shaved, and his face wore a couple of days' growth of beard, which would make him look a bit— scary, possibly.

She had finally given up tracking him and headed for her brother and the others. When she found them, Maverick had been keeping his own newly made tracks hidden and moved closer to where she'd been. Hell, she had to be a wolf.

She had brought her brother and their friends right back to Maverick's tracks—which, in the light of day, they discovered belonged to a wolf. She was tenacious. And he was certain he was in trouble. How was he going to talk to her? Convince her, if she was a wolf, that she would be safer with him than with her brother and his friends?

Maverick had buried his hiking pack in the snow some

distance from his camp, easier to be stealthier that way while he'd been spying on them at their camp. He was glad he hadn't left the tent there. She and the others had finally reached the place where Maverick and Josh had parked the truck at the trailhead, and now it was gone. He'd walked in his same tracks returning with his gear to their campsite after seeing Josh off, not realizing what a great move that had been.

Listening to them talking about how Shep was a wolf who'd met up with another wolf and left in a vehicle as men made chills sweep up Maverick's spine.

It was bad enough that he had turned a woman who might believe in *lupus garous*—though, in the tent, she had told him she didn't—but also that she and her brother and the others were trying to hunt them down.

Maverick returned to his hiking backpack, pulled it out of the snow, shouldered it, and hiked back toward where he heard them crunching through the snow on the trail. He had come up with a plan. Maybe not the best of plans, but he had to do something because this situation with Gina was bound to get worse.

"Hey, I heard you were looking for Bigfoot," Maverick said to Weston and the others, moving out of the woods and onto the trail they were hiking on.

All of them looked skeptically at him, like they didn't believe he could be one of them hunting for the same thing. They probably got a lot of harassment from nonbelievers. The stern looks they gave him made him think they were ready to pummel him if he said anything negative about their pursuit of mythical creatures.

"Yeah?" Weston asked. "Where did you hear that?"

"I was hiking and heard you discussing the possibility that some men were werewolves." Maverick shrugged. "I'm always open-minded. There's a lot we don't know about the world."

"Shep," Gina whispered. Her beautiful brown eyes were huge as she stared at Maverick, but she didn't give him away. Her heart was pounding hard, and she barely breathed. He knew she was trying to sort out what was going on.

Maverick wasn't sure the others had heard, but he had. She knew he was the dog. Or at least smelled like the dog. Or *wolf.*

"Do you own a dog?" she casually asked, but her voice had a slight tremor to it.

Luckily, no one else seemed to notice.

"Uh, yeah. He ran off after a rabbit and finally returned to our tent hours later. We figured he would. But then again, we were worried he'd lost his way or gotten himself into trouble," Maverick said.

"We?" she asked, the other men glancing at the woods as if they might be surrounded by dangerous hikers who had been with Maverick and were now just out of sight.

"My twin brother and me." Maverick had to keep up the charade. She knew there had been two men and two wolves. "You won't believe it, but we were actually looking for a reindeer near this trail."

"Reindeer?" Weston asked. "They don't live out in these parts."

"Yeah, don't I know it. My brother and I run a reindeer ranch out of Portland, and we'd done a show with the reindeer at a local mall when a couple of hikers told us they saw a reindeer running loose in the state park. My brother took our dog and our reindeer home while I made another search through the woods."

Everyone looked skeptically at him. He didn't blame them. There were three reindeer ranches in Oregon, so the chance of running into a reindeer or someone who worked at one of them hiking in the state park would be a reach. Even if that part was all true.

"The dog. But there were two," Gina said, frowning at him, and he felt as if he was under interrogation by his retired police detective brother.

"Well, Charlie and Benny, brothers from the same litter," Maverick easily said.

"What did Charlie look like?" she asked.

This got tricky. Weston and the others were sure the paw prints were wolves'. "A big dog, reddish and black guard hairs. We think they are wolf dogs, though the owners assured us they have no wolf genes. But if you saw their paw prints, you'd be certain they were wolves."

She arched a brow.

Maverick smiled. He knew she was confused, but his explanation helped explain everything she, her brother, and their friends were wondering—why he smelled like Shep, why they'd found wolf tracks, his brother having been there as well.

"Why don't you come with us while we're looking for

werewolves and then we can search for the reindeer too?" she asked.

"Sure, if you all don't mind. Even though I'm still looking for the reindeer, my brother and I believe the hikers who told us they'd seen it here in the park were probably confused and most likely had spotted a regular deer."

They all exchanged names, and then Weston and the other men headed out ahead of them.

Gina fell back with Maverick. "You and your brother carried the wolf dogs to your vehicle?" She was speaking low enough that only he could hear her.

From her scent, he knew she was definitely a wolf, and he figured she suspected he was a werewolf, the stuff of myths and legends, if she could really believe in such a thing. Now what did he say to that? He just smiled at her. He didn't want to lie. He figured it wouldn't be believable. And so far the men hadn't asked that question.

"Werewolves aren't real," she whispered.

Before hearing that, he'd thought she might believe they were.

"My brother and the others believe in them, but…" She continued, "You don't have any dogs, do you?"

They were still hiking behind the others, dropping back even farther. He didn't respond.

"Friends of ours were hunting for Bigfoot in Maine, and they saw what they thought was an Arctic werewolf shifting," she said, fishing for answers, he thought.

"Really." Maverick hoped he could keep a poker face, though his heart skipped a beat at the mention of the Arctic wolf in Maine. He definitely knew all about those guys.

"Yeah, a wolf killed one of the men, and one of the men just"—she snapped her fingers dramatically—"disappeared."

Maverick didn't comment. He didn't know what to say. He was reluctant to say too much here while the others were just down the trail, even though they couldn't hear their conversation. He didn't know how she would react if she heard the truth about what she was now. About what had happened to the other men, who happened to be their friends. She seemed to be taking all of this in stride, but she still might not believe any of it. Which was more likely.

"What do you do when you're not searching for Bigfoot?" he asked.

"I'm a zoologist."

"Really. So you study animals in the wild and in captivity?" That was good news. She had to like animals.

"I do. Whenever I return to Portland, I study animal behavior at the zoo, and I make a lot of trips through the state parks to study wild animals. But I also travel all over the world."

Which could still work for her when the new moon phase was in effect because she couldn't shift into her wolf then, but the rest of the time, she could be at risk. Even now she could be. Especially now with the full moon in full swing. What if she had to ditch her clothes and suddenly shift? Would her brother and his friends take care of her or want to eliminate her? Somehow, he had to convince her to return to the reindeer ranch with him, to remove her from the potential danger she could put herself and him in. Because he'd protect her with his life.

"You really were looking for reindeer out here?" she asked. "There shouldn't be any in this part of the world, I wouldn't think."

"Yeah, I agree with you. But that's what the hikers said."

"And you really own a reindeer ranch?"

"We do. The holidays are our busy season."

She bit her lower lip. "You smell like the wolf dog."

"I had hugged him."

"The dog bit me. Not on purpose, but his tooth or teeth cut into me, and then what?"

"You could see in the dark without using any artificial means, right?" He glanced at her hand. "You healed up quickly."

"Yeah. But the bite must have not been that bad. And it…it really was light out." She frowned at him. "You can't be beating around the bush to say I'm a werewolf."

"Wolf shifter." He hadn't wanted to say that much even, but she didn't seem to believe him. The worst that could happen was she'd think he really believed in the myth and she had reason to be concerned for her safety around him. And that was bad enough. He needed her to trust him.

She stumbled, and he caught her arm and steadied her. She stared at him. "No."

"You could track me like a bloodhound."

"Your…your dogs' footprints were easy to see."

"You smelled Shep on this trail, which verified it wasn't any other canine's trail, correct?" He knew it had to be so. He'd seen her pause, smell the air, and then trudge on. She hadn't just been following the tracks but the scent he had left behind. His scent. Not a dog's. But a wolf shifter's.

For several feet, she didn't answer him as they trudged along through the snow behind the other guys. Suddenly, she stopped in place, and he backtracked to join her. She folded her arms and looked him straight in the eye—a purely alpha posture. He loved it. "Okay, look, I don't believe in werewolves."

"Wolf shifters."

She frowned. "Or Bigfoot. I mean, maybe they all exist, but I would have to have scientific proof. That's what I am, a scientist. Myths and legends are just that. I'm willing to believe if I have proof, but I'm much more of a skeptic. Some of the so-called proof can be explained away—like with the dog prints we found that look like wolf prints. They're wolf dogs' tracks."

"Okay, I agree."

She dropped her arms and began hiking to catch up with her brother and their friends. "According to you, they're not wolf dogs but werewolves and you are one of them."

"Wolf shifters." He was glad she didn't get upset, but he wasn't sure she really believed in it. But she was smart too, and being a zoologist, she understood something about wildlife, so she might be able to handle being a wolf better. At least he hoped so.

"You're saying you were the dog in the lake who bit me and now I'm a were—wolf shifter too." She scoffed. "So you're telling me I, what? Can see in the dark? Can smell things I wouldn't be able to—I mean, you slept in the tent with me—I mean the dog did—and he was wet and doggy smelling, so of course I could still smell him? And heal faster? The scratch on my hand was infinitesimal. It was just stinging and felt worse than it really was. So naturally it was all healed up this morning."

"You heal up that fast normally? You were bleeding, and you put some liquid skin bandage on it before you went to sleep last night."

She stared at him. "How did you know I…" She quit talking and continued to walk in silence.

"You petted my head last night, told me you didn't believe in werewolves but that you were worried your brother and his friends would keep searching for them even if it killed them."

She looked sharply at him. "You were listening outside my tent? Skulking around? You were the one who unzipped my tent and then you let your dog out! Then you took off with him."

He understood her need to make up a story so that it made sense in her own reality of how things had to have gone down. "Okay, look, you don't have to believe it, but the good side is all the things you mentioned already—enhanced night vision, healing properties, sense of smell and also hearing. You might have noticed hearing things you might not have before. But the downside is the shifting issues. You'll feel like you're flushed with fever, and you'll have to strip off your clothes and shift into the wolf. It's worse when you're new and during the full moon."

She stopped walking. He turned to look at her. Gina's eyes were huge, and he returned to her side.

"What? You're not feeling hot now, are you?" That had

him worried. No way did he want her shifting in front of her brother and their friends. No telling what they'd do to her.

She shook her head, but he knew from the way she had reacted to his comments that she wasn't telling him everything. Then they began walking together again.

For a long time, they didn't say anything. He was sure she didn't believe all this, but he had to give her time. Not that they had a lot. Then he wondered if she'd shifted in her tent last night. That would be good and keep her from shifting right away again, he hoped. Newly turned wolves' shifting patterns were unpredictable at best.

She rubbed her forehead and paused again. "Can I visit your reindeer ranch?" She sounded a little meeker now, like she was really worried about whether she could be one of his kind.

"Hell, yeah. We're even having a Christmas party with—" Maverick quit speaking when the men stopped up ahead of them, crouched down, and pointed toward the woods. The Christmas party was a wolf event, and he could only invite wolves to it.

"What do you see?" Gina called out to her brother.

"Didn't Maverick say he was looking for a reindeer?" Weston asked.

"Yeah, don't tell me you found one," Maverick said, hurrying to join her brother, surprised as hell, Gina rushing after him.

"Yeah, we saw one off in that direction." Weston pointed in a southerly direction.

Maverick couldn't believe there really would be any out

here. They were at the zoo on special visits or at the reindeer ranches. It had to be missing from someone's ranch or farm.

"We'll let you go after it," Weston said. "We've got other prey to hunt."

Maverick was glad to go out on his own, but he couldn't leave Gina with the others. She wasn't one of them any longer, and she wouldn't be safe around them during this phase of the moon. The new moon phase, when she couldn't shift, wouldn't be here before New Year's.

"I'm going with Maverick," Gina said before Maverick could suggest it and hope she'd go along with it.

He was glad she wanted to remain with him and he hadn't had to convince her to stay with him for her own good, not when the other men were listening to what he had to tell her.

Her brother stared at her as if she had lost her mind.

"I'm a zoologist. Reindeer don't live here. I've got to document this. I'll be in touch," Gina said.

"Are you serious?" Weston's eyes were wide with disbelief.

"Yeah. You know this is just the kind of work I do. I'll be fine. I'll call you when we get to the reindeer ranch. I'll send pictures, even," she said.

"Actually, I can show you our webcam at the ranch." Maverick brought out his phone and then showed Weston the webcam of the property, the reindeer, and the staff feeding them. He wanted to reassure her brother that he was safe to be with.

"Let me see your ID," Weston said to Maverick, a modicum of concern in his voice—big brother looking after little sister, making sure that Maverick was who he said he was.

Maverick was glad for that. "Yeah, sure." He showed him his driver's license and a reindeer business card for bookings. "I promise I'll take care of her." Seriously, more than her brother would ever know unless they had to turn him too, which might have to happen. But now Maverick would have time alone with Gina, and he could really talk to her about the wolf business. He suspected that was why she wanted to go with him. Though maybe as a zoologist, she really did want to see the reindeer.

Weston handed Maverick's ID back to him but pocketed the business card. "You stay in touch," he told Gina, his voice stern.

"I will." She gave him a hug, and he hugged her back.

Then they split forces; the men took off north, and Maverick and Gina headed out to search for the reindeer. Maverick would need to dump his gear when they found it and lasso it.

They hadn't walked more than about ten more minutes when he could smell a reindeer's scent.

Gina asked, "Do you smell it?"

"Yeah, just like you do."

"I...I guess so." She didn't sound sure of her new abilities.

"Your brother and your friends wouldn't be able to smell the reindeer, believe me. Any more than you would have been able to before."

"If what you're saying is true—not saying I believe in any of it—I would have to learn to identify scents, I guess. I mean, I knew your dog's..." She paused.

He could see the struggle she was having with the truth He would have to shift for her, and then she would believe.

"Um, scent on the trail because I smelled it on my blanket in my tent, and finally when I saw you, I smelled the same scent. But the reindeer smells different, and I thought maybe it was him." She paused. "I still can't believe any of this. Are you going to try to capture the reindeer?"

"Yeah. And take him home to our ranch. We feed them a special diet and take care of them."

"They're herd animals."

"Exactly."

"Okay, so you seriously can't be a were—wolf shifter. I can't be one." She stayed near him as they moved through the woods, searching for the reindeer.

"I know. It's hard to believe. We're wolf shifters or *lupus garous*. That's what we call ourselves. Werewolves are seen as…so monster-like in some literature. Oh…I see the reindeer ahead," he whispered to her. He wondered how the reindeer had ended up here. He'd had a lot of experience with roping them, so as soon as he was able, he'd lasso him and then make further arrangements to move him. But the reindeer didn't seem frightened, and he suspected it wasn't wild.

Someone had to have raised him.

Maverick carefully set his backpack down and pulled his rope out.

Gina placed her backpack next to his.

Then he readied the rope and lassoed the reindeer. "Okay, we've got him."

"Wow, that was great." She frowned. "He can smell our scent. He's not afraid of us?"

"He's probably never met a wolf, but if we smell like canines, he might have been raised with them and be comfortable around them."

"Wolf shifters," she said, still sounding incredulous.

Maverick knew the wolf shifter business was going to be hard for her to believe, especially when she hadn't shifted yet, though he was glad she hadn't right now, given where they were. And what if she did and they ran into her brother and friends while Gina was running as a wolf? They'd believe he had lost Weston's sister in the woods and picked up a female wolf. That would be hard to explain.

"Now what?" she asked.

"Now I call my brother to arrange a pickup of the reindeer."

"Wait, is that a…" she said, peering into the woods.

Maverick looked to see what it was she had seen and saw a llama. "Llama? It sure the hell is." He removed his belt.

"What are you doing?"

"I'm going to put my belt on the reindeer, and if you're not afraid, you can hold onto it as if it were a collar. Then I'll remove the rope from the reindeer and lasso the llama."

"The two are friends. Look how the llama isn't moving any farther away from the reindeer than he is now. They were probably raised together," Gina said.

"I agree. Do you have a belt we can use for the llama as a makeshift collar?"

She shook her head, removing her backpack and unzipping one of the pockets. "No, but I do have a bungee cord."

"That should work." Then he pulled a carrot out of his

parka pocket and walked up to the reindeer with the carrot outstretched, and Gina pulled the bungee cord out of her backpack. Once Maverick had the reindeer eating out of his hand, he put the belt around his neck. It appeared the reindeer was used to wearing a harness. "Okay, if you'll come up here and hold onto his 'collar,' I'll remove the rope and lasso the llama."

"I've got this." She sounded excited to be in on the capture of a couple of out-of-place tame animals. The perfect mystery for a zoologist.

With the bungee cord in hand, she grasped the belt-collar on the reindeer with her free hand and spoke softly to him while Maverick tossed the rope and lassoed the llama. The llama didn't even bolt, as if she didn't want to leave her friend behind.

"This is so neat. We've probably saved their lives," she said.

"Yeah, they don't belong in the forest trying to survive. They might not have made it." Then he took the bungee cord from Gina, made a collar for the llama, and tied the rope to both of them so he could walk them on a "leash" to a pickup zone. He called his brother right after that. "Before you ask"—he glanced at Gina and smiled—"yes, Gina is one of us, and she's a zoologist, so she understands something about animals. But also I need a trailer. We found the reindeer. Not only that, but he's got a gal pal with him—a llama. They're both tame, which means we need to learn where they belong."

"A llama? I figured the hikers were mistaken. I'm glad you

found the reindeer and, uh, the llama. I'll call someone to get you. What about Gina?" Josh said.

"I'm hoping she's coming to the reindeer ranch and then the Christmas party at Leidolf's ranch."

"And the others?" Josh asked.

"They're off on a Bigfoot–werewolf hunt still."

"Okay, good." Josh sounded relieved. "I also have to tell you the couple who host the radio show? They lambasted the other ranch hands for trying to steal our show."

"Really." Maverick hoped the owner of the other reindeer ranch didn't give the radio show hosts trouble. "I hope they don't have any backlash from it, but I'm glad they outed them."

"People calling in were for us one hundred percent. They said they'd hate it if they had planned programs and someone else set up nearby to steal their business away from them. Several said they had seen us and loved our reindeer and the calves."

"That's good news. Speaking of which, I'll let them know we found the reindeer and a llama. They can air that and maybe find where they belong because the animals are probably from this area."

"Oh, great idea! Not to mention you going out and searching for the reindeer will probably show us to be the good guys."

"I agree. Thanks, Josh. I'll talk to you later." When Maverick ended the call, he phoned Andy at the radio station. "This is Maverick Wilding—"

"The man of the hour. We were just discussing the issue with you and the other reindeer ranch."

"Thanks so much. I was calling to tell you we found the reindeer you had seen."

"Hallelujah. I've got to tell my listeners." Then he paused and said, "When April and I came across the reindeer in the state park, we told Maverick and Josh Wilding of Wilding Reindeer Ranch. We asked if they could find the reindeer, and they said they would search for him. They did and actually found him."

Maverick realized Andy was currently on his talk show right this minute! "But not only did we find the reindeer"— Maverick wasn't going to leave his brother out of receiving the glory too—"the reindeer had a friend, a llama, and we're transporting them to our reindeer ranch for safekeeping until we can find their home. We would be grateful if your listeners know anything about where they might belong. If they can let you know or they can contact us, we can take them home."

"You heard the man. If you know whom these beautiful animals belong to, give us a call. Thanks for believing us and searching for the reindeer, Maverick. Calypso's ranch hands didn't believe us, and if it hadn't been for Maverick and Josh searching for them, the reindeer and llama would still be in the woods, fending for themselves. Thanks to Maverick and Josh, this story has a happier ending. We'll be talking to you soon. Signing off for now." Then Andy said to Maverick, "Okay, we're off the air."

"Thanks for alerting us about the reindeer."

"Thanks for believing April and me. We'll see you next year at your show, but in the meantime, we'll keep in touch if any of our listeners have any clues as to where the reindeer and llama belong."

"Thanks." Then Maverick said goodbye, hopeful they would get some good feedback soon. He explained what had been said to Gina.

"Oh, that's wonderful. You received great publicity, and possibly someone listening to their radio station will know where the animals belong. Wonderful."

"Yeah, it couldn't have worked out better," Maverick said as they continued to hike through the snowy woods. He and Gina had to get the animals home, checked out by a vet, and fed a proper meal. No telling how long they'd been in the woods foraging for food on their own.

But mainly, he had to get Gina to safety just in case she shifted in the state park!

―――――

Gina pulled out her phone and called her brother to let him know she was fine and where she was going next. "Hey, Weston, I'm going with Maverick to his Christmas party."

"Where is it located?"

She sighed. "Where is Leidolf's ranch?"

"It's south of mine. Leidolf Wildhaven. Your brother can check him out. He's a well-respected rancher."

"Okay, thanks, Maverick." She told her brother what

Maverick had said. "Anyway, he caught the reindeer and—get this—a llama too."

"A llama? Wow. I didn't see that. I wish I had. Were they together then?"

"Yep. We're taking them to his reindeer ranch now."

"Are you sure about this guy?"

"Yeah. I'll be fine. You know how it is when I have something I can document about animals in the wild or in captivity. This is a real mystery, and I want to help Maverick solve it. You have fun searching for Bigfoot."

"And werewolves," he reminded her.

She glanced at Maverick. "Uh, yeah, and werewolves. But you promised me you wouldn't kill anything if you found what you're looking for." God, she couldn't believe she'd be really worried they might run into real ones now like their friends had in Maine. "All right. I'll call you later."

She ended the call and frowned at Maverick. "Okay, so let's say I believe you about the wolf shifter business. When you were in your fur coat, you looked like a real wolf. Well, I couldn't imagine running into a wolf, so I figured you were a dog. But if you were a wolf shifter, you weren't some deformed wolf monster like in the movies."

"We are like real wolves, only we still have our human thought processes. You think like a human, but you have the enhanced senses of the wolf. Not only that, but if anyone checks your blood as a human, it's totally human."

She sighed with relief. "I worried about that." The coroner had said that the men the Dark Angels had killed had been poisoned with silver nitrite, but while he was doing

DNA testing, if he had discovered the men had mixed wolf and human DNA, they would have heard it on the news.

"And as a wolf, your blood is all wolf's. We also have enhanced healing abilities twice as fast as humans, and we have longer life spans. Wolves mate for life, so you can make love to a human without consequences, but making love all the way with another wolf means you're mated for life. No divorce."

"Oh, wow, I never thought there would be so many conditions."

"You'll need to stay with us during the full moon. With some of our kind, I mean. You won't have a lot of control over shifting. No driving a car or working at a job when you're around humans."

In other words, her whole life had just been turned upside down, and she was still reeling from all of this. "So about this Christmas party…"

"Yeah, at the pack leader's ranch. We're primarily red wolves."

"They're rare. I mean, real red wolves." She'd never imagined werewolves would come in all different kinds of species or subspecies.

"They are. Even with our kind. A couple of packs exist that I know of, and some red *lupus garous* have mated grays. But mostly the packs are gray wolves."

"And the Arctic wolf shifter who Weston's friends saw in Maine?"

Maverick just couldn't talk to Gina about the situation that had
happened in Maine. She was dealing with enough with learning what she'd become. "Yes. Arctic *lupus garous* exist as well."
He wasn't going to tell her about jaguar shifters. Not right now.
He suspected learning about wolves was enough for now.

"I can't tell my brother about any of this, can I?"

"No. That's the only way we can stay relatively safe, by
keeping our kind a secret. Do you have other family?" He
needed to learn all he could about her, just like she needed
to learn all she could about them.

"My parents. I have no other family except for Weston
and them. What happens if someone learns about you?"

"*Us*. You might not feel like one of us yet, but you *are* one
of us. We turn them or eliminate those who see us shifting.
No one knows of us, and we mean to keep it that way." He
was hurrying her through the woods, trying to reach the
trailhead as soon as he could.

"So the one man who vanished in Maine might be a wolf
now and he never got in touch with my brother or his friends
because he couldn't control his shifting."

Maverick didn't want to tell her that Sarge was alive until
he had time to explain about the rest.

CHAPTER 4

GINA'S THOUGHTS WERE SWIRLING AROUND HER HEAD like a blender on high speed as she considered the situation she was in. She still couldn't believe she was a wolf shifter, or *lupus garou,* but if she was, from what Maverick had told her, she wouldn't be able to do regular assignments as a zoologist during the full moon. Everything else she could explain away except for one thing—removing all her clothes in the middle of the night when it was cold in the tent and she'd been hot. No way, unless she'd been running a high-grade fever, would she have been too hot to wear her clothes. When Maverick had mentioned she would do just that—feel the heat, the need to take off her clothes, and then shift? That would be the only reason she could think of for why she was totally naked in her tent last night!

She knew there would be consequences that she didn't like. *If* she truly was this imaginary beast. She was still on the fence about it. But what worried her most was that Maverick had evaded the question of what had happened to the men in Maine. If he hadn't known, which would be very likely given how far away Maine was from Portland, Oregon, why not say so? Or if he suspected they'd been eliminated, why not say that? But he wouldn't comment as if he knew and he didn't want to upset her.

She more than worried what would become of her parents and her brother. What about their friends? It sounded as though Maverick wanted to keep her around, to acclimate her to the world of werewolves, and didn't have any intention of eliminating her, thankfully.

Maverick's cell jingled "Magical Christmas Carol of the Bells," alerting him he had a call. He gave Josh their location. "Okay, we'll take the animals to the site where we'd parked our truck. We're on our way there now." Maverick ended the call. "We'll be picked up by a friend, Jim Salsa, at the trailhead and ride down to the ranch."

They both put on their backpacks.

"All right." She took another deep breath of the air and smelled the reindeer and llama. Earlier, she'd smelled their tension, but now they appeared less anxious. They started to hike in the direction where she'd tracked Maverick's trail earlier. She couldn't quit thinking of how "awake" her senses were. She felt like she was experiencing sensory overload.

She took a deep breath. It seemed like the air out there had suddenly cleared her mind. Like the stuffing in her ears had been removed. She was now aware of the slightest of movements—the pine needles fluttering in the fickle breeze, the flitter of a cardinal's wings as he flew mostly hidden into the underbrush in her peripheral vision, the dancing of tiny snowflakes making their descent from heaven above. "I heard the plop of snow falling from a branch over there"—she motioned in the direction she'd heard it fall—"the sound of a tiny creature deep in the underbrush, the low twitter of a bird I can't see, and even the fall of a leaf." The fragrance of fir and pine, even the crisp snow, filled her nose. "Animal scents are confusing though…but I recognize the scent of a reindeer, llama, and your wolf scent too now. Not to mention I've never been able to track anything before like I can now."

"Courtesy of our wolf genetics, but hopefully the more you can connect the animals with their scents, the easier it will get for you." Maverick was pulling the animals to come with him.

The reindeer and llama balked a little at the pull of the rope.

"Come on," Maverick said, slipping another carrot out of his pocket, breaking it in half, and giving one piece to the llama and one to the reindeer.

She was surprised Maverick had carrots with him. She knew reindeer ate reindeer moss up north in alpine tundra areas, though she hadn't studied a whole lot about them. She thought studying them at the ranch would be a great experience, especially fun at Christmastime.

The reindeer and llama munched on their carrot halves. Maverick calmly talked to them like they were the best of friends and ran his hand over their muzzles with a caress. "Okay, now it's time to walk some more and hope we can make better progress."

Maverick was amazingly gifted at working with the animals, gently pulling at them to come with him, talking to them.

She really hoped this worked. "Good boy and girl," she said to the reindeer and the llama. "You're so beautiful." She noticed Maverick was smiling at her.

Then they continued their trek to where his truck had been parked at the trailhead.

Both the reindeer and llama balked again and Maverick fed them another carrot half each.

"Those came in handy," she said.

"They did. We had some for our reindeer during the show, so we brought them with us in case we spotted the reindeer in the woods. The hikers never said anything about a llama."

"But you were running as wolves."

"To cover more territory, sure, but we had the carrots at the camp, and I took them with me when I went to look for you, just in case I ran into a reindeer."

That was a surprise to her. "You were looking for me, not the reindeer?"

"I had to make sure you hadn't been turned. When I was in your tent, I thought you had been cut by the ice, not that I'd bitten you. I smelled your blood, and I smelled the liquid skin bandage you put on. I had so much lake water in my mouth, and I was so frantic to get out of the water before I expended all my energy, I didn't actually taste your blood. But then the more I thought about it, the more I worried what if I *had* accidentally bitten you? I couldn't stop thinking about it, not knowing if you were one of us, and if you were, what I would say to you and not say to you because I didn't want to scare you."

"Especially in front of the others."

"Right. Knowing what we are and what you are now too, maybe we can...date? If you're not seeing someone else right now."

"I'm not." She thought he was cute, and she sighed. "So what does dating you entail?"

He glanced at her and smiled, looking pleased she was taking him up on his offer. "Dining out, movies, dinner and dancing at a wolf-run club—"

"A wolf-run club? Ohmigod, this is just so unreal." And fun too. At least she hoped she would have a good reception from other wolves. What if they didn't like that he'd accidentally turned her? She didn't go out very much, but if she enjoyed his company, she was really looking forward to the dating bit.

"You can have an in-depth study of reindeer at the ranch and observe all kinds of wildlife that make their home on our acreage and on Leidolf and Cassie's property. You can go on wolf runs with us when you can shift, and that will give you a whole new perspective on wildlife, believe me. We have a lot of celebrations at the pack leaders' ranch that you can enjoy."

"That sounds like fun. What are you going to do about my brother and my parents?" Everything else sounded like a boon, but the part about her family was still a real concern.

"We need to talk to our pack leaders about it. My take on it is we turn them. But turning people has consequences, as you probably already realize. They'll have to leave their jobs, unless they're doing remote work. They can choose to join us and make new friends with our wolf kind, and we can help them through the changes. It's one thing to accidentally turn someone, but another to purposefully do so. How would your parents feel about it? How would Weston come to terms with it?"

She didn't say anything for a long time. How could any of this truly be real? "I'm not sure about my parents. They are pretty open-minded, but this is pretty far out there. My brother?" She laughed. "He would think it was great. He would no longer be looking for werewolves, and I'm sure he would love knowing they are for real and he was one of them. But still searching for Bigfoot? He probably wouldn't give that up. In fact, he might believe he'd have a better chance of tracking one down with a wolf's enhanced senses."

"He could no longer go on hunts with his human friends, except for during the new moon phase. Wouldn't they wonder why?"

She sighed. "Yeah."

It seemed to take them forever to reach the trailhead where a truck and trailer were waiting for them. A man smiled and waved when he saw them.

Maverick introduced Gina. "This is Jim Salsa."

"You're a wolf," she said, surprised, already recognizing his wolf scent, but not exactly the same as Maverick's or her own, she realized. Just how many were there? She couldn't believe she could now identify a wolf by scent, as if she had a magic ability all of a sudden—a werewolf detector. If her brother knew that, he'd take her with him on all their hunts!

"Yeah, like you are." Jim gave Maverick a questioning glance.

"Uh, she's newly turned." Maverick sounded a little guilty for it.

She didn't want him to feel guilty about it. Maybe she should have felt upset that her world was topsy-turvy, but she really didn't. Maybe because she'd only experienced some of the good things, not the bad. She felt new avenues of exploration had been opened up to her with her enhanced senses. Belonging to a secret society of wolves was uniquely appealing to her.

Jim helped Maverick load the reindeer and the llama into the trailer. "So you know you're a red wolf and so is Maverick. I'm a Mexican gray wolf, a subspecies of the gray wolf. My parents and I were born and raised in the States, but we're all from Mexican gray wolf stock."

"That is so cool." She knew Mexican gray wolves and the Arctic wolves were a subspecies of the gray wolf, but not that wolf shifters could be every subspecies as well.

"How in the world did a reindeer and llama get out here?" Jim asked.

Maverick shook his head. "We have no idea, but they're both tame, so I need to learn where they belong. But, hey, thanks for helping us out."

"No problem. Wolves aid other wolves whenever we can."

"Well, we owe you one."

Maverick took Gina's backpack and put it in the back seat of the pickup truck. She climbed in next to it, and he put his gear beside her and then climbed into the front seat of the cab.

"So how are your twins doing?" Maverick asked Jim as they got on the road.

"They're a handful. I thought they'd just eat and sleep and poop, but now they're running around and getting into everything."

She and Maverick chuckled, but then she realized that Maverick had a twin, and now this man had twins too? Which made her think of wolves and how they had multiple births of anywhere from four to six in a litter. Some had fewer, but some even had more.

"You have multiple births?" she blurted out.

Jim laughed. "How newly turned is she?"

Maverick let out his breath. "Since last night."

"Oh, damn. *Newly* newly turned. Okay, yeah, we do, just like wolves, but our human genes seem to have something to say about it, so we generally have one to four kids, but rarely more than that."

She wasn't *ever* having kids.

The guys talked about ranching for a long time, and she finally fell asleep in the truck, probably because of all the getting up in the night over raccoons and such. And then getting up earlier than she normally did on a hike.

She dreamed of running as a dog or a wolf that looked like Maverick and then falling into an icy lake before she heard a new voice that woke her fully from her slumber.

Maverick's lookalike twin—Josh?—opened the back door of the cab and smiled at her, but it was a worried kind of smile. Was Maverick in trouble for turning her? It was an accident, and he hadn't meant to.

"I'm Josh, Maverick's older twin brother." He pulled Maverick's backpack out of the truck, handed it to him, and then offered his hand to help Gina out of the truck. She got out, and he pulled out her backpack.

"My mate, Brooke, and I have the house over there." Josh

motioned to one of the ranch houses. "You can stay with us or with Maverick at the main house."

Josh and Brooke's home was a beautiful, one-story brick house with a large wraparound porch to enjoy the views and featured large windows too. Gina looked at the breathtaking, panoramic vista of the Cascade Mountain range and the cheery ranch houses, three of them, a bunk-house, pastureland, forest, corrals, and barns, and even a Christmas tree farm.

The reindeer stables and ranch houses were decked out in Christmas lights, the corrals covered in garland, red bows, and pre-lit Christmas wreaths too. A large irrigation pond was off to the south, and way off in the distance a river snaked across the property.

"That's Randall Anders's home. He's the ranch manager. And then we have the bunkhouse for the ranch hands," Maverick said, motioning to another lovely home made of brick with a big porch and windows to show off the view.

One of the ranch hands greeted them and took the rein-deer and the llama into a separate barn.

"We have a vet room in that barn," Maverick explained, "where the reindeer and llama will be checked out."

"Oh, that's good. This is lovely. I never imagined it would be so Christmassy. It's just magical and beautifully deco-rated." She couldn't wait to see all the Christmas lights at night. She'd expected just a regular working ranch where they took the reindeer to special events, but nothing like this.

"Thanks. The reindeer *are* magical, and we wanted to have a special showcase for them throughout the year. We have special Valentine's couples' events as well. Groups come here to see the reindeer frequently," Maverick said.

"Our vet will come out to check on the animals," Josh said.

"That's good," Maverick said.

"After lunch, Leidolf and Cassie want to meet with you," Josh said to Gina. "You're welcome to go with her, Maverick."

Now that meant they were going to get down to business. She would learn what the pack leaders wanted to do about her parents and brother. She wished her family could choose for themselves, but she suspected that wasn't an option.

"Did you want to have lunch with us?" Maverick asked Josh and Jim.

Jim declined. "I've got lunch plans with my mate and the kids." They thanked him again, he got into his truck, and then he drove off the reindeer ranch.

Josh bowed out too. "I have lunch plans with Brooke at the antiques shop. See you all later for the Christmas party."

"See you, Josh," Maverick said, and then he escorted Gina into his house.

The first thing she noticed was the open living arrangement in the house, and she loved it. Against one wall was a floor-to-ceiling stone fireplace and a beautifully decorated mantel with garland and brass reindeer, red bows, and red berries. The ceilings were pine vaulted, the Christmas tree seven feet tall, covered in all kinds of reindeer, from plaid fabric to crocheted, porcelain, and crystal, and red-and-green-plaid bows and multicolored Christmas tree lights. Really cute.

They set their backpacks on the floor. He helped her out

of her parka and hung it on a coat rack and then did the same with his.

"I love your reindeer décor."

"Thanks. We've been getting them from fans, friends, and family for years. Would you like lobster rolls for lunch?" he asked as he headed to the spacious, open kitchen.

"That sounds delicious." She figured he had premade lobster rolls, not as good as fresh ones, but when he pulled out lobster meat, mayonnaise, lettuce, celery, lemon juice, and parsley, she realized he was making them from scratch.

She admired the custom cabinetry in distressed maple wood, the granite countertops and marble backsplash, and the granite-covered island that separated the kitchen from the dining and living areas. He had double ovens and double fridges that looked like he was used to entertaining. It was so nice compared to her little apartment in Portland.

She watched him combine all the ingredients, minus the lettuce, in a bowl, coating the lobster with mayonnaise and then placing it in the fridge to chill.

He pulled out split-top potato-bread rolls, buttered the tops, and sprinkled some salt on top. Then he toasted them butter side down for four minutes in a pan, removed them, and set them on reindeer-decorated plates. How adorable.

He placed a lettuce leaf on top of each and then spooned out lobster salad on each of the sandwiches.

She found glasses for water, filled them up, and brought them to the table, appreciating the centerpiece—a big red candle surrounded by holly and red berries and trimmed in a ribbon of green. Once they were seated and she'd taken a bite of her lobster roll, she was in heaven.

"Okay, so I'm really going to like having you for a boyfriend as long as you make meals this good."

He laughed. "I guess fixing lobster rolls was the right move."

"It sure was." She licked some mayonnaise off her lips. "You know you're going to have to turn into Shep again just so I can believe this is real."

He chuckled. "I can do that. Right after we eat."

Once they finished eating and putting the dishes away, Maverick said, "Normally, we strip off our clothes and shift, no big deal. Everyone has been doing this since they were born."

She took a deep breath, rubbed her arms, and exhaled, feeling anxious about this. "Unless they are newly turned. I just kind of figured that all werewolves began as humans and then were bitten, but I'm not sure how the first one came about."

"Exactly. We're not sure either. So I can go in another room and shift and come out, if it's all a little too much for you to handle, but—"

"I need to see you do it." She couldn't envision it no matter how much she tried, and she was still afraid of what might happen.

"I figured that. You won't have bones breaking or any kind of painful experience to deal with when you shift. Heat fills our muscles, our bones, and we shift in the blink of an eye, like magic. If you're not watching closely, you'd miss it," he reassured her.

"Oh, no pain, I like the sound of that. I could imagine all the cracking of bones and howling in pain. And shifting quickly? That's great news."

"Yeah, we seem to be engineered that way to help us exist as only a myth in a human world."

Then she frowned. "You really were born this way?" She'd never heard of that in any mythologies she'd read. Then again, what she'd read was all fiction.

"Yeah."

She kept thinking he'd turn into a mindless beast, so she had to remember what Shep had been like, sweet and gentle. He had left her alone and hadn't harmed her in the middle of the night. Then Gina frowned. "You didn't hang around for long in my tent, right?"

"No, as soon as everyone was sound asleep, I was out of there." Then, before she could ask him any further questions and delay what he was about to do, he stripped off his clothes.

Oh, God, he was a veritable hunk, and she eyed him with intrigue.

She couldn't help it. He was exquisitely sculpted, hot, beautiful. She'd wanted to see the transformation of man to wolf, but she wanted him to take his time at it so she could enjoy seeing more of his beautiful body.

He gave her another moment to see him like this. Was he showing off? She was totally impressed, and she appreciated that he was giving her another eyeful. And then he shifted—a blur of forms, exquisite, magical.

Wow, that's how he looked turning into a wolf? She loved

it. Nothing horrifying or scary about it. She swore the transformation was like art in motion.

As a wolf, he approached her and licked her hand. She petted him, thinking just how beautiful he was as a wolf. "Shep, not a German shepherd at all. A beautiful red wolf. Okay, shift again. I barely could see you shifting the first time. It happened in the blink of an eye."

He shifted again. "I told you so."

She admired his human form a little too much, felt her cheeks heat, but she just had to see if it happened as fast the second time. "Okay, shift again."

He smiled, and without another moment's hesitation, he shifted into his wolf.

Oh, wow, that was beautiful. She had worried that if she had to turn wolf, she would be struggling with it and would quickly be seen and outed. "Okay, shift again." She loved how he humored her. He was a good sport.

He shifted again. But this time once he was back in his human form, he took her into his arms and hugged her. "I'm sorry I turned you, and I'll do everything to help make up for it."

She kissed him then, just a sweet kiss on the lips, not sure if he was ready for more...yet. "I never believed in werewolves, but when you said you were one, I never expected you to be so...hot."

He smiled, pressed his mouth to hers, kissed her lightly, and then pressured more until she opened her mouth to his and their tongues caressed.

"Hmm," she said. "I'm really going to like dating you, I

think. Before we get too carried away, I guess we need to see your pack leaders." That worry about her family kept niggling at the back of her thoughts. Not to mention the full moon was in force and that worried her more than she cared to admit.

"Yeah, we do." He kissed her lightly on the mouth again, as if to ensure that she would like dating him, and then he grabbed up his boxer briefs and pulled them on. "Are you ready to meet them?" He finished dressing in a hurry.

"I am." She figured she really didn't have a choice and it was better to get this over with.

Then he took her out to his garage to get his pickup and showed her his 1957 red-and-white Corvette, and she loved it.

"This is really lovely. It must have cost a fortune." She was impressed and wondered if the reindeer ranch made enough money to afford the classic car and the beautiful ranch.

"Brooke inherited a Ferrari, the Corvette, and the 1940 Ford pickup we use for displays from her great aunt, so Brooke gave this car to me for a Christmas present."

"That is a really nice Christmas present, and I bet it's fun to drive," she said as they got into his truck and headed down the road.

"Yeah, it's great when it's warmer and I can take the top down."

"I bet." If they were still dating each other by then, she'd love to try it out.

When they finally arrived at Cassie and Leidolf's ranch, she admired the acres of trees and meadows and mountains, a main ranch house and bunkhouse, and several other homes and barns. She imagined the bachelor males lived in the bunkhouse.

Cassie and Leidolf welcomed them into the main ranch house, both of them smelling like red wolves—which amazed her to no end that she could tell that—and they were both lovely redheads with expressive green eyes.

"We're so excited to meet you," Cassie said. "I'm a wolf biologist myself and go on lecture tours all over the country, spreading the word about wolves."

Cassie had made them cocoa and Black Forest cake just to welcome her, and Gina really appreciated it. They sat in the den with a view of the mountains, forest, and pasture-land to enjoy their dessert and drinks.

"That sounds great." Gina was all for spreading the word about different animal species and how important they were to the ecology. "I've done that too about other species. I'm a zoologist."

"Maybe we could do it together sometime."

"I'd like that." Gina couldn't believe how normal every-one she'd met seemed. It wasn't anything like what she'd envisioned real werewolves would be like.

"So we need to discuss what you want to do now that you're one of us," Leidolf said, getting down to business. Gina envisioned a pack leader would be just like him. In charge, wanting to set the rules right from the get-go. She figured Cassie would be too when she needed to be, but she was friendlier.

"Maverick and Josh both invited me to stay at their

homes," Gina said, "to study the wildlife and the reindeer. So I'll be happy to do that. Plus Maverick has offered to take me on some dates, so I'm looking forward to that. I just have to say that a lot of this doesn't seem that real because I haven't shifted. Sure, I have heightened senses and all, but that isn't like actually turning into a wolf. It still seems unreal."

Leidolf said, "You can turn into a wolf at any time, except during the new moon phase, but for new wolves the phase of the full moon will have the strongest pull on you."

Gina glanced at Maverick. He hadn't exactly mentioned that part to her, had he? Just about the full moon.

"Yeah, it can affect you at any phase of the moon other than the new moon," Maverick said.

"That's why we want new wolves to stay with us so we can help them through all this," Cassie said.

That wasn't good. No wonder Maverick had come back to search for her. What if she hadn't agreed to go with Maverick and she had turned in front of her brother and their friends? That would have been a major disaster.

"Maverick says you have an older brother and parents," Leidolf said.

"Yes, and we're really close."

"Okay, well, my recommendation is we turn them as well," Leidolf said. "We don't take a situation like this lightly though."

"In other words, you usually don't turn a family," Gina said. "You would terminate them instead?"

"Only those who are out to harm us. We work hard to

ensure humans don't catch us shifting. And we try not to turn anyone accidentally. In any event, we would take your parents and brother in as well, but how do you think they'll handle it?"

"I believe my brother would be thrilled. I can't be for certain, but I think so. Mom and Dad, I have no idea. They're open-minded about a lot of things, but I'm not sure about this."

"They'll have to leave their friends behind," Cassie said. "Being with humans doesn't work out well for newly turned wolves. For those of us who were born *lupus garous* and who have very few human genes in our roots, we're known as royals who can shift at will, even during the new moon. Royals can blend in even more with the population because of this."

"Okay, so then how do we work this? Both of my parents are retired. They'd talked of moving from Corvallis to Portland because that's where I was working as a freelancer."

"One thing they'll probably enjoy, we have increased longevity and healing abilities. I'm sure they'll appreciate that," Cassie said. "Why don't you bring your parents out to the reindeer ranch to see your new boyfriend?"

Gina glanced at Maverick. She really liked him, but she hoped his biting her didn't mean he felt he was stuck mating with her. Then she frowned. "And then you'll turn wolf and bite them?" She felt like she was setting her parents up to be ambushed.

"We have a more civilized way to do it. But I'm afraid we

can't discuss what we are with them and give them a choice," Leidolf said. "I was thinking more of letting them meet Maverick, see his setup at the reindeer ranch, see that he and the rest of the ranch hands and Maverick's brother, Josh, are stand-up guys."

Gina figured they couldn't talk to her family and give them a choice. It was hard to come to terms with all this. "And my brother?"

"Invite him at the same time. Just make sure no one else comes with him," Cassie said. "The fewer who are involved, the better. Oh, and we have our Christmas party in a couple of hours. Why don't you get settled, clean up—since you've been camping and hiking and you'd probably like a hot shower. Then we'll see you both back here with the reindeer for the party."

"In the meantime, you can think over what we've said and tell us what you want to do," Leidolf said.

Gina was surprised they wanted her to help with the decision-making in this case. If she had her parents turned, she felt like she would be betraying their trust. But if she tried to stop seeing them, they'd worry she'd joined a cult or something and try to have them investigated. With her brother, he was already fascinated with searching for were-wolves, and she thought he'd be all right becoming one, but maybe not.

"If you would ever like to stay with us, you're welcome to," Cassie said. "Come, see the rest of the house."

Gina appreciated that Cassie was trying to make her feel comfortable. Cassie showed Gina the master bedroom and five more bedrooms, all well furnished, each having its own bathroom, sitting area, and patio to enjoy the view of the lands and mountain range.

When they reached the living room, the place was just as elegant with leather couches, Persian rugs, crystal chandeliers, and oil paintings of the Oregon coastline. All around the room, brass wolf sculptures were displayed in various poses—from resting in packs to nuzzling each other or snarling at one another.

"It was nice meeting you both," Gina said, really liking both of them.

"Likewise," Cassie said and gave her a hug.

Leidolf smiled and said he enjoyed meeting her and looked forward to seeing more of her at pack events.

Then she thanked them for the cocoa and cake, and she and Maverick said their goodbyes and left.

"I know it's a lot to think about," Maverick said on the drive back to his ranch.

"I just don't want to force something on my parents that they'll hate. Then they'd be angry with me for instigating the whole thing. But we've all been really close, and if I just distance myself from them, they'd investigate to learn what was going on, afraid you and my new friends were holding me hostage. Maybe they'd think that I joined some weird cult out on a ranch. Who knows what they might do?"

"You don't have to make a decision right away."

She let out her breath. "What's the other way they can be turned other than a bite?"

"A wolf's saliva introduced into their bloodstream."

"Okay, at least that seems more civilized. But then you'd have to discuss this with them to get their approval."

"Which we can't really do. I mean, we could discuss it with them, but if they said no, we'd have to bite them."

She sighed. She could imagine them saying no and it being forced on them. "You know you could just take me home and I can get cleaned up there."

"Your hiking backpack is still at my house."

"Oh, true."

"Where do you live exactly?"

She gave him the address of her apartment, which was about 45 minutes from where he lived.

"Okay, we'll drop by my place, get the backpack, and I'll take you to your place. You can shower, change, and then we can go to my place. I'll shower and change, and we'll take the reindeer down to the ranch."

"That will work. I worried that Cassie and Leidolf smelled that I hadn't showered in a while and that's why she suggested it."

He smiled. "No, you're good. She just knows we were camping and hiking and you'd want a nice hot shower. Me too."

"I do. I just forget everyone can smell scents so much better."

"You smell like a wolf, and that fragrance trumps all."

"Okay, thanks."

When they arrived at the ranch house, he grabbed her backpack while she waited in the truck. Then he joined her, and they were off again.

"Are people dressing up for the party?"

"Everybody wears everything to these events."

"I don't want to be totally underdressed in front of everyone." She thought about it and figured he might have some pictures of last year's Christmas party. She reached out her hand for his phone. "Show me pictures of past Christmas events." She didn't trust that everyone didn't come dressed for the occasion. Though what did she know about werewolves when they partied?

"You don't trust my word?" He smiled at her, appearing amused more than anything, and handed his phone to her.

She thought he was brave to give her access to all his photos, but mostly they were of the reindeer and visiting groups at the ranch or out on tour. None of him hugging on a woman in any of them. Then she found the Christmas pictures.

She flipped through them and saw several people dressed in Christmas sweaters, some in skirts, others in jeans, so he was right. They wore a variety of clothes from casual dressy to casual.

"See? They wear a little bit of everything."

"You're right. The women dress up a bit more."

They finally arrived at Gina's apartment, and she led him inside. Luckily, she'd picked the place up. He set her backpack on the living room floor. She would do a load of laundry after the Christmas party.

"Grab anything you'd like to drink from the fridge. I'll be just a few minutes."

"Take your time. We're not in a real big rush."

But she knew they were because they still had to return to his place, he had to shower and get dressed, and they had to take the reindeer with them, and drive back to Leidolf's ranch. So she was going to make this as quick as she could.

Still, she felt so grimy, and she didn't want to leave the shower once she was in it. She couldn't help thinking of him lathering up in his own shower after seeing his rock-hard body. She finally dried off and started yanking clothes out of her drawers and closet. She thought she knew just what she wanted to wear, but after trying on four sweaters, three shirts, and three skirts, she was totally exasperated with herself. She was never this indecisive!

It all had to do with wanting to make a good impression on him and on the other wolves too. But especially on Maverick.

But then she sat on her bed in her underwear, suddenly feeling overwhelmed by the whole thing. She needed a breather from all this wolf business. Time alone to think about all the consequences she faced. If she had to do it all over again, knowing what she knew now, would she have attempted to save the wolf?

She loved all animals, and if she'd known he was a wolf shifter? She would have done it anyway despite how crazy her life was bound to become.

Yet she was having second thoughts about going with Maverick to the party, of seeing all the other wolves, of facing the reality of her new worldview.

Truthfully, she didn't know what she would do. What if

meeting the pack members at the party was a total disaster tonight? Or she had to strip and shift while she was there? Or even on the way there?

CHAPTER 5

STILL SURPRISED GINA WAS TAKING THE WOLF BUSINESS so well, Maverick didn't want her to feel she didn't have any control over her life or that he was now in charge of it, but he had turned her, and it was his ultimate responsibility to watch over her. He'd listened to her showering, and though she said she'd be quick, she had taken a long, hot shower, and he knew just how she felt. After camping, he always wanted to take a long shower to clean off the sweat and grime, to feel the heat penetrating his skin too.

Then he'd heard her bringing out clothes, trying on some, starting over again. He wanted to tell her whatever she wore, everyone would love her in, but she sounded indecisive. Worse, when he figured they really needed to hit the road so he could manage a quick shower, he heard her sitting on her bed and everything was silent.

Then he heard a sob. Ah hell. He felt like he was two feet tall, and he walked across the living room where he'd been pacing, unable to stop himself because he had been anxious about arriving back in time, and knocked on her bedroom door. "Gina? Do you want to talk to me?"

"No, I..." She sobbed again.

"Can I come in?"

"I'm not...not dressed." She paused. "You might have to

help *me* figure out what to wear too. I'm really not good at it." She chuckled through tears.

He figured she wasn't concerned about what to wear to a Christmas party but how to face a bunch of wolves in a wolf pack at a Christmas party.

If the roles had been reversed with Gina and him, Maverick would probably have felt the same way as her—overwhelmed and unable to make a decision of any magnitude.

"I'm going to step outside for a moment and call to get someone else to take the reindeer to Leidolf and Cassie's ranch so we have a little more time."

"No, I'll…I'll be ready in a moment." But she didn't move from the bed, and he figured she was having an identity crisis.

"I'll be right back." He headed outside and called Josh, needing to express the concern he was feeling.

"Hey, is everything all right?" Josh asked, sounding like he already suspected trouble.

"Yeah, I took Gina home to shower and put on something dressier for the party. She's feeling unsettled about everything."

"Okay, I knew you wouldn't have called while she was visiting with you unless you were concerned about something. Are you afraid she'll want to skip the party?" Josh asked.

Maverick sighed. "Maybe."

"Look, we'll get the reindeer to the ranch. You stay with her and make sure she's all right. I'm sure it's probably just sinking in. She needs to think about it on her own without anyone influencing her. But you need to be there for her, waiting in the wings until she can sort things out."

"She's worried about her family and what to do concerning them."

"Exactly. Don't worry. We'll have lots more parties. She's under a lot of pressure. If you come late, you come late. If you don't show up, we'll understand."

"I don't want her to feel like I'm dominating her life."

"I have every faith in you. Everything will be fine."

Then they finished the call, and Maverick was glad he'd talked to Josh. His brother always felt the same as he did in so many ways and made him feel better about the situation.

But when he went to the apartment to open the door, he realized it was an automatically locking door and he was locked out in the cold without his parka!

━━━━━━

Feeling overcome, Gina thought of not going to the party. But she figured she would have fun if she could see everyone as human and not as a bunch of werewolves—just as long as she didn't shift during the festivities. And she really did like Maverick and wanted to be with him. She wiped away her tears and hurried to choose just anything so she wouldn't make Maverick wait on her any further when he needed to shower at his home and dress too. Her phone rang, but it was in the living room, and she needed to get dressed, so she ignored it for the moment. She'd call whoever it was back. Probably her brother, checking up on her again.

She donned a red sweater, red boots, and a maxi red-and-green-plaid skirt and left the bedroom, surprised when she saw Maverick wasn't there. Then she grabbed her phone and checked her messages. Maverick said he'd locked himself out of her apartment.

Oh, God. She realized his parka was lying on her couch. The poor guy.

She texted back: Coming!

She grabbed her dressier coat, his parka, and her keys, stuffing them in her coat pocket, and then hurried to open her front door. "I'm so sorry. I didn't even think about the door automatically closing on you when you left."

He pulled her into his arms and kissed her. "Are you all right?"

Tears sprang into her eyes again. Here he was freezing, and all he could think about was how she was feeling. She hugged him. "I'm terrified. But let's go so you can shower and dress."

"You're terrified that you'll shift?" he asked, getting the truck door for her, taking his parka from her, and then climbing into the cab.

"Yes, of course. And meeting a ton of wolves."

"They'll love you. That's one thing about wolf packs. No one is a stranger. And people shift. No one thinks anything of it. I know it's impossible for you to see that, but it's true."

He was right. It was impossible for her to believe that.

She glanced at his back seat. It was clean, so she supposed she could climb back there and remove her clothes if she had to. And turn into a wolf. If she turned at his house while he was showering, she'd just stay there, and he could go to the party without her if he wanted.

"What about the reindeer?"

"Josh made arrangements to take them down to the ranch. No problem. We all help out when wolves need it."

"I'm sorry."

"Don't be. Everyone understands."

They finally reached his ranch house, and they hurried inside so he could get a shower and change. When he came out, he was wearing a red sweater and plaid scarf, jeans, and cowboy boots and all smiles. He looked so Christmassy. She hadn't ever dated a guy who dressed up for anything, and she was glad she'd gone home and changed into dressier, warmer clothes for the fun, since he had too.

"You look great," she said, giving him a hug and kiss before they took off again.

He kissed her back, tonguing her mouth, showing her he wanted more. But she didn't want to come to the party super late and be the center of attention.

Though when they arrived at Leidolf and Cassie's ranch, everyone greeted them as if they were celebrities. So much for blending in with the crowd.

Thankfully, she was fine all the way there. Now if she could just get through the party without shifting. She thought the whole place looked like a magical Christmas setting: reindeer, lights, everyone dressed up, Santa, and the kids waiting in line to sit on his lap. Even the llama and her companion were there. It was just wonderful, and she would have so missed out if she hadn't come to it. If this was what her family had to look forward to, she thought they would really enjoy it. Most of all, everyone looked normal!

Looking thrilled to be with her and finally relaxing—she couldn't believe how she could smell emotions in people so much—Maverick pulled Gina into a hug and kissed her forehead. "I meant to tell you you're beautiful and I'm so lucky to be dating you."

She smiled. "Can we go to that wolf club to have dinner and dance tomorrow night?"

"The Forest Club? You bet. But for now, we can grab something to eat and dance if you'd like to—here."

"Oh, absolutely. You didn't mention that part."

Kids were playing tag and other games while Maverick and Gina went to the long tables to fill their plates with goodies. "Did you make anything for the buffet?" she asked.

"The French dip roast beef sandwiches. They were really quick to make, fifteen minutes and they were done."

"Okay, after having your delicious lobster sandwiches today, I have to try these first."

He smiled. "Thanks."

"Were you worried I wouldn't return?"

"I worried that you might be feeling anxious about everything."

"I won't deny that it's a lot to think about. But I'm not going to do this on my own." She hadn't had to think very hard about that. Even though she wasn't able to turn into a wolf yet, she could just imagine the difficulties in dealing with the process all by herself.

"Good." Maverick sounded super relieved.

She smiled at him, glad he was the person he was. She figured she could have ended up with a wolf who wasn't that into her or who was even already mated, and he would have been her mentor instead. So she was glad Maverick was the one who had turned her.

They took their plates to a table where several others were already sitting and enjoying the meal, including Josh and his mate, who made introductions.

"So glad to meet you, only I hope you're all right with what happened between you and Maverick," Brooke said.

"It was an accident and couldn't be helped. Besides, I tend to look at the positive side of things." Except for the minor meltdown she'd had when she was trying to figure out what clothes to wear. "I think as a zoologist, it will really help me to understand animals more as I study them."

"True," Brooke said. "As you get used to smelling different scents, you'll also smell the difference in their emotions."

"Oh, yes, I've already noticed that." She was glad Maverick was much more relaxed. When she'd been trying to figure out what to wear, she'd heard him pacing across her living room floor.

"You know, I could take you to the zoo, if you don't think you'd experience sensory overload. But you could smell the various animals and catalogue their scents that way. You would catch up on what we learned when we were young," Maverick said. "Maybe we can go after the new year, when the new moon is out."

"Oh, I'd like that. I've been there a number of times. But this would be so much different." Then she bit into the sandwich Maverick had made first. "Ohmigod, this is delicious."

"Thanks." He smiled.

She glanced around at the other tables filled with people eating and having fun. A man sitting at a table in another row caught her eye and made her gasp. Everyone else looked up from eating their food and glanced at Gina.

Gina felt chilled when she saw Sarge—the man who had supposedly seen the white wolf shifter in Maine—alive and most likely a wolf shifter like the rest of them here. She turned to look at Maverick. "You knew about the men in Maine. My brother's friends. The ones who were looking for Bigfoot and saw an Arctic wolf shifter. Why didn't you tell me you knew?"

Maverick instantly looked sheepish. "You might know that the one went to prison for murdering two men and a wolf killed one of the werewolf hunters. I'm sorry. They caught some of our kind, caged them, and planned to murder them after already killing the other two men. They wouldn't give up their plan to expose our kind and eliminate us all. Sarge was the only one who was willing to become one of us and give up on the notion of being a werewolf killer. I should have told you, but you've had so much to deal with already. I was waiting for a better time to bring it up," Maverick said.

"Even so, you should have told me before."

"I'm sorry. I planned to. Then we were planning to come here, and I just didn't think about it again."

"They were real people."

He sighed. "With a vendetta to kill us. And they had murdered two shifters too," he reminded her.

That worried her. That her brother and his friends might feel like the other men had. "Sarge was accepted into the pack?"

"He had to earn that respect. He was a killer like the rest of them. A self-professed Dark Angel."

"Yeah, I learned what they were calling themselves after that. My brother and his friends didn't ascribe to that. The other men even had Dark Angel tattoos."

"No longer for Sarge."

She raised a brow.

"He had to remove it," Maverick said. "We can't wear tattoos. Can you imagine anyone finding us in our wolf coat wearing a tattoo?"

"They wouldn't think you were a wolf shifter."

"Not unless they were your brother and his friends."

"Okay, gotcha. Or they'd think someone owned the wolf and tattooed him."

"Right. We try to be all wolf when we're a wolf." He glanced at her pierced ears.

She touched them. "No."

"Yeah, no jewelry."

She sighed.

"You could lose your jewelry if you suddenly had to shift, but earrings? That could be problematic."

"I'll still have piercings." It was a good thing she didn't get more than a piercing in each ear. Who would have ever thought she'd have to worry about being a wolf with pierced ears? "Anything else I should know?" Gina didn't really want to hear anything else like that.

"We can polish our nails, but in the shift, the polish is gone, at least," Brooke said. "And hair dye? It vanishes with the shift."

"Oh, my mom has been a bleached blond for years. She won't like turning white." One con for turning her mom.

"The increased longevity and faster healing abilities will most likely make up for it," Brooke said.

Then there was a commotion down below the ranch at the front gate, and Leidolf was on his phone, getting into a truck with a couple of other men and heading down there to speak to the visitors.

"I wonder what that's all about," Josh said.

"Probably someone attempting to trespass," Maverick said.

Gina got a call, pulled out her phone, and saw it was from her brother. "Yeah, Weston, what do you need?" He was probably just checking on her to make sure she was still okay.

"You. We're at the ranch where you're supposed to be at a Christmas party, and the guys and I wanted to join you. But the men at the gate said we didn't have an invitation to come to the party," Weston said.

She knew her brother had given up his search for Bigfoot to make sure she really was safe, and she appreciated him for it. She hoped he hadn't ruined their Bigfoot hunting trip by coming here, but if they had known the truth—they had found the grand prize, a whole pack of werewolves—what would they think then? "It's a by-invitation-only party."

"So invite me and Patterson and Bromley." Weston wouldn't let it go.

"Okay, fine. I'm coming. I'll meet you at the gate." Gina ended the call. How could things get so messed up? She wasn't going to ruin everyone's party because of human gate-crashers, even if Weston was her family and the guys were her friends too.

"I'll take you down there," Maverick said.

"Thanks. And no, I'm not going to try to change Leidolf's mind about letting them in," she said to Maverick as they got into his truck and headed down to the gate. "If I even could. You have enough trouble keeping your secret. This is your place, free from humans. Besides, they're only here because they want to make sure I'm safe after I took off with you."

"But they're going to wonder why we don't allow them in."

"I'll go home with them."

Maverick sighed. "I don't want that. And I hate to mention it again, but there's the possibility you could shift in front of them. Further, it's up to Leidolf and Cassie as to what they'll allow."

When they reached the gate, Maverick and Gina got out of his truck.

Leidolf was waiting to hear what was going to be said. And two other men—part of the pack, she suspected—were standing nearby, appearing to be serving as gate guards.

"Okay, I guess you guys are here to take me home." She made a move to get into her brother's truck.

"No, we were just going to join you. We didn't want to spoil the party for you." Her brother had the decency to look a little apologetic, shoving his hands in his pockets, his expression glum.

"They can stay," Leidolf said, surprising her.

But then she worried. Did Leidolf intend to turn the men as soon as they joined the party? She could envision a bunch of wolves shifting and biting the men, forget doing the gentler approach. And what if she suddenly had to shift? Then they would really want to turn them.

Leidolf headed back up to the party, and she figured he was warning everyone to be on their best behavior. She felt bad about that. She would have preferred leaving, though she had wanted to dance with Maverick, spend lots more time with him, and enjoy the festivities. She appreciated that her brother and his friends had been concerned enough to track her down, but she was also annoyed with them for barging in an all-wolf party that she had thoroughly been enjoying—up until now.

CHAPTER 6

ON THE DRIVE BACK TO THE CHRISTMAS PARTY, MAVERICK knew Leidolf had done what he'd done to try to mitigate the situation between Gina and her brother while not arousing too much suspicion of what was going on here. Before they ran into Sarge—which was Maverick's own mistake for not telling her already about him—he called Leidolf to warn him.

"You might want Sarge to return home before Weston and his friends see him and give him the third degree."

"Already done."

"Okay, good." Then they ended the call.

Leidolf was a good pack leader, and Maverick figured he'd thought about it, but better safe than sorry.

"I'm sorry they came here and messed up everyone's fun," Gina said to Maverick, sounding truly regretful.

"No one's running as wolves until later tonight. And since you haven't been able to shift yet, though I'm really surprised you haven't, I'll take you home before that, and your brother and his friends will have to leave."

"Actually, it would be better if I made him take me home so that he has to leave. I'm afraid there's no getting rid of them otherwise. Are you ready to dance?"

Yeah, he certainly was. "Absolutely."

After they parked back at the ranch house, Maverick took Gina's hand and led her to the dance floor while Gina's brother and their friends went to eat. A couple of men talked and joked with them, making them feel welcome, though they were also serving on guard duty.

Maverick hoped it wouldn't come to having to turn them tonight at the party. He didn't want Gina to see wolves attack the men. It would be the only way to turn them though, he was thinking.

But then Gina slipped her arms around Maverick's neck and pressed her lips on his chin, capturing his attention. He bent his head, and their mouths connected in a long, lingering, smoldering kiss. For the moment, he forgot about everything else but her.

She finally came up for air and looked into his eyes, her dark-brown ones glittering with sensuality. "Wow, is it just you, or is it because of my new wolf senses that your kisses are so hotly stimulating?"

"It's you and me—us. And being wolves. You are much more attuned to the subtleties of our actions and reactions, to changing scents, to even the pheromones that are telling you to go for it and not to hold back." He certainly was all for pushing for more.

"And making love?" she asked, sliding her hands up his body.

"It would be much more intense because you can sense more. At least that's what newly turned wolves tell me."

"But you can't make love."

"Not all the way unless you want to mate a wolf. Most of the time when we meet the wolf we want to be with permanently, it's decided fairly quickly, like wolves in the wild do."

"Hmm, that's good. Like other animals do after a ritual courting."

"Right."

Suddenly, another man was at Maverick's side. Ethan Masterson, a DEA agent, extended his hand to dance with Gina. Maverick really didn't want a bunch of bachelor males to dance with her, but it was important for her to discover if someone else suited her even better than him. "This is Ethan Masterson, and Ethan, I'm sure you already have heard that this is Gina." Maverick had dated other wolves, but none of them had fascinated him like she did. None had made him want to get to know them better.

He allowed Ethan to dance with Gina and stepped off the wooden platform to watch. Josh joined Maverick on the sidelines and slapped him on the back. "I think that's the hardest part—letting someone you're really developing feelings for be with other wolves who are eager to convince her that they might suit her better."

"Yeah, I don't want it to happen, but if she truly falls for another wolf, it's important she ends up with the right mate for life. It's not just about what I want. And being newly turned, she's going to have a hard time deciding, most likely." Maverick kept his eyes on her though.

Then Gina's brother came up to talk to Maverick, and Maverick introduced his brother. Josh shook his hand, a look of speculation in his hard gaze. He tended to be wary of people he didn't know in general, courtesy of his wolf nature and the criminal cases he used to deal with.

"I guess you know why we're here," Weston said, watching his sister dancing with Ethan.

"To ensure your sister is safe with me," Maverick said.

"Yeah. So why are you letting some other yahoo dance with her?" Weston asked, sounding astonished.

"He's a friend, and he knows she's with me." There was no explaining the way of a wolf pack without becoming one of them.

Weston folded his arms and shook his head. "I've never seen Gina so taken with a man right off the bat like that—to agree to go with you on a hike through the woods, then to go to your place and with you to a Christmas party afterward. She's really cautious about being with men. Any man."

"She's had trouble in the past?"

"Yeah, she has, which was why I was worried about you with her. She acts as though the two of you have a history. Do you have a history?"

"No, but she's really excited about studying the reindeer at the ranch."

"It appears to me there's a hell of a lot more to it than that."

Maverick thought Weston had good wolf instincts for being human. Josh slapped Maverick on the shoulder as if to say this problem was all his to deal with tonight. "I'm going to dance with my...uh, wife."

"Sure thing, Josh."

Josh shook Weston's hand again. "Good to meet you."

"Likewise," Weston said.

Then Josh walked off to take Brooke's hand and pulled her close, kissed her, and then hauled her off to dance.

"Where is Gina staying tonight?" Weston asked.

"At her home. We haven't talked about the logistics of her studying the reindeer at the ranch yet, but she's welcome to stay at the ranch. Josh and I both have a house, and both of us have offered for her to stay at either of them. Josh and Brooke also have a home in town, so she could stay at their ranch house on her own, if she'd like, and then she wouldn't have to commute."

Weston nodded, appearing satisfied Maverick wasn't keeping Gina at his place tonight, though Maverick wished she would stay with him.

"Excuse me, before someone else tries to fill up Gina's dance card, I need to take charge of the situation." Maverick shook Weston's hand again and then strode through the dancing couples to take over from the other wolf. Maverick smiled down at Gina and pulled her tight against his body as they danced together again.

"I saw my brother talking to you. I wondered if you might need rescuing." She tilted her head up to face Maverick, inviting a kiss. "What did he say?"

Maverick kissed her, licking her lips and deepening the kiss. She seemed to enjoy the intimacy and met him move for move.

Then he finally answered her question. "He was worried about you. Does he always worry about you when you see some guy?"

"I rarely go out. Work consumes my time. And when I do date, it's a lot more conventional. Not running off with a man I don't know into the woods to find a reindeer and then go home with him."

"Hmm," Maverick said, adjusting his body against hers for a better fit, a more intimate contact. "Wolves aren't very conventional. So until he's turned, he could see a lot of changes in the way you do things—aside from the shifting."

"I suspect so. I was afraid you had abandoned me," she said, their bodies rubbing together in a sensuous dance.

"Hell, no."

She smiled. "Good." Then she glanced at her brother and his friends, all of whom were still eating and drinking. "You know if you turn my brother or someone in the pack does, he and his friends might be really angry that shifters killed their other friend."

"I didn't have anything to do with it. I was here the whole time. It was an Arctic wolf pack that did it."

"And Leidolf?"

"He was there, yes."

She glanced back at her brother. "Knowing my brother, he wants to dance, but it seems the females are all taken."

Maverick kissed her cheek, his hands sliding down her arms in a gentle caress. "We have some single women in the pack, but just like with you, the wolves want to make their interest known, and they certainly don't want some human interloper to monopolize the she-wolf's time."

"They don't have to worry about Patterson and Bromley. They don't like to dance."

"So what's the situation with them as far as family goes?" They needed to know if turning the men was even a viable option. If they had lots of close family, it wouldn't be.

"Both the other men have nothing to do with their

families. That's why they hook up with Weston to go on these long Bigfoot hunts."

"Your brother said you've had issues with men in the past so he was surprised you seemed so eager to be with me."

She laughed. "He did, did he? Yeah, I have. For me, picking up the wrong kind of guys happens on occasion. But then I met you."

"And I bit you."

"It was to be expected when you were so frantically trying to save yourself from the frigid water."

Another wolf came up to dance with Gina, and Maverick bit back a growl. He was having a wonderful time with Gina, and he didn't want to give up another minute with her. But to look like a nice guy, he conceded and noticed then that Weston had managed to dance with a she-wolf. The other wolves were really watching the situation though. They probably realized that Leidolf wanted Gina's brother and parents turned, so they had to play nice for now.

When the dance ended, Maverick got back in with Gina—a lovely slow dance, waltzing to "It's the Most Wonderful Time of the Year"—and he was making the most of it. She was making him hot for her, and he really wished she'd stay the night with him. Then the last dance to "I'll Be Home for Christmas" ended, and he really didn't want to end it there.

Finally, Cassie said, "Thanks to everyone for coming tonight and for helping to set up the party. We had a grand time."

"Are you sure you don't want me to take you home

tonight?" Maverick asked Gina, holding her hand and caressing it lightly. "I still worry about you shifting."

"Yeah. I'm sure the other wolves will hang around to do their night thing, and my brother and his friends will stick around then too. This way they'll have to leave to take me home. And if I shift, I'll just have to bite them all."

He smiled, imagining the chaos, but losing the smile when he thought of them crashing the vehicle.

"I'll come by in the morning to see the reindeer, but tomorrow night, I want you to take me to the wolf dinner-dance club," she said.

He smiled down at her. "You have a date." He kissed her and then led her to the table where her brother and his friends were drinking punch.

Maverick shook the men's hands.

"See you around," Weston said.

Probably a hell of a lot more than Weston planned, if they ended up turning him.

───────────

"I know you're annoyed with me for coming to the party. But I was just worried about you," Weston said as he drove her home.

"You could have called." And then she wouldn't have to worry about shifting. "Can you turn the heater down?"

"The truck is cold still." Weston glanced at her. "You could have been coerced. I had to see for myself."

"You watch too many thrillers. I'm fine. I was fine. And you've met Josh, his brother. Everyone's nice, okay? Are you going to return to the park to search for Bigfoot?" She wanted to turn the conversation off the wolves, Maverick, everyone.

"Tell her. She needs to know," Bromley said.

"Tell me what?" She didn't like the anxious tone of Bromley's voice and glanced back at him in the back seat.

"We saw lots of wolf tracks at the ranch," Weston said.

"What?" Her heartbeat was pounding hard. She was glad they couldn't hear it. And she felt a flush of warmth running through her veins. Concern, not shifting, she told herself.

"When we got out of the truck to speak to the guards, we saw wolf prints all over the place. And then they were up at the ranch house. There were so many boot prints that had obliterated some of them, but we saw enough of them to know something was going on," Patterson said, agreeing with Weston.

She had to tell Maverick right away. Not that her brother and his friends could tell the world that werewolves existed at the ranch if that's where they were going with this. Maybe she was only thinking that because she was so aware of the truth.

"Okay, so the wolf dogs Maverick and his brother own probably were at the ranch." She hoped they would concede that was all there was to it.

"Maybe. Or the wolf dog we rescued from the lake wasn't a wolf dog but a werewolf. Though I hadn't figured one would look like a real wolf. But maybe that's how they keep their secret so well," Weston said. "Besides the fact we had seen the wolf prints at the campsite and they vanished and then two men walking in hiking boots were the only visible prints after that."

"Don't let on to Maverick or any of the others that we have our suspicions about the ranch, that they're werewolves," Patterson said. "Weston said you were going to the reindeer ranch to study the reindeer."

"I don't believe werewolves are real for one second. Maverick and Josh have a couple of wolf dogs. Maybe others have more of the litter at Leidolf's ranch. That's a lot more viable reason than a couple of ranches run by werewolves." She'd never thought she'd be having a conversation like this with her brother and their friends when they were right about all of it.

"All right, but just don't breathe a word of our suspicions to them," Weston said. "We don't want to get you into trouble. I know I can't convince you to not go there. Not when you love studying animals as much as you do."

She sighed in an exaggerated manner. "They're human, just like us."

None of them said anything after that, and she figured they had made up their minds already.

Then Weston drove her up to her apartment door, and she got out, trying not to look like she was in a rush. She thanked him for the ride and said goodnight.

"Call me tomorrow. Look for those wolf dogs at the reindeer ranch and send me photos," Weston said, as if he was going to prove they were real wolves and not just wolf dogs.

He would need DNA evidence to prove that. She knew he wasn't going to give up on the notion he'd found a pack of werewolves. That decided it. If she'd been able to shift, she would have bitten her brother right then and there! Maybe if he were turned, he could convince his friends there was nothing to it or they'd have to turn the whole lot of them.

She waved goodbye, unlocked her apartment door, and went inside. She'd missed seeing the lights at the reindeer ranch, to her disappointment. And being with Maverick further too. Then again, she could see the ranch all lit up tomorrow night.

She tossed her coat on a barstool and called Maverick. "Hey, I'm home. But I have some worrisome news. My brother and our friends think all of you are werewolves."

CHAPTER 7

"ARE YOU OKAY, GINA?" MAVERICK ASKED AS SHE TOLD him about the conversation she'd had with her brother and his friends. That was what he was most worried about—how she was dealing with all this. He felt like she was a new wolf out on a limb, all by herself, even though everyone in the pack would help her. But still, she was alone right now.

"I was ready to bite my brother." She sounded serious and annoyed.

He laughed. He really hadn't expected her to say that. He thought she was going to fit right in with being a wolf if she could deal with the shifting issues satisfactorily. "I'll tell Leidolf and Cassie what you learned, though they may still be enjoying a wolf run."

"I'm afraid my brother and his friends aren't going to let this go. And if they truly believe you're a werewolf, I'm sure he's going to be watching me—*us* closely. Don't be surprised if they all end up at the reindeer ranch to see your 'wolf dogs' next. And then everything's going to be just as he said it was. You and Shep are one and the same. You both can't exist at the same time."

"He'd do that too, wouldn't he?" Maverick could see where Gina was coming from.

"Yeah, he's serious about this."

"If they do a surprise visit, that will work out better for us."

"How?"

"We'll turn them then. If we invite them to anything else, the reindeer ranch, Leidolf and Cassie's ranch, what do you think would happen?" Maverick asked.

"Weston and his friends might believe it was a setup." She sighed. "So what are we going to do?"

"It's on me to take care of this. I believe we'll have to turn them at the reindeer ranch if they show up unannounced and insist on seeing the wolf dogs. But we'll have to do it when we don't have any visitors. They may only come when they feel it's safe and filled with visitors though. Let me call the pack leaders and I'll get right back to you."

"Okay, thanks, and I'm sorry for my brother and his friends getting involved in this."

"I'm the one who should be sorry since I turned you in the first place."

"You couldn't help it."

"You...don't have any urge to shift yet, do you?"

"I thought the truck's heater was on too high, but other than that, no."

"All right. Well, I'll call you back in a few minutes." When Maverick called Leidolf, he got ahold of him right away, and Maverick was glad he was back from the wolf run.

"Okay, then we'll turn the men if they show up at your ranch. You've got your ranch hands, but I'm going to send a couple more men over there to work at your ranch in case her brother and the others show up. I've spoken with Sarge. He said he knows these guys. Sarge said they were more interested in discovering a new species and getting credit for it by proving that we exist, not in killing us. They were even against calling themselves Dark Angels like the others had. So Sarge vouches for them, and he wants to help in any way that he can."

"We don't know for certain if they'll show up at the reindeer ranch, but we'll let you know if it happens." Maverick was glad Sarge wanted to assist them in this. Once they were turned, it could help that he had been a former friend of theirs.

"Sure thing."

Maverick called Gina back. The decision was out of his hands. They would take the necessary action if Weston and his friends dropped by for a visit and indicated in any way that they suspected he and his friends were wolves.

"Okay," Gina said, sounding like she knew they had no other choice.

"I'll see you in the morning."

"See you after I have breakfast."

"'Night, Gina." Then Maverick called his brother.

"I'll tell Brooke I'll be at the ranch all day to help out if you need to turn the men."

"Thanks, Josh. See you tomorrow." Maverick finally went to bed, his hands on his chest, looking up at the ceiling, not believing how one little trip into the woods looking for a reindeer could get him into so much trouble and potentially turn so many lives upside down.

Gina was so happy to have met Maverick. He was the first guy she'd really taken to and could imagine being with for the long term. She showered, went to bed, and thought about the way he had kissed her, full of intrigue and lustful need, just like she had felt about him. And dancing hot and heavy with him? She was ready for more of that tomorrow night at the Forest Club. She was excited about going to the reindeer ranch tomorrow and spending the day with him. Just working with the reindeer and him was enough to make her feel like she was living a magical year-round Christmas dream.

She turned off her bedside lamp and closed her eyes.

In the time between sleep and dreams, she felt herself getting hot, yanking her comforter and plaid flannel sheet aside, and sitting up in bed. But the heat wouldn't subside, and she had to reduce the fever rushing through her muscles and bones. She jerked her pajama top over her head, and then she pulled off her pajama bottoms. The heat pervaded and then suddenly...vanished.

She felt comfortably warm, leapt off the bed, and paced, not sure why she was doing so or what was bothering her. She walked around the apartment a few times. Maybe she'd heard a sound, something waking her.

After walking for what seemed like forever and unable to settle back down, she finally jumped into her bed, hoping that would help. She was determined to sleep and curled up against her pillow, still too warm for her flannel sheet and comforter, leaving them off for the moment.

When the day dawned that morning, Gina felt on top

of the world, stretching, and realized that under her flannel sheet and comforter, she was naked. What the…?

She tossed her covers aside and found her pajama bottoms shoved deep under the covers near the foot of the bed, probably from when she was tossing and turning in the night, and her pajama top on the floor. She frowned, not having any kind of recollection of having removed her pajamas last night.

Despite the late hour that her brother and their friends had dropped her off after the Christmas party, she had awakened early again like she had on the campout, as if this was her new morning clock—a wolf's internal wake-up time since they loved the dawn and dusk so much. She thought about the day she'd spend at the ranch again, eager to help with the chores so that the reindeer would see her as one of the ranch hands, like when she worked and studied tame animal behaviors.

She quickly dressed in jeans, a warm wool sweater, and hiking boots, and hastily made an over-easy egg, two sausage links, some cantaloupe, and a slice of toast smothered in the blackberry jam she'd made after gathering wild blackberries on a previous hike through the woods in August, when the berries were ripe. After eating wild blackberry jam, nothing tasted like it. Every bit of it she breathed in, enjoying its delicious bouquet. It was just amazing and so much wilder than she'd ever remembered. She smiled. Hopefully, her parents would appreciate some of the enhanced abilities they would have. After a good night's sleep—well, maybe not really all that good—she was feeling better about them becoming wolves like her.

She made some lavender honey tea, and when she sipped some from her Santa gnome mug, it had a delightful effect on her palate. She bit into her toast and practically hummed her pleasure. Ohmigod, it was bursting with flavor. She swore she could taste the wildness of the woods imprinted on the blackberries! Ordinary food and liquids she'd eaten and drunk in the past were embodied with so much more flavor now that she was a wolf.

She got a call and thought it would be from Maverick or her brother, but it was from her apartment manager. What did she want?

"This is Ms. Prescot. One of your neighbors said you had a big dog at your apartment."

"What? I don't have a big dog. I don't have any kind of a dog."

"He said the dog barked several times and he thought you'd never get him to shut up. You know the new policy we have. Anyone who hasn't registered their pet with us prior to signing the earlier lease agreement can't have a pet now."

Which she didn't think was fair. Maybe new renters, sure. But she hadn't agreed to that when she had signed the lease. And she didn't have a dog! It had to have been some other dog barking.

She glanced back at her bedroom. Ohmigod, had she shifted? Was that why she had pulled off her pajamas in the middle of the night?

She thought back to when she was on the campout and how she'd planned to take Shep home with her. She figured now that wouldn't have worked if he'd been a real dog. But now she worried that she would shift in the middle of the night and howl!

"Well, I don't have a dog, cat, or any other pet in my apartment. You can come and check it out at any time." But not if she shifted. This could be a total nightmare! She hadn't lied. She wouldn't have a dog in her apartment, she'd have a *wolf* there instead!

"Your neighbor recorded the dog's barking." Her manager played it back for her.

"Okay, whatever. I don't have a dog."

"We can terminate your lease agreement if you violate the lease."

"*My* lease said we could have pets. Merry Christmas." Then Gina hung up on her. So much for having a super great start to her morning. But she was rattled that she could have turned into a wolf in the night, not known about it, and barked her fool head off.

Then she called Maverick. "I'm ready for you to pick me up."

"I'm on my way."

"Bye." She figured she'd tell him when he picked her up that she might have shifted last night, unbeknownst to her.

Then she frowned. Maybe she had shifted the night before too in the tent and that's why she wasn't shifting during the day. That would be good if she could control it to a degree, as if shifting without her knowledge was having any say in it.

She quickly packed a red sweater dress and high-heeled boots to wear to the dinner-dance club and a bag with more clothes to wear for working and looking Christmassy enough for tour groups or exhibitions. She hadn't planned to stay with Maverick overnight until she had no control over the shifting, but if that had actually been her barking last night—how would she know, she didn't recognize the bark because she'd never barked before—then she didn't want to be evicted because she had a dog—wolf, whatever. And she could just imagine an irate manager coming to her apartment in the middle of the night to see her as a wolf. Then again, she guessed she was going to have to move out of her apartment anyway because the shifting issues weren't going to just go away in a month's time.

Twenty minutes later, Gina heard a knock at her door, and she opened it to see Maverick smiling at her. She seemed to brighten his day like he brightened hers. A piece of straw was caught on his worn and stained cowboy hat, and he was wearing chaps, blue jeans, cowboy boots, a plaid flannel shirt, and a vest. He looked like a real cowboy, and she really liked that look, she realized.

"I'm excited about working with you today." She pulled her suitcase toward the door, and he hurried to get it for her.

"Good. I'm looking forward to it. We've got a couple of tour groups coming in today, but also we are taking three reindeer calves to show off to three preschools in one of the communities. So you'll have your pick of what you want to participate in."

She loved how he was including her as a participant and not just an observer. "I definitely want to see the preschoolers with the calves."

"Okay, good. The preschool visits are this morning. You can also see one of the tour groups come to visit the ranch later in the afternoon."

"Great." She glanced back at her apartment complex and saw a man watching her from the window. The neighbor who had reported her for having a dog? No dog here, she wanted to say to him.

Before she climbed into the truck, Maverick gave her a hug and kiss, and she tongued him in a fun-loving way. "Very nice start to my day." With Maverick. The business with the barking dog was another matter.

She climbed into Maverick's truck while he put her bag in the back. As soon as he joined her, she asked, "Would a wolf bark just to…uh, well, bark? Don't they howl?"

He started the engine and took off. "We can bark, howl, yip, yelp, woof, whine, squeak, just all kinds of sounds, depending on the situation and our reaction to it."

She pondered that. She wondered if she'd been sitting at the door barking to be let out so she could run free.

"You've decided to stay with me tonight?"

"Uh, yes. My apartment has a new policy about not letting people have pets who didn't have them when they signed their lease agreements. But back then pets were allowed."

Maverick smiled. "So you were worried you might shift and bark in your apartment."

"No, I'm worried I did it already. Last night."

Frowning, he glanced at her. "You don't…remember?"

She sighed. "No. I don't even remember dreaming about it. But one of my neighbors said I had a dog, and it was barking last night. He even recorded it, but I wouldn't recognize the sound, of course."

"Hmm."

"So I figured rather than get an eviction notice, I'd better stay with you tonight."

"I'm glad you are, and I think you should stay longer. But if you shifted last night, maybe you shifted in the middle of the night the evening before as well."

"I considered that too."

"Okay, so that would explain why you're not shifting during the day." He took a deep breath and let it out. "I was worried about it."

"Yes, that's good, isn't it?"

"Yeah." He smiled at her. "I was afraid you would never shift."

"That's not a real possibility, is it?"

"Not that I know of, unless you hadn't been turned. But you have all your other enhanced senses, and you smell like a she-wolf, so we know you were turned."

"Okay. Oh, and I know why I love your food so much. I mean, it tastes really great, but I'm tasting more of the flavors now with being a wolf. I could be a professional taste tester."

He chuckled. "You could be."

"Of course, if it's something that isn't really great, I'm sure I'll be able to taste that too."

"Yeah, that's the downside to smelling and tasting bad things. How are you feeling about things as they are?"

"Much, much better. And about turning my parents too. I need to give them a call." Then she got a notification her mom was calling her, and she said, "Speaking of which, Mom is ringing me." She took in a deep breath and let it out. "Hi, Mom. I meant to call you last night, but I got in so late from a Christmas party, and then I was up so early this morning—"

"Weston said he was worried you were involved with a bunch of werewolves."

Gina's heart skipped a beat. Her parents humored her brother's searches for Bigfoot and werewolves, but they didn't believe in them—she didn't think. "Uh, yeah, he told me that last night."

"He said there were wolf tracks all over the ranch where you were. Is it safe?"

"Sure. They have a couple of really sweet wolf dogs."

Maverick glanced at her.

She smiled at him and patted his leg with reassurance. "Did Weston mention that I slept with one in my tent? He was well-mannered. A beautiful dog. Or wolf dog." Suddenly, Gina thought back to the fact that Maverick had slipped out of her tent while she was sleeping. That no one had unzipped it and let him out. He had been naked, and she had never even seen him! She imagined she would have screamed her head off and woken everyone in camp, but he would have shifted and turned into his wolf and fled. Her brother and their friends would have thought she'd had a nightmare! Still, she realized she would have seen Maverick in the dark when the others might not have.

"Yeah, a wolf dog," her mom said. "They can be dangerous."

Okay, so her mom hadn't suddenly begun to believe werewolves existed.

"Just don't let any of the wolf dogs bite you because you might turn into one of them," her mom joked.

It was too late to heed her mother's advice, but she knew her mom was only humoring her. "Oh, did Weston tell you I'm going to be studying the reindeer at Maverick's ranch? We'd love to have you come and have lunch or dinner sometime and see it. I think at night would be the most spectacular time because the whole ranch is lit up in Christmas lights. I haven't seen them after dark yet, but I will tonight. Maverick and I are dating, if Weston hadn't told you." Though she hadn't exactly told him that either. But she assumed he'd figure as much.

Maverick smiled at her.

"You just met him," her mother said.

"Yes, and I'm studying the reindeer at his ranch and the wild animals on their acreage that make it their home too. I'm going with Maverick to show off some reindeer calves to preschoolers this morning even, but we're having a dinner date tonight."

"Oh. Reindeer calves? I'd love to see them."

Her mom and dad loved animals as much as Gina and her brother did. "Let me ask when it would be a good time for Maverick to have you over. He's an amazing cook too."

"Like your dad."

"Yeah, just like that. Different kinds of dishes though."

"All right, just let us know when and we'll add the date to our schedule."

"Okay, perfect. I just arrived at the ranch. I'll talk to you later." She didn't want to mention that Maverick was

driving her to his home. Then the questions would begin—
questions she couldn't answer.

Maverick drove them across the cattle guard at the ranch
and pulled up next to the main house.

She got out of his truck, and he joined her, pulling her
in for another hug and then kissing her with gusto. "Wow,"
she said, coming up for air. "Now that's what I call a good
morning greeting."

"Yeah, well, we're dating, so no holding back. Thanks for
telling your parents that."

That was what this was all about. She had made it official
with her parents. Wouldn't they be surprised to learn she
was moving in with him because she figured she was bound
to get evicted over the barking wolf business if she stayed in
her apartment any further—unless it was the phase of the
new moon.

"With you, it works." With other guys she'd dated, it
wouldn't have. There was just such a draw between her and
Maverick that she'd never felt with any other man. Even
now she smelled his pheromones—and hers—coming
into play. That didn't happen when she was dancing with
Ethan or the coroner last night. She smiled at Maverick
and then got serious. "I talked to my parents about getting
together for lunch or dinner. I think dinner would be nice
so they can see the whole ranch lit up in Christmas lights.
I guess if I suddenly shift when my parents are here, that
would decide it."

"I agree. I was going to suggest having them over.
Tomorrow night then? We'll have a tour group out both

tonight and tomorrow night, but I have ranch hands who can run the show or Josh will. So no problem."

"Oh, sure, I didn't think about that. I guess with all the Christmas lights and the reindeer, it would make for a big draw."

"It does. Come on, I'm getting the calves ready to go to see the preschoolers."

"My mother said that Weston told her you all were werewolves." Gina followed him to the stable.

"Oh? I didn't think your parents believed in werewolves."

"They humor us about going on the hunts. She was worried about the wolf dogs though. I told her I slept with you, um, the wolf dog, and he was safe. Somewhat."

"Uh, yeah, after I bit you. Then I was perfectly harmless."

"You cut me with your tooth. You didn't really bite me."

"True."

Then she helped Maverick load the reindeer into the trailer. She was so excited about this. "What time do you want to have my parents over?"

"How about six? What do they love to eat?"

"Any fish. Salmon, steaks too, but fish would be great. They like just about any side dishes. I'll help you make them."

"We can do that."

Then they got into his pickup truck, and she called her parents. "Will six tomorrow night be good for dinner for you and Dad?"

"Yes, that would be perfect."

"Okay, great. We're taking the reindeer calves to the preschool now. I'll talk to you later."

"Tell Maverick thanks."

"I will." When she and her mom ended the call, she told Maverick, "My mom thanked you. And by the way, I never invite my parents to dinner to meet my boyfriends, so they know you're someone special already."

He smiled. "Good."

"But I worry about my brother if he wants to see a photo of your wolf dogs. I'm sure my parents will want to actually see them in person too, to make sure they are safe to be around."

"Well, a lot of red wolves look similar to the human eye. We could just have a couple of wolves on hand to play the part of our wolf dogs."

"Okay, and maybe make it the same two for future encounters. I mean, my brother and his friends saw you as a wolf when you were wet, not all fluffed out. They might not realize you aren't the same one as the ones we'll showcase. Not to mention, they never saw your other supposed wolf dog. So they have no idea what he looks like."

"True."

When they reached the first of the preschools, Gina was so glad she'd been given this opportunity to help with the reindeer calves. They set up a corral for the calves while the preschool teachers, children, and staff came out to visit with the reindeer. It was such a heartwarming experience, watching the three- to five-year-olds visiting with the reindeer, petting them, talking to them, giggling.

She enjoyed watching Maverick explain all about the reindeer to the boys and girls. "Both male and female reindeer grow antlers. Males are called bulls, females are cows, and the babies are calves. The two female calves have thin antlers still. They're named Silver Antlers and Jingle Bells, and the male calf is Glistening Hooves. He shed his antlers earlier this month."

Which meant that Santa's reindeer crew were all females, Gina was thinking, but she noticed Maverick didn't mention that.

After the kids had pictures with the calves—even the teachers and staff had to have theirs taken too—they went back inside while Maverick and Gina packed the calves into the trailer. They took them to two more preschools before Maverick got a text, which he shared with Gina.

"Brooke wants us to drop by with the calves and show them off at her antiques shop. She and Josh will take care of them while we grab some sandwiches at the bakery across the street for lunch. Then we'll take the calves home. We regularly set up a couple of adult reindeer at advertised times at the antiques shop to draw visitors. But Brooke wanted to have the calves there since we were so close by and then we could break for lunch."

"Oh, that sounds really nice."

When they arrived, Josh hurried out to help Maverick with the calves while Gina went inside to see Brooke. A couple of customers were perusing merchandise, and Brooke hurried to give Gina a hug. "Thanks so much for bringing the calves."

Hearing that the calves were there, the two shoppers went outside, excited to see them.

"You're so welcome. They're so cute, and it's been a lot of fun to see the kids with them."

"We might get some more traffic here. I already made an announcement about their appearance. I have a lot of fans who watch my posts to see when I have sales, new items, and reindeer visits."

"Oh, that's good," Gina said.

"And I've made friends with the owners of the bakery. Sarah and her husband, Gerry Burns, make great sandwiches, soups, cakes, cookies, and pies. You'll love their food."

Maverick came inside then and ran his hand over Gina's shoulder. "Are you ready to go to the bakery?"

"Yeah, I sure am."

They had lunch there, sitting in front of one of the large floor-to-ceiling windows, watching over the antiques store and all the rest of the shops lining the road. Several people, young and old, were going into the antiques shop or through the back gate to see the reindeer.

"The reindeer are sure a great draw," Gina said while she ate her brisket sandwich topped with caramelized beer onions and blue cheese with a side order of potato chips.

"They are. A lot of the people who come to shop in the area learn about the reindeer and then spend more time at her store and the other businesses. So they all make a lot of sales from the venture and help pay for the reindeer when they are on exhibit. We don't normally have the calves on display, just the adult reindeer." Before Maverick took another bite of his Christmas crab and avocado roll, he explained how his brother had met Brooke when one of their reindeer calves ended up in her courtyard.

Gina laughed. "I love hearing how they met."

"Yeah, almost as wild as how we met."

"Searching for reindeer, only not your own this time. Seems to be a pattern there. Brooke wasn't kidding about the food here."

"I haven't had anything at this bakery that I didn't like."

After lunch, Gina shopped at the antiques store, loving the crafts and antiques, while Maverick was outside talking to customers about the reindeer calves. Gina picked up several Christmas gnomes, delighted to add to her collection she'd grown over the years.

Then Maverick came back inside to join them.

"Did you see all the lovely handcrafted signs in the shop? They are all Maverick's handiwork, if he didn't tell you about it. Even the signs at the ranch are his work, which is why I asked him to make some for my shop." Brooke served them wassail and sugar cookies from the bakery across the street.

"Oh, I love them." Gina looked up at Maverick. "You didn't tell me you were so artistic."

She swore he blushed a little, his ears tingeing red. "It's just a hobby of mine. I usually run out of people to give them away to, so this was a great way to share the signs with others." He ran his hand over Gina's back in a soothing caress.

She liked how intimate he was all the time with her.

"They sell really well," Brooke said, "and I don't have to pay for the stock."

"Well, they're beautiful." Gina thought he could even make her a gnome sign: GNOMES LIVE HERE or some such thing.

It was finally time for Gina and Maverick to leave with the reindeer calves. They'd stayed later to give Brooke's customers more time to come to see the calves. And then they said goodbye to Josh and Brooke and drove back to the reindeer ranch.

"We have a group tour when we get home, and then we'll go to the dinner-dance club."

"That will be great. It's been such a wonderful day already."

"It has been, and I've enjoyed every minute of it with you."

"Same for me."

"You haven't had any urge to shift during the day?" he asked.

"Not yet. Not at night that I know of either. Is that unusual? What if I can only shift in my sleep?"

"Well, for everyone, it's a different experience."

At the reindeer ranch, a couple of ranch hands were taking care of a tour bus of people asking them questions about the reindeer. Gina and Maverick put the calves in one large stall, the reindeer happily worn out.

Three other calves were in the WHERE THE MAGIC BEGINS corral where kids were petting them.

She listened to the ranch hands' spiels, fascinated.

Then the tour moved to the stable, and the tour group got to see each of the reindeer, Christmas music playing overhead. Everything was already lit up, and when the sun went down, the whole ranch would be even more spectacular. She couldn't wait to see it and for her parents to visit with the reindeer to see just how magical it was.

The lights inside the barn made it look just like Christmas. Little colorful lights twinkled over each of the stalls, and each had a hand-carved sign with gilded letters displaying the name of the reindeer. Each stall was trimmed in gold, and the whole barn was painted red inside, including the siding and stall gates. Up above, the ceiling was blue, covered in painted stars and the full moon.

She looked up at it, thinking she should be shifting out of control by now.

Everyone coming into the barn was in awe. She loved it. What a fun place for visitors and how neat it would be to work here on a regular basis—with Maverick.

After the tour group ate a variety of cinnamon, chocolate, and Christmas cookies, drank hot cocoa topped with whipped cream, and took pictures with the adult reindeer and calves, they left.

"We'll have another tour group after sunset, but we'll see the Christmas lights even better when we return," Maverick said.

"I look forward to it. I'm going to grab the dress I brought to wear to the club and change."

"I'm going to change too."

When they reached the house, they went inside and peeled off their parkas. "I'll show you to your suite. My brother and I both had master bedrooms with baths when we built the house and a couple of extra guest bedrooms to spare."

Then they each changed into their dressier clothes, her in the guest room and him in his master bedroom. They finally met in the living room. He smiled at her. "Beautiful."

"I could say the same about you." She frowned then, having forgotten all about her brother and hoping he hadn't caused trouble for the ranch hands while she and Maverick had been in town. "My brother didn't show up here while we were at the schools, did he?"

"No. The ranch hands were aware of the problem, and Leidolf sent extra ranch hands just in case we had issues. We have two dedicated hands who will serve as 'wolf dogs' at a moment's notice."

"Okay, good. Maybe Weston and his friends will quit believing that werewolves run this ranch and Leidolf and Cassie's."

"Do you think they will?" he asked, helping her into her dressier coat.

"No. Once they believe something, they'll exhaust all avenues to explore the notion."

"Then we'll remain on guard. Are you ready to go?"

"I sure am."

They drove off in his pickup, though she wanted to ride in his Corvette—then she'd feel like a '50s-era princess being escorted to the ball. They finally arrived at Forest Club, which lived up to its name. She studied the building covered in a thatched roof, giant maples towering over the parking lot at irregular intervals making it appear like a dwelling in a forest, the whole surrounding area forested.

"I love it already," she said.

"It's a real hot spot for wolves." He guided her into the club, where dark oak tables set under fake trees covered in real bark and mossy-green chairs and booths made her feel as though she was in a real forest.

Each of the booths had tree-bark walls separating it from the other booths for privacy, and the tables were also secluded from each other by a stand of trees or massive tree trunks, though most had a view of the open dance floor.

"This is really fun."

The club's ceiling was painted black as night, and sparkling white lights made it appear as though the stars were overhead. The music beat a rhythm made for dancing, and she was ready. She saw several of the wolves she'd seen at the Christmas party, and she really was feeling like she was part of the pack.

A waitress seated them, gave them menus, smiled, and left the table so they could choose what they wanted for dinner.

"She's a wolf," Gina said, looking at the menu.

"Right. The whole staff is. Everyone who dines and dances here is a wolf. The restaurant is known for its excellent steaks," Maverick said.

"Okay, then I'll get the petite filet."

"I'm going to get the rib eye. Would you like a cocktail or wine?"

"I think I'll get a cocktail after we dance and when our meals are served."

"That sounds good." Then the waitress returned, and Maverick ordered their meals and waters, then reached out his hand to Gina, and escorted her to the dance floor.

She loved dancing with Maverick. He was so sexy. And this time, no one seemed to be coming up to dance with her, and she was glad for that. Not that she didn't want to meet other wolves, but she wanted to be with Maverick like this, bodies pressed together, no one else intruding on their time. Lost to each other. Whispered words. Sweet and sizzling kisses. She could dance with him like this all night long.

But after four dances, they saw their meals delivered to their table, and she realized just how hungry she was.

"Let's go eat so we can dance some more afterward," he said.

"Yes, I'm hungry." If she had shifted last night and had gotten it out of her system until she went to bed tonight, she was glad for it because she wasn't feeling any urge to do so. And she wanted to do a whole lot more dancing with Maverick tonight.

CHAPTER 8

MAVERICK WAS HAVING A GREAT TIME WITH GINA, GLAD SHE liked to dance with him just as much as he enjoyed dancing with her, but man, their pheromones were on fire. He motioned to the waitress. Gina ordered a marzipan dream cocktail, and the description sounded so good—amaretto, vanilla, and bourbon, drizzled with chocolate syrup, and dark-chocolate sprinkles floating on the foamy top—he decided to order one for himself.

The waitress said, "Be right back with them."

"Do humans ever come here?" Gina asked, cutting into her steak.

"You have to have a reservation, and the way that works, the place is only open by word of mouth, no online reservation numbers available."

"Wow, okay."

Then their cocktails were served, and Gina took a sip of hers. "This is delicious. I wondered why no one else is asking me to dance."

He smiled. "We're on a date. At the Christmas party, the bachelor males figured it was a safe bet I'd be willing to let them dance with you. But on a date?" He shook his head and then took a sip of his cocktail. "Unless of course you want to dance with someone else."

She smiled. "No way. You have way hotter wolf moves than any guy I've ever danced with."

He laughed. "I feel the same way about you."

"You mean if any woman tried to steal you away from me—"

He patted her hand. "You're stuck with me."

"Good thing. This drink is totally dreamy."

He agreed. "Yeah, that was a super choice."

He was glad she was staying with him after this, since he worried she would have more trouble with shifting. He couldn't believe she'd shifted last night, didn't recall anything about it, and had been barking like a dog, getting herself in trouble with her neighbors and her apartment manager. He was concerned about making a good impression on her parents tomorrow night too. He seemed to be doing everything right with Gina so far though, and for that, he was grateful.

Then they heard a commotion near the entrance to the club.

He could see three men and two women had arrived at the club, and the hostess said, "I'm sorry, you have to have a reservation. We don't have any tables available."

The music was still in full swing, and the wolves were still dancing with each other.

The newcomers' voices elevated.

"We can pay," one man said.

"I'm sorry. We're booked. You have to call ahead for reservations," the hostess insisted.

"How much is it going to take to get a damn seat here?" one of the human males asked, pulling out a credit card.

He appeared to be used to getting his way. He wouldn't get his way here.

"We're full," the manager said, coming to the hostess's rescue.

"What about that table?" the man persisted, pointing to an empty table.

"It's reserved," the manager said.

Then another couple arrived, and Maverick smiled to see it was Leidolf and Cassie. A table was always set aside for them in recognition of their pack leader status.

"Is there some trouble here?" Leidolf asked, smelling the tension in the air like the rest of the wolves could and knowing the humans were causing problems.

The five humans glowered at Leidolf, the man in charge of the group staring him down. Leidolf was a total alpha wolf, and he waited for the man to say anything further before he did anything.

"Okay"—the man turned to the manager, losing the staredown with Leidolf—"so I'll make reservations." He gave Leidolf a cutting glare, acting as though Leidolf couldn't be as important as he was.

"We're booked. You'll have to make a reservation online. We don't do that here."

Waiting for this to be resolved, Leidolf and Cassie stood their ground. Everyone in the club was tense; several of the men, including Maverick, were ready to leave their seats quickly to force the humans out of the club if they needed to.

The guy finally conceded. "Fine. We'll make a reservation. Online." Under his breath as he and the others in his party turned to leave, he muttered, "And leave a bad review for this place."

Before they exited the club, they gave Leidolf and the manager one last cutting glare and finally left.

Cheers went up, amusing Maverick. Gina smiled. "Wow, that was intense."

"Yeah, Leidolf allowed Weston and your friends to come to the Christmas party last night because they're your brother and friends, you're one of us, and we'll probably end up turning them, but we don't have to allow non-wolf types into one of our wolf-only establishments."

"What about them leaving a bad review for the restaurant?"

"It's not listed anywhere online. Everyone knows about the restaurant by word of mouth. The wolves don't share about the place with humans. They can't make a reservation because only the wolves have the number."

Gina smiled. "Very clever."

"Occasionally, we get passersby who see the place, the crowd of vehicles, and drop in like that to check it out. It only happens a couple of times a year or else they'd have a bouncer checking patrons at the entrance."

"Well, this is a fun place, and the steaks and the rest of the food are fantastic." She took another sip of her cocktail. "And this is divine."

Which was just why he'd brought her here.

Once they finished dinner and their cocktails, they headed back to the dance floor.

She was an accomplished dancer, and she stirred his loins on the dance floor like no one else had ever done. This had to be one of his favorite activities with her, and he fully intended to have more dance nights with her. Though he enjoyed being with her while doing just about anything.

At the reindeer shows, she'd been letting him do all the talking, but he hoped she'd like to share about the reindeers too when she felt more comfortable doing so.

But right at this moment, this was what he wanted, her in his arms, their bodies snug, her arms wrapped around his neck, moving to another nice, slow dance. They ended up dancing until the club closed for the night, and as late as it was, he was really glad she was staying at his place.

They said goodnight to several couples in the parking lot, including Leidolf and Cassie, and then Maverick and Gina got into his truck.

When they arrived home, she said, "I'm exhausted. Late night, late to bed last night, rising really early this morning, and the same the morning and night before. Who knows what I was really doing last evening all night long."

He wanted to sleep with her, but he figured they wouldn't sleep much if she was in bed with him, and she needed her rest. "Then I'll kiss you good night, and in the morning, we'll have breakfast before we do another show."

"Okay, that sounds good." She wrapped her arms around Maverick and hugged him close, her delectable body making his stir into action again. She kissed him with hot-blooded passion, and he kissed her and hugged her back with the same desire, wanting in the worst way to take her to bed with him.

But then they ended the kiss, and he knew this was only the very beginning for them. At least he certainly hoped so.

When he retired to his bedroom, he texted his brother:

Have you ever heard of anyone who doesn't shift for three days, except shifting in their sleep during the night?

If she did it tonight, he wanted to know about it as soon as it happened.

Josh texted: That's a new one on me.

That's just what Maverick was worried about.

─────────────

Seven days until Christmas, Gina was thinking, as she took a quick shower, dried off, and then pulled on her red-and-green-striped pajamas and slipped into bed. She loved the guest bedroom, Josh's master bedroom suite, all browns and tans and touches of aqua. The Western theme with the rugged oak furniture, the pictures of reindeer in the field, the Cascade Mountain range serving as a backdrop. The reindeer flannel sheets kept her warm, and the embroidered patchwork quilt was really pretty. She turned off her bedside lamp and then closed her eyes. For a long time, she lay awake, wanting to feel the shift coming on, if it happened, trying to sense any change in her body temperature. The last thought she had before she fell asleep was hoping her parents liked Maverick as much as she did when they came to dinner.

And then the next thing she knew she was burning up, wishing the heater would be more uniform and not so up and down. She'd been comfortable before this, and she couldn't help it, but tossing the covers aside didn't make any difference. She was still burning up. And then she started stripping out of her pajamas.

Suddenly, she was comfortable again.

When she woke that morning, she stared at her bare shoulders, realized her body was naked, and she couldn't believe it. She pulled the covers aside and got out of bed, and this time she looked at the sheets. Telltale wolf fur was clinging to the flannel bottom sheet. Unless another wolf had slept on them and the washing machine hadn't removed the fur, that was hers. She couldn't imagine she was shifting at night and didn't remember a thing about it.

She smelled breakfast cooking—ham, hash brown potatoes, and eggs. She dressed and then headed out of the bedroom to join Maverick.

He smiled at her, and she went into the kitchen and gave him a hug. "Did you miss me?" he asked.

"I think I shouldn't have slept alone."

"Did you…" He hesitated and frowned. "Did you shift?"

"I think so. Unless someone else left wolf fur in the bed."

"The sheets have been cleaned since the last person used them. And he wouldn't have been in the bed in his wolf coat."

"Sorry. I shouldn't have been either. And you're right. I only smelled me on the sheets."

"Well, hot damn. That's good news then. It means you most likely won't shift again until late tonight since we got in so late this morning." Then he dished up their breakfast and frowned again. "Did you sleep at all? I tried to stay awake in case I could hear you shifting. I would have heard you bark or howl. I guess you didn't."

"If I did, it sure didn't wake me either. Just like the last time at my apartment."

He made her a cup of peppermint tea. "At least your bedroom door was closed so you couldn't go running off."

"Yeah, but what if I had gone to your bedroom and joined you in bed?"

"Now that would have been welcome."

"If I'd been a wolf?" She couldn't believe he would be okay with that.

"Yeah, as either would be great."

"Okay, good to know." She wasn't sure she would be comfortable joining him in bed as a wolf. "Breakfast is outstanding." She took another sip of her tea.

"Thanks. I should have asked you what you wanted to eat, but we got in so late last night, I didn't think about it."

"Well, it's delicious. So what are we doing today?"

Maverick and Gina fed the reindeer after breakfast. She was petting them, getting to know them, and he was glad she was having such a great time with them. They took over the morning reindeer tour after that. She even began talking about the reindeer to the tour group as if she'd always worked with them.

While she was talking, he watched the easy way she handled questions, leaning against the corral fence, looking so relaxed, using her hands to help tell her story, reaching over to pet the reindeer. She even was talking to the visitors about the llama. Gina was so pretty; her dark hair tossed in the breeze, and he wanted to run his hands through it and kiss her smiling lips. She laughed with joy when some of the visitors joked with her. Maverick couldn't stop thinking about how he wanted to convince her to join him in his bed tonight. Not to make love, unless she wanted to. He was definitely up for that. But because he really wanted to see her shift, and at this rate, if she didn't bark or howl to alert him, he didn't think he'd ever witness her change.

They worked all the rest of the morning, taking a break for a light lunch, and she said, "I love my parents, but I'm so tired after all the short nights of sleep, I hope I don't fall asleep during dinner tonight."

He chuckled. "I'll make the meal tonight. You can just relax and talk to your parents and have a Christmas cocktail."

"No way. If I relax and combine that with a cocktail, I'd just pass out."

He smiled. "Do you want to take a nap this afternoon while I go out and finish some work?"

"No. I'm having way too much fun. I just hope we don't have too late of a night again."

Then they headed back outside, and she began cataloging the reindeer's and llama's behavior on her notebook—watching the animals as they interacted with each other and with the ranch hands and visitors, measuring the stalls, and analyzing their feed. He admired her determination to keep on trucking, no matter how tired she was, especially since she really didn't have to do so.

Even so, he told Randall to handle things earlier than he normally would have so they could go inside, clean up, and get ready for her parents. Later, they went inside to shower and dress for her parents' arrival. He and Gina met in the living room, and he cupped her face and kissed her. "I loved watching you speak to the tour group, answering their questions, petting the animals."

"Thanks." She slipped her arms around his waist and kissed him more, their tongues connecting, tasting, teasing. "I love seeing you work with the reindeer, wearing your sexy cowboy clothes and directing your wolfish smiles at me. It makes me want to just drop everything I'm doing and haul you right to bed. Speaking of which, if I do get in bed with you tonight, are you sure you wouldn't have any issues with me if I suddenly turn into a wolf?"

Then he realized that was what she was really worried about. "I would be honored with your presence, no matter what form you're in. Seriously."

"Okay, good." Then she glanced at the oven clock. "They should be here soon."

They heard a car pull up outside.

"It's amazing how I can hear vehicle engines now and can recognize them the next time I hear them." She went to the door. "Yep, it's them." She took a deep breath and exhaled and opened the door. "Mom, Dad, don't you just love the ranch?"

"Oh, my, yes," her mom said, giving her a hug.

Then she gave her dad a hug and took their coats. "Mom, Dad, this is Maverick Wilding, and Maverick, this is my mom, Faye Hutton, and my dad, Reggie Hutton."

Maverick greeted them, shaking Gina's dad's hand, and

then her mom gave Maverick a hug. He hadn't expected it but appreciated it. "What would you like to drink? How about caramel white Russians?"

"Yes," Faye said.

"Oh, that sounds good. I'll help you make them," Gina said.

"Sounds good to me," Reggie said. "So how many acres do you have out here?"

"Four thousand," Maverick said, starting on the drinks.

"That's a nice spread," Reggie said.

"The place is beautifully lit up in Christmas lights," Faye said. "It's just magical."

"Yeah, and you have a beautiful home," Reggie said.

"Thanks, we love Christmas, and we do well enough. We're going to have salmon, asparagus spears, and potatoes for dinner if that sounds fine to you all?"

"Yeah, just what we love," Faye said.

Brooke had picked up the salmon earlier that day for them so it would be fresh. He just hoped they cooked it up perfectly, her parents enjoyed the meal, and he didn't make any major mistakes. He'd never considered he might be trying to impress human parents and show them that he was just who their daughter should date and even mate at some future time.

CHAPTER 9

GINA HAD MIXED FEELINGS ABOUT HER PARENTS COMING here for dinner. She knew Maverick didn't plan to turn them tonight, but she figured it was inevitable, and she normally didn't keep secrets from her parents—especially secrets of this magnitude that would affect them so drastically.

She truly hoped her parents would like Maverick and that he would like them. She was used to going to the movies with them on occasion, even taking trips with them and eating out, plus taking shopping trips with her mother. She didn't want to miss out on all that.

Her mom and dad were dressed to impress, and so was Maverick. She appreciated that he had dressed up for her parents. Her previous boyfriends wouldn't have for any gathering, no matter what it was.

"It really is a beautiful ranch," her mom said, and Gina knew right away she really did like it. "I didn't expect it to be so whimsical."

"Yeah, everything here looks first class," her dad said.

Okay, they already accepted him, probably because of the beautiful ranch and home.

"You have a couple of other homes out here?" her dad said, as Maverick served them caramel white Russians.

"Our ranch manager has a place, and my brother and

sister-in-law have a home here. Josh and Brooke often stay in town in their house behind the antiques shop though."

"Oh, I love antiques stores." Her mom took a sip of her drink. "This is so good."

"I'll have to take you there," Gina said. "Brooke has the cutest things."

"Weston said you have a couple of wolf dogs," her dad said.

"They're staying with Josh and Brooke at their home in Portland," Maverick said.

Nice save. Smiling at Maverick, she figured he didn't want to have to text the ranch hands so they would hurry up and shift and show themselves in their wolf halves at this point.

"The ranch is owned jointly by you and your brother?" her dad asked.

Gina figured that her dad wanted to know how well off Maverick was or if the holdings belonged to both brothers and he wasn't as well off as he appeared.

"We both own it, though I run it because Josh works most of the time with Brooke at her store. Before that, Josh had been a police detective with the Portland Police Bureau, and then he retired. Brooke actually inherited more acreage adjoining our property, and she has a home on that that she rents out."

"Oh, Dad, you have to see Maverick's car," Gina said. "It's beautiful. A classic '57 Corvette."

Her dad instantly perked up. She knew that would get his attention.

"I'll show it to you after we start the dinner," Maverick said.

Then he and Gina started the asparagus and fondant potatoes in a frying pan with olive oil. She cut the potatoes into cylinders, browned them on both ends along with the asparagus, and then slowly roasted them in the oven with butter, veggie broth, and rosemary.

"That will take about thirty minutes. Do you want to take a walk through the stable and meet the reindeer and see my Corvette in the garage?" Maverick asked.

"Yeah," her dad said. "That would be great."

"I sure do," her mom said.

"You'll love the llama too. Gina and I found a reindeer and the llama together in the woods at the state park," Maverick said.

"Oh, no. They were all right though?" Faye asked.

"Yes. The vet checked them over, and both were in great health."

Then they headed outside, and Maverick led them to the stable where all the reindeer were bedded down for the night. The night tour group was just getting into their bus to leave. Her mom and dad were smiling at all the fancy carved signs, the lights, the reindeer and calves, and even the llama in the stall with the reindeer, happily lying down together like best friends.

"Oh, they're so cute," her mom said.

They finally went to see the classic Ford truck and then the Corvette. Her dad had to sit in the car and place his hands on the steering wheel. He looked like he was in heaven.

"Sometime, I'll let you drive it," Maverick said.

"That would be great," her dad said, looking like a kid in

a toy shop, his bright smile contagious. Then her dad got out of the car, and her mom got behind the steering wheel. "This is really nice."

"The same goes for you—driving the car," Maverick said to Faye.

Gina glanced up at him, and he wrapped his arm around her shoulders and smiled down at her. "You too."

Then Gina's dad and Maverick started the salmon steaks on the grill under the patio cover.

"Come on, Mom, we'll finish the rest of the meal." Gina and her mom went inside.

"Oh, Gina, honey, I like this new boyfriend of yours."

"So do I. He's a great dancer." And kisser! And he had a super-hot body. She loved how he was with animals, loving them just like she did. "A super cook too."

"He's a dreamboat. Your dad approves of him just because of his car."

Gina laughed. "Yeah, I figured he'd love that." But what would they think if they knew he was a wolf shifter? And he and his pack planned to turn her family?

She so wanted to talk to her mom about wolf shifters, to tell her they were real and all the good things about them. She knew she couldn't, but she really, really wanted to. If she did, then what? Her mom wouldn't believe her. At least Gina figured she wouldn't.

Then the men came in with the salmon steaks, and Gina served up the potatoes and asparagus. Once everyone had glasses of water and a wine glass filled with pinot noir, they took their seats to eat dinner.

"So how do your wolf dogs get along with everyone? And are there more than just the two?" her dad asked, his dark brows arched, and he was looking like a protective father.

Gina wanted to groan out loud. If her brother hadn't crashed the Christmas party, none of this would have come up.

"We took in two wolf dogs that the owner swore didn't have wolf genes, and some of our friends took in some others of the same litter. But they're good dogs. They're good with the reindeer and with the horses and cattle on the other ranch. Sometimes they can be a little stubborn, but they get along great with each other, and they do really mind us when we give them commands. They grew up with the reindeer herd and the horses." Maverick didn't sound in the least bit perturbed that her dad was questioning him about it further, for which Gina was glad.

"Well, you know your brother, Gina. He was so excited—and concerned—that you were associating with a pack of werewolves that when we told him we were invited for dinner, he insisted we ask about the wolf dogs. Weston said he always knew you didn't believe in Bigfoot or anything but went along on the hunts because you enjoyed hiking with him and his friends so much. So he worried you could be in the middle of a pack of werewolves and not even realize it," her mother said.

Gina smiled, but she felt so insincere. She patted Maverick's shoulder. "Maverick is the best thing that's ever happened to me. So if he's a werewolf, I'm glad to know him."

Her parents laughed and went on to other topics to Gina's relief.

After enjoying the spectacular lighting display one last time—her mom even taking a few phone pictures as it illuminated the ranch houses, stables, corrals, and Christmas tree farm—Gina's parents finally said their good-nights and left.

"Sorry about all the interrogation about the wolf dogs."

"No problem. I think they liked me well enough." Maverick sighed with relief.

She smiled at him. Before now, she wouldn't have even heard his nonverbal response. "You passed my parents' inspection with flying colors. With my dad, it was the offer of allowing him to drive your car. He'll take you up on it, too."

Maverick laughed. "I'd be happy to loan it to both of them for some test drives. Anything that will help them adjust to the changes in their lives once we have to turn them, the better. Now the question is: my bed or your own for the night?"

"I don't know. I need to check out how nice your bed is first." She smiled up at him and loved how his expression instantly brightened.

━━━━━━━

"Hopefully, my bed meets with your expectations." Maverick genuinely liked Gina's parents, and he was so glad he'd met them. They seemed to really like him, but would that all change if the pack turned them? He was also thrilled Gina wanted to stay with him in his bed tonight. "Don't worry about the business with werewolves and all. Your parents don't believe in them. I got the impression they were amused by your brother's claim that I'm part of a werewolf pack."

"I agree."

He set her bag on a chair in the bedroom as she checked out the bed first, plopping down on her butt in an exaggerated way. She was such a fun person to be with.

Then she lay down and sighed. "Okay, this is perfectly acceptable."

He was glad, though he suspected she would have stayed with him even if it hadn't been perfect.

She got up from the bed. "I need to take a shower."

"Bathroom is in there."

She took his hand and led him in there, surprising him. "Keep me company?"

He sure would and didn't have to be asked twice to do so. He pulled off her sweater, revealing her red-lace bra and creamy breasts. Then he leaned down and kissed the swell of her breasts, his hands stroking her smooth shoulders, before he moved his mouth to hers and kissed her on the lips. They were pliant, eager to ramp up the energy and passion already igniting between them.

Kissing his mouth back, she slid her hands from his shoulders and ran them over his chest, their pheromones even now telling them they were on the right track. Their hearts were thundering, their blood heating as he reached behind her and unfastened her bra, sliding the straps down her arms and dropping it on top of her sweater.

But then it was her turn, and she began to unbutton his plaid shirt, one torturously slow button at a time, twining her tongue with his, continuing to kiss him in a lingering and methodical way. His boxer briefs were already stretching with his rigid erection, and he wanted her to hurry up with his shirt so he could ditch his pants and boxer briefs and hit the shower with her.

She was in no rush, making him fight the urge to plead with her to hurry it up or he'd take over from her to finish unbuttoning his shirt instead.

"I love your buttons," she whispered against his mouth, the seductive vixen.

He wished he'd worn a pullover shirt instead. "I'm glad you were only wearing a sweater. Well, and a bra."

He ran his hands over her breasts, enjoying the plump feel of them in his hands, the nipples peaking against his palms, rigid, feeling sexy against his skin. Her lips were lightly moist, sinful, and she was still working on his buttons! She slipped her hand under his partially unbuttoned shirt to run her fingers over his pecs and smiled against his mouth.

He couldn't wait any longer and began to unbuckle his belt. She leaned down and kissed his chest. And then she finished unfastening his shirt buttons and slipped his shirt off his shoulders. She began kissing his shoulders, her lips like satin on his skin, and he stroked her bare shoulders and then kissed them with reverence. Every inch of her was delectable.

He moved his fingers down to unfasten her jeans and then unzipped them and slid his hand down her panties, feeling the wetness between her legs. He smiled. She was as ready for him as he was for her.

He had never expected to turn a woman into a wolf and feel the incredibly strong desire he had for her. Not just wanting sex with her, but something deeper emotionally.

He pulled her jeans down just as she seized his waistband and began to pull his pants down too, like they were conducting a synchronized, intimate dance move. He kicked his off and pulled hers the rest of the way down, and then he slipped her socks off her feet before yanking his own off.

She reached into the glassed-in shower to turn on the water, and he pressed his frontside to her backside, rubbing his engorged cock, still confined in his boxer briefs, against her, his hands on her hips as she gyrated against him. He groaned, not expecting her seductive move.

He slid his hands up her belly to her breasts and gave them a gentle squeeze, kissing her shoulder at the same time, and she shivered. Then he slid one hand down her tummy and under her waistband, finding her mons, and began stroking her clit.

She moaned, and he pulled her hair aside and licked her neck. She was soft and warm, and her heart beat like crazy. So did his, the musky smell of her sex sending him into overdrive.

Hot, hot, hot, and the water was steaming things up. He slid her panties down, and she kicked them aside. He was going to yank down his boxer briefs, but she turned and pulled them down, his cock springing free, and she smiled in appreciation. Then he removed his boxer briefs the rest of the way, and he joined her in the shower, shutting the glass door, the steam enveloping them.

They were kissing again, the water running down their bodies while they rubbed against each other, unable to get enough. This was so nice, hot, riveting, and they were both totally primed.

He cupped her bottom, moved between her legs, and rubbed his cock against her, wanting to go all the way, but he couldn't. *They* couldn't. Still, the raging desire was there, and he desperately wanted to fill her all the way. He'd never felt that way about a she-wolf he'd dated.

Gina was truly special. She ran her hands over his rigid nipples with just her palms and then leaned down and kissed them, licking them, teasing them with a gentle pull of her lips.

Then she slid her hands over his abs and his pecs, kissing him at the same time, as if memorizing all of him in this moment.

He was trying to control his growing need to mate with her and claim her for his own. He was sure no other she-wolf would do. But he also knew she needed time to come to that conclusion—if she did—about him too.

Then he slid his hand to her mound, found her clit, and began to stroke. This would have to do for now. Though he desperately wanted more, he would hold off for as long as it took for her to want him too. She lifted her leg around the back of his, rubbing her foot against his leg, opening herself to him for better access. Her hands gripped his arms as if she couldn't stand on her own because he had taken her under his spell to such an extent.

Good, because she had certainly done that to him.

She arched her back, and he leaned forward to kiss her, slip his tongue into her mouth, continuing to stroke her until she was barely breathing. Her fingers were digging into his arms, and then she came, crying out, "Oh, yeah, Maverick."

And then she smiled up at him, kissed his mouth with passion and possession, her arms wrapping around his neck, her feet both planted on the shower floor, but she was rubbing against his cock again, teasing, tantalizing him.

God, this was good with her like this. He was about to grab the bodywash when she pushed him gently back against the shower wall and began to kiss him, her hand on his shoulder, pinning him to the wall, and her free hand on his cock, stroking him. Hell, yeah, he was going to make her his mate. He would do anything to make her want that to happen.

Maverick was sooo hot. Divine, sexy, loving, and Gina couldn't believe how he put her needs ahead of his own. She'd never had a man do that with her before, and she really thought the world of him for it. She was still thrumming with blissful climax as she kissed him to kingdom come and stroked his erection. She loved smelling the scent of him, of the water and the musky smell of their sex, of his manly and wolfish fragrance. She reveled in hearing his heartbeat pounding like hers was, the sex so much more real, definitive. All her enhanced senses reeled from the overload. It was wonderful. Maverick hadn't told her about that part of the wolf equation.

His hands combed through her hair, making her feel cherished so she wasn't forgotten. No, not in the least as his tongue lingered on hers. Then he pumped himself against her hand, and she took that as a cue that he was about to come, to keep stroking faster, firmer. And then he let out a howl and released. She smiled, and he pulled her close and rubbed his body against hers, as if he was marking his scent all over her, just like she was doing the same with hers on him.

Then he reached behind her to the shower shelf and pulled a bottle of bodywash off it, poured some in his hand, and then gave her some. He put the bottle back on the shelf, and they began soaping each other up. Now this was pure pleasure too.

They rubbed their soapy bodies against each other, laughing, smiling, kissing. This was so much fun. Then they used some shampoo, and she lathered up his hair, and he did the same with hers. When he did it to her hair, it felt so inti-mate, and she loved it.

Before the water turned cold, they began rinsing each other off with the showerhead, but when he put it between her legs to rinse her off, she jumped and laughed. "You are so bad."

He laughed. Then she got him back. They finally grabbed a couple of towels and dried each other off. Once done, she used her hair dryer to blow-dry his hair, and then he dried hers. After they were finished, they raced each other to the bed, the air in the room cool, the perfect temperature for sleeping close and cuddling. They dove under the covers and settled in together, snuggling, sighing, kissing.

"I thought I'd never say this, but I'm glad I fell in the lake and you tried to save me."

She smiled up at him. "I'm glad you saved me before I fell in the lake! You didn't tell me that as a wolf I'd have the hots for you to this degree."

"I didn't know that you would. I only knew that I did."

And then they closed their eyes, but she couldn't stop thinking about all this. About being a wolf, being with him, wanting more. Was it all just so new to her that she really didn't know what she wanted? That any wolf would make her feel this way because of her extraordinary senses now? She had to be realistic about this and give them a chance to really get to know each other. So why was she already wanting to say "I do" in a wolf mate sort of way?

———

It took Maverick forever to get to sleep last night. He had been so wrapped up in enjoying the intimacy with Gina he hadn't wanted it to end. He knew he had to encourage her to see other wolves if she wanted to. Before she came along, he had seen other wolves. She needed that too so that she knew if he or some other wolf was the right one for her. But he was so lost in his feelings for her, he didn't want to give her up to anyone. He needed to talk to his brother about it, to get someone else's objective opinion. He was afraid he was way too biased when he thought of her seeing anyone else.

The light had already dawned, and being cuddled against

her was just too good to give up. He could have stayed in bed all day with her, if he didn't have a job to do.

But he was worried about her as far as this business of her turning into a wolf soon. Being so newly turned, Gina could turn into a wolf at a moment's notice. He was glad she had stayed with him overnight because of it. Not to mention how much he enjoyed her company—beyond the sex play they'd had.

She stirred and looked up at him and smiled. "Waking up with a wolf is a new experience for me. The last time we were together—you were a wolf in my tent one moment, and then you abandoned me."

He chuckled. "For good reason. You intended to take me home with you, which I appreciated, but I knew my brother was trying to find me."

"Oh, he might have come upon the camp and worried we had hurt you."

"Exactly. That's why I had to take off as soon as everyone was asleep, to find my brother and assure him I was all right. Are you ready to get up and have breakfast?"

"Oh, yeah. I'll make it." She hurried to get out of bed and dress.

He climbed off the mattress and grabbed some clothes out of his closet. He didn't bring up the issue of the moon again, but she hadn't shifted last night, and he was concerned about it. He didn't want to worry her. In the event she started to feel strangely, he'd have to hurry her to the ranch house safely before anyone saw her though.

"I feel fine," she said as they reached the kitchen.

He made coffee and heated water for her tea. "Okay, well, if you feel like your muscles are warming and your whole body is feeling like it needs to change, let me know and I'll get you back to the house pronto."

"Right. You've told me that already." She grilled up some veggies—mushrooms, onions, and bell peppers—while he chopped up ham and cheese. They made omelets filled with the mixture of veggies and ham and cheese and then sat down to eat them.

"Sorry." He didn't want to keep reminding her, but he had trouble not mentioning it. He also knew she said she'd make breakfast, but he enjoyed cooking meals with her, and she seemed to like that he did.

"I appreciate that you are worried about me. And I'm trying not to overthink it too much because it might not happen, and I don't want to miss out on enjoying each and every day."

He was glad she was looking at it that way, not dreading the shift—like he was. How would she feel the first time it happened and she was fully awake? Would she be all right with it? Freak out? He had no idea, and she wouldn't either until it happened—when she was fully awake.

"Yeah, I just worry about it since you're so newly turned. I keep feeling it might happen at any time now." He drank some of his coffee.

"You're not used to being around someone so newly turned, are you?" She forked up some of her omelet. "I'm sure you still feel responsible for me."

"Right on both counts. I want you to have the best

experience with your first time. Well, and every time after that, but at least if you have a good experience the first time, you'll be less apprehensive the next time." Hopefully.

"I guess I didn't shift last night," she said, sounding disappointed.

"Not to my knowledge, unless you shifted while I was completely dead to the world, then shifted back before we woke, and you don't recall any of it."

"I wouldn't know. The only reason I knew something was up the other times was because I had stripped off my pj's in the middle of the night. Since I wasn't wearing any last night, I could have shifted and would never have realized it."

"I think I would have woken if you had, unless I was really sound asleep about then." He truly wished she had shifted, but he didn't think she had.

They finished breakfast and took their plates into the kitchen, but before he could put the dishes in the dishwasher, she pulled him into her arms. "No matter how it happens, it will be the best experience ever."

He kissed her upturned lips and sure as hell hoped so. He could see having a tour group here when she suddenly wanted to strip off her clothes and shift. And she'd panic and feel totally unsettled over the whole thing. He'd be just as panicked while trying to get her to safety. But he knew she wouldn't go for being locked up in his house day after day until she could get the shifting out of the way for a few hours.

CHAPTER 10

ALL MORNING, MAVERICK AND GINA WORKED WITH THE reindeer. She enjoyed the tour group visits, and everything was going fine. Gina had mixed feelings about shifting. She wanted to feel what it would be like to be a wolf, but she supposed it would be better and safer at night. Still, when she was working hard, moving around a lot, she'd work up a sweat and then worry she was going to shift suddenly. It happened again, and she paused, listening to her heart beating hard from exertion, but what if she was going to shift? She sensed her body cooling down in the frigid air. Maverick stopped feeding the reindeer and glanced at her.

She smiled. "I'm hungry. Are you?" And if she was going to shift, she could have lunch afterward.

"Yeah." He sounded relieved.

She smiled, gave him a hug, and then raced him to the house, and he was looking worried all over again.

She and Maverick finally reached the house, went inside, and decided to have grilled chicken sandwiches for lunch. "I wasn't shifting, by the way."

Pulling the bread out of a cabinet, he smiled at her. "I figured that out."

Then her phone rang. Her brother was calling, and she assumed he was going to be questioning her all over again. Normally, she loved talking to her brother, but now? She felt she was going to give herself away. "Weston, are you on your way home from finishing up the hunt?"

"Yeah, we extended it a bit, and I dropped off the guys. We didn't find any sign of Bigfoot."

She didn't mention anything about werewolves, not wanting to get into that discussion with him again.

"How are things going with you? Are you still at the reindeer ranch?"

"Yeah, I'm having a great time."

"Mom and Dad said they had a really good time there last night. They didn't get to see the wolf dogs though."

Oh, brother. She knew he'd get to that. She was going to help Maverick make lunch, but he shook his head, indicating she should concentrate on the call instead.

"Yeah, they were with Josh," she told her brother.

"And today?"

She looked at Maverick.

"Here," he mouthed to her.

Wondering if he'd misjudged what was being said, she frowned at Maverick.

He nodded.

She sighed. "They're here now."

"Cool. You can take pictures and send them to me then."

"When I have time. We're having lunch."

"They're outside then?"

"With the ranch hands," she improvised.

"I'll let you go then."

"See you later." Then she ended the call, breathing a sigh of relief. "He's the first one I want to turn."

Maverick smiled and brought the sandwiches to the table, and she served them water.

"He's still asking about the wolf dogs?" he asked.

"Yeah, he won't give up."

They heard a truck pull up in front of the house, and she got up from her chair and looked out the window. "Ohmigod, I don't believe it. Weston is here."

"If you want me to shift, I can, and I'll just turn him."

She laughed. "What about the wolf dogs?"

Maverick was already texting someone on his phone. "Two, coming right up."

She was so glad for that. "Will they come into the house?"

There was a knock on the door.

"I'll get it," Maverick said. "And yes, the wolves will come to the house. Just for your information, they've been fed already."

"Okay, maybe he won't notice there are no dog dishes in the house."

Maverick answered the door. "Hi, Weston. Gina didn't say you were coming for a visit. Would you like a grilled chicken sandwich? We were just sitting down to eat."

"Yeah, sure, that would be great, thanks. I didn't mean to come at lunchtime exactly, but I just left the other men off at their homes, and I wanted to see the ranch. From what Gina said, you've had a lot of tour groups so I figured one more tourist coming to see the reindeer wouldn't be too much of a problem."

Gina was already getting her brother a glass of water.

"No problem. You're welcome." Maverick made up another sandwich and delivered it to the table.

Then they all sat down together to eat.

"Dad mentioned seeing the Corvette." Weston lifted half of his sandwich to take a bite.

Gina wanted to laugh. So that's why her brother was here?

"Yeah, you can see it after lunch," Maverick said.

She noted he hadn't offered for Weston to drive it.

Two wolf dogs barged through the wolf door and headed to the table to greet everyone. She smelled that they were two of the ranch hands. It was still so foreign to her to think they were one and the same as the men she had greeted and talked to when they were doing ranching duties.

Weston was petting both of the wolves, checking out their wolf paws, but then he had to take a picture of them, as if he had to prove that if he saw others, he'd know they weren't the same as these two.

She glanced at Maverick to see his take on it. A sliver of a smile curved his lips.

Then the wolves went into the living room and curled up near the fireplace.

After Gina and her brother and Maverick finished lunch, they went outside, both wolves following them out the door. Maverick showed Weston his Corvette first since he knew that was what would really interest her brother.

"Have a seat." Maverick opened the car door for him.

Weston hurried to climb in, sat behind the wheel, and steered it as if he was on the road. He adjusted the rearview mirror, and she was thinking how Maverick would have to readjust it again.

Then Maverick took him to see the reindeer, though a

tour group had just offloaded. Some of his ranch hands were taking care of them, the wolves sticking close to them, waiting for Maverick to tell them when they could shift back. But Maverick didn't, and she figured he was afraid Weston might want to see the wolves before he left.

Maverick gave Weston a private tour of the stables while the tour group was outside.

"They all look the same to me. Do you still have the one that you found in the forest up north?"

"Yeah, I've checked with the other reindeer ranches. He doesn't belong to them. I've checked with the zoos too, but no one seems to have lost a reindeer," Maverick said.

"So what are you going to do with him?" Weston peered into the stall that housed the llama and the reindeer. "You have a llama too. I'd forgotten that."

"That's the pair we found at the state park. We'll keep them and take care of them like they are our own and continue to try to track down where they belong. My brother's former police detective partner is still with the Portland Police Bureau, so he's checking with his sources too."

"They seem to be best pals," Weston said.

"Yeah, they were most likely raised together."

Then Gina suddenly felt strange, and she knew she was in trouble. Heat began filling her muscles and bones, and she moved close to Maverick and reached out her hand and squeezed his arm. "I've got to use the bathroom. I'll clean up the dishes too from lunch."

He said, "Sure. See you in a bit."

But she didn't let go of his arm and squeezed tighter while her brother was talking to one of the reindeer in a stall. She raised her brows, hoping Maverick got her message. She didn't have to go to the bathroom. She had to turn into a wolf.

She hurried off then. She figured Maverick wished he could go with her and reassure her for her first time. But she needed him to keep her brother away from her. She hoped she could just turn back at will, but what if her brother wanted to leave and say bye to her and she had just—vanished?

She couldn't worry about that right now and hurried out of the stable.

Weston glanced in Gina's direction. "Where's Gina going?"

She heard him because of her enhanced hearing despite having left the stable already.

"To use the bathroom and then clean up the dishes from lunch."

She finally reached the house and threw open the door to the house, feeling panicked, like a fever was filling her with heat. She stripped off her clothes as soon as she slammed the front door shut, hoping Maverick wouldn't let her brother come into the house and find her clothes strewn all over the place. She would never do that—*normally*. But she couldn't help it. She was so afraid she'd shift and still be wearing her clothes.

Then she pulled her panties off at the last minute. She went to grab her clothes and take them into the master bedroom, but suddenly she felt like she was changing, and the next thing she knew, she was standing on the floor on four furry paws. No matter how much she thought she'd be ready to face this, she wasn't prepared for it at all. She couldn't talk, except to bark. Or howl, which of course she wasn't about to do.

Again, she felt panicked. She paced. How long would this last? What could she do now?

Her clothes! She grabbed her panties with her teeth and ran them down the hall to Maverick's bedroom. Not having hands to work with, she had to find another way to do things. For now, her teeth did the job. She returned to grab her bra. She needed to take more of a load at a time, but every time she tried to grab two articles of clothing, she couldn't manage, losing the other. Giving up on it, she grabbed her bra again and raced down the hall to the bedroom. Then she ran back to the living room and grabbed her jeans, but she kept tripping on the pant legs on the return trip. Man, this was a job. Next time she had to shift, she hoped she wouldn't have to hurry like this.

She managed to get both socks in a mouthful, squinching up her nose a bit because of the idea she'd had the socks on her feet earlier, even though it seemed different to be carrying things in her mouth as a wolf. Then she managed to carry one hiking boot into the master bedroom and dropped it when the front door opened.

Ohmigod, no! Her heart was doing double time. She went into the bathroom and stared at herself in the full-length mirror. She thought she was a pretty red wolf with a black-tipped tail swishing behind her, but her brain couldn't embrace the idea that she and the wolf were one and the same.

Then she heard Maverick and Weston talking in the kitchen. "Want a beer?" Maverick asked.

Are you kidding me? Maverick hadn't understood that she'd actually shifted?

She sat on her rump, annoyed. Then she realized she'd better try to shift back. But no matter how much she tried to convince her body to turn back into a human, it wasn't working. Okay, so, yeah, this was frustrating. She was glad the other times she'd shifted, she hadn't known about it.

"Where's Gina?" Weston asked.

Her heart skipped a beat.

"She came in to use the bathroom," Maverick repeated. "She was up really late last night. Maybe she lay down to take a nap."

"I wouldn't think she would until I left. Well, you have quite a setup here. It's really a nice ranch."

"Thanks. We enjoy it."

"And so does my sister from the sounds of it."

Maybe Maverick wanted her to join them as a wolf and bite her brother. Or maybe she was supposed to pretend to be one of the wolf dogs, though she guessed that wouldn't work because they were supposed to both be male.

"I'm going to go check on her," Maverick said, and she could hear him walking down the hall toward the master bedroom. He walked into the bedroom and shut the door.

She peered out of the bathroom at him, and he smiled

broadly, appearing pleased with the way she looked, even though she hadn't wanted to turn into the wolf while her brother was here, of all things. She was glad Maverick felt that way about her when she was a wolf though. Animals in the wild partly selected their mates because of their appearance, and in some cases, the males had to do unbelievable feats to win the female's attention. She did wonder if *lupus garous* were the same.

Maverick was carrying her other boot and set it on the floor next to the one she'd managed to bring with her. "You're beautiful, you know?" He gave her a big hug.

Then she licked his face to thank him. It seemed a natural thing to do, and she was amazed how some of the wolf traits that she wasn't born with would be so innate. This was an adventure and a half. Everyone should have this experience. Then she thought about her pierced ears. She wasn't wearing earrings because of the fear of shifting and having them still in her ears, but were the holes in her ears still showing?

She pulled away from him and returned to the bathroom to look at herself in the mirror again, only this time concentrating on what mattered. Her pierced ears. No holes! Or so tiny they weren't noticeable because of the fur on her ears. Yay! One obstacle overcome.

He joined her in the bathroom. "You can stay in here and pretend to be napping or come out and greet him as a new wolf dog he hasn't seen before. Or you could, if you want to, bite him. Make him one of us."

She perked up her ears. Seriously? Maverick wanted her

to bite her brother? Well, she'd been saying she should all along. Maybe her brother had said something to Maverick out at the stable that made him realize they truly needed to turn Weston earlier rather than later.

She nudged Maverick's hand. She would go with him and try to feel out the situation on her own.

She walked over to the closed bedroom door and looked back at Maverick. She hadn't thought of all the repercussions of being a wolf—like the fact that closed doors were impenetrable barriers.

He opened the door for her and walked with her down the hall. She felt like running down it ahead of him but at the same time staying behind him for cover. Her feelings were all over the place. In her mind she was walking in a wolf's body, with a human brain that couldn't let go of the way she felt people would see her—as Gina, human.

When she reached the end of the hall, she stopped dead, afraid to show herself to her brother. Afraid he would see her as Gina—eerily transformed. What if he was horrified to see her if he really believed she was a wolf shifter now too?

Maverick waited with her for a second, petted her head, raised his brows at her, watching her to see what she wanted to do. Appreciating him for that, she pushed at the back of his leg. She wanted him to go first.

She wasn't sure, but she thought she'd feel better if Maverick started talking to Weston in the beginning. Then she'd come out, and he could introduce her.

"You want me to go in first?"

She nodded.

He leaned down and hugged her and kissed her on the face. She licked his face again. Then he walked into the living room. "Do you want a refill on the beer?"

"Where is Gina?" Weston asked, frowning, sounding a little worried.

Maverick glanced back at her.

Oh, oh, he really wanted to call her out?

She came out at a trot, and Maverick waved at her. "Gina. Wolf shifter extraordinaire."

Weston laughed.

Her brother didn't believe it now?

"Seriously. I can shift and show you my wolf form if you want, and you can decide who bites you, or we can do a non-bite method," Maverick said.

Weston stood up from one of the couches and smiled. "Yeah, sure, go for it. You can both bite me if you think it works best that way."

Was her brother serious? She didn't think so. She thought that he was playing along with it. Where was her brother going to stay if he had to shift and didn't have any control over it? Had Maverick even thought of that?

Maverick started stripping off his clothes. Ohmigod, he was going to do it. There was no turning back.

Weston was still smiling. He glanced at Gina. "So you turned my sister?"

"I accidentally turned her, yes."

"When you were kissing?" Weston wasn't being serious at all. This was going to be a rude awakening for him.

"We can't turn someone when we're in our human form. We have to share saliva in the bloodstream to make the turn possible, but only when we're in wolf form." Maverick was still pulling off his jeans. "I turned her when she was trying to pull me out of the lake water. I cut her skin accidentally with one of my teeth."

"Okay." Weston definitely was playing along, not believing any of this.

Gina drew closer to Weston, still not sure if Maverick was going to go through with shifting in front of her brother, but if he was, then this was it. She wasn't sure she could bite him. The others were right. Making a choice to turn someone was a lot different than accidentally turning a person.

Maverick reached for his boxer briefs waistband and Gina moved even closer to her brother, nudging his hand, and he ran his hand over her head in a firm caress. She was just a dog, or wolf dog, to him. About the time that he did, Maverick pulled off his boxer briefs and shifted into his wolf.

Weston's eyes were huge, his jaw hanging. He didn't cry out. He stood there like a statue, as if he couldn't believe what he was seeing and he was frozen in time.

She waited for Maverick to indicate to her what they should do. Maverick was eyeing her brother, giving him a chance to react. Weston was still as death, looking like he didn't know how to react to what he had just seen.

Then Maverick rushed forward, just as she was about to open her mouth and bite her brother.

Maverick bit her brother's hand. Weston cried out,

yanking his hand away and stepping back from him as if
he was afraid Maverick would bite him again. She figured
Weston might have now realized what he had gotten himself into with all his probing into what Maverick and his kind
were.

Frowning, Weston was favoring his hand. "Damn." But he
was just staring at Maverick, like he couldn't believe that he
was right about Maverick and the others being werewolves.
Or that Maverick bit him. Or even that his sister was already
one of them.

Gina wagged her tail. There hadn't been any going back,
she had figured, though she really had planned to bite him
instead so it would be on her and not Maverick.

Maverick woofed at Weston, and then he shifted again
to prove to Weston that the blur of forms he had seen
was truly what he thought—that Maverick had been a
human and then a wolf in the blink of an eye. He was a
wolf shifter.

Then Maverick shifted into the wolf again.

Weston sat down hard—or fell was more like it—on the
couch behind him, sinking down in it, looking gobsmacked.
"Hell. I can't believe it." Then he glanced at Gina. "Shift
back."

Maverick shifted and began getting dressed. "Okay, so
did we make you a believer yet?"

Weston tore his attention away from Gina and frowned.
"I can't believe your kind really exist."

"Your kind now too. You're officially one of us. We
thought you believed we were werewolves already." Maverick

went into the kitchen, got a first aid kit out from under a cabinet, and then returned to doctor Weston's hand.

"My kind now too," Weston said, watching Maverick clean the bite wound. "My kind now too?" It was finally sinking in that Maverick had turned him.

"Yeah, that's what you wanted, isn't it? To find our kind? You can't tell anyone else about us, but now you're one of us and don't have to hunt for us any longer."

"Hell. I, well, I didn't really think you were real. It was fun believing it, but… I mean, how can any of this be real? It's like something we've always wanted to discover but never truly believed we would." Then Weston glanced at Gina. "Gina's not changing back." He sounded worried.

Maverick bandaged Weston's hand. "That's the issue you'll have also in the beginning. But mostly around the time of the full moon." Maverick took a seat on the couch, and Gina sat next to him on the floor.

She didn't want to shed wolf fur on the couch.

Maverick ran his hand over her head and back and began explaining all about *lupus garous* and the pack. He told Weston he'd talked to Josh, and Weston was welcome to stay at Josh and Brooke's house for now so that he wouldn't run into humans if he couldn't control his shifting.

Gina suddenly felt the heat filling her body again, and she tore off to the bedroom. She loved seeing Maverick stripping out of his clothes and showing off his beautiful body before he shifted. But no way was she shifting and appearing naked in front of her brother. She wondered if she would ever be able to strip in front of others in the pack and not feel insecure.

When she reached the bedroom, she immediately shifted. This was unbelievable. She thought her brother was taking the news in good stride though. At least she hoped so.

She put on her clothes and then took a deep breath and headed back to the living room. Her brother was just sitting there, looking a little shell-shocked.

"Okay, so you were right, Weston. Are you happy?" Gina asked, approaching him and giving him a hug.

He hugged her back. "Hell, Gina, I knew it! Well, at least in my vivid imagination, I did."

She smiled and sat down with Maverick on the couch. "Yeah, keeping it from you was getting harder because of all your inquiries about the wolf dogs."

"Wolf dogs that were actually wolves... I thought so, though I thought they would be a little bigger." Weston glanced at his bite wound.

"We're red wolves," Maverick said, "not the bigger gray wolves."

"I hope you are...okay with it," Gina said, really meaning it. She hated the idea of terrifying her parents by biting them like that though.

"It's going to take some getting used to. What about our parents?"

"We can't be around them if we're having shifting issues, unless we turn them. Mom's not going to like that when she dyes her hair, it will go away once she shifts. She also won't like that she can't wear her wedding rings."

Weston raised his brows in question.

"You should see how fast the need to shift occurs. Well, I

guess you did. But with us, since we're newly turned, we have no control over it. I didn't think I'd make it in time to even reach the house from the reindeer stable so I could yank off my clothes and then turn wolf. I had to carry my clothes back into the bedroom as a wolf so if the two of you came into the house, you wouldn't see my clothes lying all over the floor. You wouldn't have known what to think," she said. "So if Mom were to do that outside sometime? She could lose her jewelry. Except for during the new moon phase."

"Gotcha."

"I'm sure they would miss their friends."

"But they would miss us even more," Weston said.

"Yeah, exactly."

Maverick was on his phone texting away, and she glanced at his cell to see whom he was texting. He said to her, "Leidolf and Cassie. And my brother. I need to let them know we have a new pack member."

"Pack member. It still seems so unreal. Part of me—" Her brother smelled the air. "I can smell things more. Scents are...much more defined. But it doesn't seem like I'm really one of you. That you two are either."

"Wait until you don't have to turn on a light at night," she said. "I kept thinking it was light out when we were camping, and I hadn't even used a flashlight."

"Hell, you were a wolf on the campout," Weston said, as if all of this was sinking in a little further. "That's why you were sitting in the dark. And probably why you got up so early too."

"Yeah, I don't remember ever shifting though."

"We have to turn Mom and Dad," Weston finally said,

as if he had come to the same conclusion as she already had.

But she was glad at least that her brother felt the same way as she did, and that made it easier to turn them.

"Okay, Leidolf and Cassie Wildhaven, our pack leaders, want to know if you want to go down there to see them or stay here and they can come here," Maverick said. "If you go to their ranch, you can meet more of the pack members. Yes, you've already met some, but it will be a different experience for you now that you are one of us."

"I won't be an outsider," Weston said.

"More than that. You'll be able to smell people's scents and make connections you need to make. They have plenty of land, 30,000 acres, for you to run freely on as a wolf, be yourself, not worry about anyone seeing you if you have to suddenly shift. And we have others who were more newly turned a year or more before you were." Maverick finally told him about Sarge and the others.

Weston raised his brows. "Damn, so learning about you could have deadly consequences."

"Yeah. But like I said, your other friends were killers, bent on destroying our kind. Sarge made amends, and he serves as the accountant for the pack. So he'll be glad to see you and reminisce over old times, I'm sure. He can speak to you about how it is to be newly turned also and answer any other questions you might have," Maverick said.

She loved how patient Maverick was with her brother, how he did everything to make him feel like part of the pack right away. She hadn't been sure Maverick would be that way with anyone else. She suspected he had treated her in that manner because he was interested in dating her—and because he'd accidentally turned her.

"Yeah, I'd like to go down there and see everyone. I really had a great time at the dance. And maybe I could see more of the gal Dorinda I danced with." Weston smiled.

"Okay, well, let me tell you right now there's a shortage of females in the pack, in most packs. So the bachelor males can feel really territorial about having a new member of the pack target one of the eligible females. That said, if a she-wolf really likes you, the males will not fight you over her. That all has to do with mating for life. We have to be really sure she's the right one for us, and vice versa."

"And you and Gina?" Weston asked, motioning to Gina.

Maverick squeezed her hand and smiled at her. "We're definitely dating."

"Can we drive down in the Corvette?" Weston sounded hopeful.

"When there's no snow on the ground and when we don't have three occupants for the car. It only has two bucket seats. And just so you know, we have 4,000 acres at the reindeer ranch where you can also run as a wolf." Maverick got up from the couch and grabbed the empty beer bottles to dump them in the recycle bin. "We'll have to take my truck. When I do let you drive, when we don't have another passenger, if you have the urge to shift at all, you would have to tell me right away, pull the car onto the shoulder of the road, and you can strip off your clothes and shift in the car."

"It's a deal. I might even be able to stay with Sarge then down at the ranch," Weston said.

"You can do that. I'm sure he'd be glad for the company. What about you, Gina? You do want to come with us, don't you? I'd prefer you come too."

Gina didn't know about riding in the truck down to the ranch. Now that she'd shifted out of the blue during the day, she wasn't sure she wanted to risk doing the same on the way to the ranch.

"Now that you've shifted, you should be okay," Maverick assured her.

But she wasn't sure if she wanted to see her brother overcome with panic if suddenly *he* had to shift in the pickup. Nor did she want to see him naked. That was definitely something she wasn't ready to deal with—wolves getting naked, all except for Maverick, and that was a given.

"Come on," her brother said. "You have to come too."

"All right." She said to Maverick, "I thought you wanted me to bite my brother. I was surprised when you did it instead."

"I wanted you to make the decision about your brother completely. But then I realized if I bit him instead of you, he'd have more of my royal root's genetics, and it could help more with his shifting issues like it does with yours. I've never turned anyone before you, accidentally or otherwise, so this is a new experience for me."

"Oh, okay. You're right. There are so many matters that Weston and I have to learn about as we go through this journey." Gina got up from the couch, and when Weston rose to his feet, she gave him another hug. "I'm glad you're a wolf like me now." It made her feel better that at least her brother's situation was resolved and they could share this journey into the previously unknown world of werewolves together.

"What about Bromley and Patterson?" Weston asked.

"You're going to have to convince them the wolf dogs run all over the ranches. That you were mistaken about wolf shifters," Maverick said as they pulled on their parkas and headed out of doors.

They got into the truck, and Gina opted for sitting in the back seat, just in case she had to shift again.

"Okay, I can do that." Weston buckled his seat belt. "They should trust me. But what if my getting so cozy with all of you after claiming you are werewolves and then saying you're not makes them suspicious? So much so that they're afraid I was turned against my will?"

"Then we'll have to turn them," Maverick said. "Though if we can avoid it, we really only want to turn those we have to. And in Gina's case, it meant her family. Your family."

"Also, they might just figure you're getting friendly with everyone on the ranch because I'm dating Maverick now," Gina said.

"What about Sarge?" Weston asked.

"Don't tell them about Sarge," Maverick warned. "We don't want him having to explain what had happened to him in Maine. Even though he has a made-up story to use, it's best if your friends don't know about him or he might slip up about his concocted story."

"Okay."

Though Gina knew her brother didn't like to have to keep a secret about that either. "Now you know what it feels like to keep quiet about all this. It's not easy."

"Yeah, I can see that now." Weston was quiet for quite a bit of the drive, probably thinking about all the ramifications he had to face with being turned. "Man, your car is a real treasure. I can't wait to ride in it." For a while, Weston mulled over things in silence again. Then he finally spoke up. "I'm a software engineer, and I work out of my home, so I guess I can still do that."

"Yeah, as long as you don't have to go to in-person meetings or have videoconferences when you are having shifting issues," Maverick said.

"I can do that."

"And you can't go out like this unless you have someone with you who can take over for you if you get into trouble," Maverick warned.

"Yeah, I got it."

But did he? After having shifted herself when she was fully aware of it, she really was feeling more of the impact of having had no control over the shifting. Sure enough, as they drew closer to the ranch, her brother suddenly started to strip off his clothes in the truck.

"Feeling really hot here. It doesn't hurt though." Weston sounded thrilled that he was going through the process, not anxious like she'd been.

She was glad for it.

Seconds later, Weston was sitting as a wolf on the front seat and howled his delight. Maverick chuckled.

Smiling, Gina admired him. "You are a beautiful wolf."

He howled again, and she loved that she could now recognize his voice as a wolf. She had to try her howl out the next time she was a wolf too.

As soon as they arrived at the ranch house, Gina got out of the truck and let Weston out.

"If you want, some of our wolves who are available can run with you," Maverick said.

Weston woofed what sounded like his approval.

She wished she could too, but she couldn't summon the need to shift at all. And she realized that was the first time she'd even really wanted to turn wolf.

Leidolf came out of the house and smiled. "Looks like our newest pack member is finding his wolf half to his liking."

"Are there any other pack members who are available to run with him?" Maverick asked.

"They're coming," Cassie said, hurrying outside. "Several are eager to run with a new pack member and make him feel perfectly welcome."

Just then six male wolves raced out of the bunkhouse and greeted Weston, surrounding him, licking his face, and he greeted them in the same manner, as if he had been born to this way of life. Gina loved it and again wished she could be a wolf to run with her brother. But she was glad Maverick didn't go running with her brother. She would have felt left out.

Then the other wolves ran with Weston, and Gina watched, thrilled that he was having such a good time, nipping at them and racing through the snow-covered pasture toward the river and woods.

Change! Turn! Shift! She wanted so badly to run with them and play too. She hadn't imagined it being like that. She wondered if she would feel the same way when the new moon phase appeared and she couldn't shift.

They watched as another man drove an all-terrain vehicle after them, just in case Weston needed transport back to the ranch house.

"Are you all right?" Maverick asked, taking Gina into his arms, and she realized she was lost in thought as she watched her brother disappear off into the distance with the others.

CHAPTER 11

MAVERICK WAS AFRAID GINA WAS UPSET WITH SEEING her brother racing with the wolves, but she turned her face up and smiled at him, and she seemed perfectly pleased Weston was a wolf. "Thank you for turning him so I didn't have to, especially since your reasoning is right on track. I wanted to run with my brother in the worst way. With you too. Thanks for not running with my brother until I can."

"I wouldn't have left you behind. He has enough new friends to be with as it is, and when we can run safely together—at my ranch when we have no tour groups there or here—I'm doing it."

"How are you feeling about all this?" Cassie asked Gina.

"A little overwhelmed after shifting earlier, worried about doing that again in public. But out here? I so wanted to run with my brother and the others, and I still love being a wolf," Gina said.

"Good. You'll get more used to it as time goes on. Come inside, both of you, and we'll have some dessert," Cassie said.

Then they went inside to have fudge cake and cups of coffee in the sunroom.

"Unfortunately," Cassie said to Gina, "we can only give you advice about what to do around this time of the month—don't wear jewelry, be with someone when driving a vehicle, airline trips are out. This is such an individual thing, and it

yone differently. As a non-royal, you won't ever
shift during the new moon, and it can take months
to get a handle on shifting during the full moon. The
the month you'll have a little more control over it."

Cassie's right. At least part of the problem has been
olved as far as Weston being one of us now though,"
Leidolf said. "But you didn't turn Gina and her brother's parents yet, did you, Maverick, when they had dinner at your
place?"

"No. We were trying to show them we're the good guys
first," Maverick said.

They sat down in the sunroom and watched the scenery
for any sign of the wolves. But they didn't see any yet.

"How receptive do you think they'll be now that they've
met Maverick?" Leidolf asked.

"My dad loves his car," Gina said.

Leidolf laughed. "Okay, good. We'll keep your brother
here as long as he wants to stay."

"One of the wolves is Sarge," Maverick explained to Gina
as the group of wolves ran past the sunroom window.

"Oh, wow, okay. I would never have recognized him.
Well, my brother said he wanted to stay with him here, so I
guess that will work," Gina said.

"It will," Maverick said. "But if your brother wants to
return to the reindeer ranch, he can stay in Josh and Brooke's
house until he knows what he wants to do long term."

"If that's settled, what is the next step with your parents?"
Leidolf asked.

"We'll turn them," Gina said, reaching over to squeeze

Maverick's free hand. "Maverick will have to do it so they have more royal roots."

Cassie said, "Good. I'm still thinking of us doing it in a more civilized manner with your parents so it's not so terrifying. Maybe we can tell them about it, show them about your shifting, and then if they don't agree to taking the more medical approach, Maverick will have to bite them. What are you going to do about Christmas?"

"Weston and I are supposed to have Christmas at Mom and Dad's place," Gina said.

Maverick hadn't even thought about Christmas where her family was concerned. This would be a new experience for all of them.

"That's the time of the waning gibbous," Cassie said. "Then New Year's Eve is a new moon phase, and we have a big New Year's Eve party here, and your parents can come here for it. If we've turned them by then, they won't have any shifting issues."

"That would be lovely. They don't go anywhere for New Year's Eve, so I know they'd love it. We should have my parents come to your home for Christmas," Gina said to Maverick. "If they have to shift like my brother and I did, at least they'll already be where they need to be—among their new kind."

"Absolutely. Would they be receptive to having Christmas at the ranch?" Maverick asked.

"Yeah, because they think we might be becoming a couple and they would be happy to help make that happen."

"That works for me. Josh and Brooke will be having

Christmas with us also. My brother and I and Brooke no longer have any family, so we're it for each other."

"Oh, wow, okay, so my parents will have to adopt the three of you."

"Yeah." Maverick smiled. "That would be nice. They'll need to meet my brother and sister-in-law too."

After his brother had married Brooke, Maverick had never expected to meet, well, turn a woman who had parents and a brother. He'd been kind of thinking when he met the right wolf, she'd be on her own like Brooke had been. But he was glad to have more family, and he knew his brother and sister-in-law would be too.

"What happens if my brother unexpectedly shifts out in the snow?" Gina suddenly asked.

"That's why a couple of men followed them in an all-wheel Jeep Wrangler to pick him up, and they'll have spare clothes for him," Leidolf said. "We have a lot of experience dealing with new wolves."

"Okay, good. I wasn't a wolf that long after I shifted this last time. And of course I was in the house, so I haven't run as a wolf yet either."

"Yeah, we've got it covered." Leidolf got a call. "Yeah?" He looked up at Gina and smiled. "Okay, see you in a few." He put his phone back on the chair. "Your brother shifted, and he's dressed and on his way here to join us."

"Oh, wonderful," Gina said.

"Oh, good," Cassie said. "We can give him some cake and coffee too."

It didn't take long before Weston arrived at the house,

wearing his own clothes that he must have changed into in Maverick's truck, and everyone greeted him. Gina gave her brother a hug, and Maverick shook his hand, smiling. "Well, how was it?"

"Oh, man, that was the thrill of a lifetime," Weston said.

Gina smiled at him, and Maverick heard her sigh in relief. He rubbed her back, and she relaxed a little. He guessed she'd been worried about how her brother would have felt after turning into his wolf and running with the others.

"That really was an experience and a half. Smelling all the scents, hearing so much more, seeing things I never would have, and being so low to the ground it's like someone had shrunk me in size. But also running like that for miles and so fast was totally cool." Weston sat down with them in the sunroom while Cassie brought him a cup of coffee and some cake.

"Thanks so much. I guess as wolves we can still eat chocolate." Weston took a bite of his cake.

"Yeah, as a human, you can eat anything you normally eat. As a wolf, you can crunch into uncooked bones that you couldn't as a human. If you ate chocolate as a wolf and you shifted quickly enough, you would be okay. I wouldn't recommend eating chocolate as a wolf otherwise," Cassie said.

"Good to know. I hoped you would come running with us," Weston said to Gina.

"I wanted to, but I couldn't call on the ability to shift."

"Next time you can do it," Maverick said, hoping that it would happen when they both shifted at the same time. "Or one of these times." All he knew was *he* wanted to run with her as a wolf.

"Are you staying with Sarge at this ranch?" Gina asked.

"Yeah. He has plenty of room for me, and he said I could stay with him as long as I like."

"That's great," Gina said.

"And you?" her brother asked.

"She's staying with me," Maverick said before she could answer.

She smiled at him.

They finally got ready to leave, and she hugged her brother goodbye and thanked Cassie and Leidolf for everything.

Then they left, and Maverick was feeling good about all of it so far, though still concerned about turning her parents. He thought about having Christmas with them and turning them then—*here's your Christmas gift. Merry Christmas.*

"Is it really fine with you and your brother and sister-in-law if we have Christmas at your place?" Gina asked on the drive back to the reindeer ranch.

"Yeah, it sure is."

"Okay. My parents will be delighted about going to the New Year's Eve party. We have another problem though. What about Christmas Eve dinner? We would always spend that time with my parents too."

"They can come out to the reindeer ranch and stay overnight. Then they can have both meals with us."

"Okay, that could work. Otherwise, I was afraid we would have a problem with them wanting to have us over for Christmas Eve dinner."

"Right. And both you and your brother could possibly

shift. As long as they are fine with staying with us, we should be good."

"What about shifting issues for my brother and me when our parents stay overnight at your place?" she asked.

"I've been thinking about that. There's no way to plan for every eventuality."

"I still want to go to the zoo so I can see the animals and learn their scents so when I'm out running in the wild, I can distinguish all the scents I'm smelling from each other. I think after New Year's Day will be great. But I'm also going to time how long between shifts I can expect to go."

He hated to tell her they couldn't predict a need to shift like that for the recently turned. But he wanted her to know the truth so she would be better prepared, though even then he assumed anytime that she would have to suddenly shift would be a shock to her for some time to come.

"I would do that too, though shifting can be unpredictable, particularly in the beginning and during the time around the full moon."

"Oh, okay. I was hoping there was more of a scientific approach to this."

"Like your studies of animals."

"Yeah." She sighed and leaned back against the seat. "My brother couldn't have been happier to be a wolf."

"And you?"

"I love it. The shifting when I'm least expecting it is a problem, but otherwise, I am fine with the rest of it."

"We need to bring more of your clothes here, now that you're staying with me."

She didn't say anything for a moment. "My apartment's lease is up in thirty days."

"You can move in with me. We're dating, and you'll feel more comfortable at the ranch while you're having trouble with shifting. And we can run whenever we want after the tour groups are gone. I'll get us whatever we need at the store. Otherwise, I'll have to drive you home each day and pick you up now."

"True. Besides, I can't be barking at the apartment, and you have to prove to me you're the right one for me."

He smiled at her. It was mutual, but he really liked her. He was so glad that the woman he had accidentally turned was single and someone he enjoyed being with.

"Okay, look, since I've shifted already, maybe we should go ahead and get my stuff now before I have to shift again."

"Let's do it. And when we get to the ranch, we can run tonight if you can shift."

She smiled. "I would really like that."

Then they went to her apartment in town, and he went inside to see the neat little place, cheerfully decorated in gnome art, a small Christmas tree on a table featuring more of the Swedish Christmas gnomes. "You're really okay with staying with me?"

"Yeah, moving from my little apartment to a nice big ranch house with lots of acreage, most definitely. Wolf parties like the last one, wolf runs on your ranch and at Cassie and Leidolf's ranch? The exquisite meals you prepare? Yeah, I can live with that." She brought out her suitcases and laid them on the bed.

"What can I do to help?" He wasn't sure if she wanted him to pack her clothes.

"Food. Pack up everything in the fridge. I have sacks under the kitchen cabinet next to it."

Then Maverick got a call, and he saw that it was Andy, the radio talk show host, and he answered it.

"One of our listeners said that he knows of a man by the name of Chester Hopper who had a reindeer and llama that he raised together. He died of a massive heart attack, and his son, a man by the name of Danny Hopper, took over his farm. When my listener contacted Danny, he said his father had a reindeer named Rudolph, and Lucy the llama, but both were gone when he took over the farm. He assumed his father had found homes for them before he died." Then Andy gave Maverick Danny's contact information.

"Thanks, we'll check with him then."

"Good luck and let us know what you discover. Our listeners are waiting to hear what happens to the reindeer and the llama."

"Sure thing. Merry Christmas," Maverick said.

"Happy holidays to you."

When Maverick got off the phone with Andy, he said to Gina, "We might have found the farm where the reindeer and llama belong."

"Oh, that's great. Though I adore them and hope we can keep them."

"The new owner didn't even know they were missing, if they had belonged to his father, so maybe he will be glad to let us keep them." Maverick called Danny and explained who he was. "Do you have pictures of Lucy and Rudolph?"

"I'll check and see. You say you manage a reindeer ranch?" Danny asked as he shuffled through papers in the background.

"Yeah, near Portland, Oregon."

"Then you can provide the perfect home for Rudolph."

"We can. And we'd be happy to keep him and Lucy here. We just need to ensure they had belonged to your father and not someone else who might be frantically searching for them."

"I understand. I just found their photos on my dad's phone. I'll send them to you in an email."

Maverick gave him his email address and waited for the pictures to come through, and he showed them to Gina.

She nodded. "They're the same ones."

Maverick agreed. "Okay, it looks as though they're your father's reindeer and llama. Are you sure you want us to keep them?"

"Yeah. I'm planning to spruce up the farm and then sell it. I would've had to have found homes for them anyway."

"All right, well, they have a good home with us. I'll send you some pictures so you can see how they're doing." Maverick wasn't sure if Danny even cared, but it appeared his father really treasured the pair. Maverick sent five pictures of Rudolph and Lucy, showing the kids and adults visiting them and loving on them and them being with other reindeer and then cuddled together in their own special stall.

"They look like they got a real upgrade in their accommodations and lots of special attention. I'm grateful to you providing for them then. My father would have approved."

Then Maverick had him sign some paperwork online to say Danny did indeed own them and was giving the animals to him.

Afterward, Maverick let Andy know so he could tell his listeners that the one who had called him about Lucy and Rudolph was correct and now they were permanently in their new home at the Wilding Reindeer Ranch.

"That's great," Andy said. "We'll let them know."

Then they ended the conversation, and Maverick assisted Gina with packing up her grocery items. "I'll give notice on my apartment too," she said. "No sense in dragging this out. And we can move the rest of my stuff to the ranch after New Year's Day."

"Sure, we can do that."

Once they were back at the reindeer ranch, he helped her bring her clothes and food into the house. "Are you sure you have enough room for me to hang up my clothes and such?" she asked as she put her milk in his fridge.

"Hell, if I don't, I'll thin out my clothes so you'll have all the room you need."

She laughed. "Okay, I think you are absolutely the perfect boyfriend."

He was glad he had said the right thing then. They needed to finish putting her groceries away, but otherwise, he was planning on taking her to bed with him. He'd help her sort out her clothes tomorrow.

But tonight, he wanted to share the intimacy again with her after a quick dinner. She helped him put the rest of the food away quickly, and he hoped she was doing so because

she was also eager to make love to him. Then he made them
a quick and easy dinner of tuna and cheesy noodles.

They finished dinner, and then she grabbed his hand
and hurried him off down the hall. He was certain it wasn't
because she was eager to sort out her clothes.

Unless she was in a rush because she had to shift!

When they reached the bedroom, all Gina could think of
was having wild and crazy sex with the hot wolf, so glad she
had decided to take the plunge and move in with him, but
Maverick seemed worried about her.

"I'm not shifting," she said. "But I'm definitely ready for
some hot loving."

"Me too." And then he began pulling off her sweater, and
she wriggled the rest of the way out of it.

He sat her on the bed and tugged off her boots, and
then she grabbed his hand and pulled him onto the bed and
switched places with him, but she had more trouble removing his boots. She finally managed to get one off. When she
pulled the other off, she fell on her butt and laughed. Then
she straddled his legs and pushed him back against the mattress. She wanted to make love, but she wanted to play too.

She hadn't imagined ever being that way with a man
during sex. But Maverick made her want to explore all kinds
of different avenues of lovemaking with him. And for now,
she was having fun.

He smiled up at her, his eyes taking on a lustful glaze, his heartbeat already pounding. She was amazed at how much she could hear with her enhanced hearing. She loved knowing how her actions were turning him on. She was amused he was wearing a pullover shirt today, no buttons. She liked his button shirts, tackling each button at a time, feeding into the anticipation. But this was nice too as she ran her hands over his shirt and slowly pulled it up to expose his flat belly. Then she kissed it and licked his belly button. He smiled at her.

She slid his shirt up further, pressing kisses over his chest until she reached his pebbled nipples and licked, kissed, and nibbled on them. He moaned and ran his fingers through strands of her hair. She pulled his shirt over his head and tossed it, and it landed on top of the bedside lampshade. Whoops.

Then she had her hands all over his beautiful chest, carved exquisitely from all the ranching duties he was involved in. She wondered if she helped him out with them all the time, she'd build up her muscles too.

Then he pulled her closer to him and kissed her mouth, her lace-covered breasts pressed against his bare chest. He wrapped his arms around her, holding her close, exploring her mouth as she tongued his too.

He was such a consummate kisser, but she loved how he seemed to enjoy sliding his hands all over her, her arms, her back, his hands cupping her face, and their mouths sought each other's again.

His hands drifted to her back, and he began unfastening her bra and then pulled it off her. Instantly, she felt so free and sexy now that they were bare chest to bare chest.

She pulled away from him to unbuckle his belt and then unfastened his jeans, running her fingers along the zipper, relishing how aroused he was. She yanked at his jeans to pull them off. When she finally managed, she grabbed one of his socks, tugged it off, and then tossed it and pulled off the other, dispensing with it.

Maverick quickly flipped her onto her back and then began to pull off her jeans, her socks, removing everything but her panties.

He ran his hand over her belly and kissed her cheek. "So hot."

She smiled at him and looked down at his boxer briefs stretching over his arousal. "You are too."

Then he slid his hand down her panties and inserted a finger into her, feeling her wetness. Yeah, she was wet and ready for him. He slid her panties down her legs, and she reached up to pull off his boxer briefs. And then he was kissing her again, rubbing his leg against her mons, their lips melded, sensuous, heated.

She felt hotter, her blood pumping hard from the thrill of it all, and she had to keep telling herself it was just that she had the hots for him, not that she was going to shift. She realized that heat felt different, more bone-deep, actually, thankfully.

He deepened his kiss, and she savored the feel of him, the taste and smooth texture of his mouth and tongue and lips, inhaling his heady scent. She strained against him, feeling driven to want him inside her now. Not having sex with him all the way was wreaking havoc with the instinctual need to make it happen. Was that even normal this soon after meeting him? After being turned?

He began touching her feminine bud with exquisite strokes. Her breath hitched. He was building the pressure, and she felt lost in him, the heady feeling of his touch sending her soaring heavenward. Her need intensified, and she arched against his skillful fingers. He kept up the strokes, faster and firmer. She couldn't hold back and cried out, not knowing if she could last much longer just courting him and not declaring him her mate so he could bury himself deeply in her, stretch her to the max, and make her climax with him.

But she was ready to stroke him to climax next, and she eagerly moved him onto his back and took charge.

Maverick was so into Gina, he wanted to go all the way with her, but he had to rein in his own raging desire. She stroked his cock, and he was reveling in her velvet touch. He knew this would have to suffice for now, no matter how much more he wanted with her, but man, he wanted to mate her, wanted to push into her and make love to her in the worst way.

She moved around to kiss him while still stroking him, and he cupped her head and kissed her with pent-up longing. He smelled her she-wolf scent and her sex, and all of it enticed him to want to slip into her slick, sweet sheath and take his fill of her, feeling her ripples of climax squeezing him.

And then he was coming in a burst. She smiled and pulled

him into her arms and kissed him lavishly on the mouth. Being with her meant everything in the world to him, and his imagination took him to the future when he could be with her all the way. Then he moved her onto her back and climbed off the bed. Time for a shower. He lifted her off the sheets and carried her into the bathroom.

"You sure know how to do this right," she said.

He sure hoped so. Then they were soaping up, kissing all over again, and getting a lot more than a shower out of the bargain.

When they were all dry and settled back in bed, snuggling together, she said, "So as a zoologist, I study all kinds of animal behavior, including courting and sexual behavior."

Maverick smiled. "Now you're studying *lupus garous'* courting and sexual behavior."

"I am, as an aside. And you're one hot specimen of a wolf. But I have to say when it comes to courting me—you are way ahead of the rest of the wolf bachelors in the pack."

CHAPTER 12

GINA FELT EXQUISITE WHILE SHE WAS LYING AGAINST Maverick after having the greatest time together in bed. Other guys she'd dated hadn't wanted the intimacy during the night when they were sleeping like he had. She wondered if Maverick being with her, snuggling all night like this, was due to their wolf halves—like animals that would curl up together, bonding.

It was so nice, extending the glorious way she felt through this connection. She didn't want to let go and sleep, wanting to feel this moment for all time. But sometime in the night, she left the bed in a fog. That's the only way she could explain it as her body warmed after leaving the warmth of Maverick's body and the covers of the bed. The air surrounding her was cool, and then she was warm again, but she was lower to the ground as if she were crawling on her knees but still standing on her feet—all four of them.

She moved through the ranch house as if in a dream, barely aware of her surroundings, shrouded in mist, her shoulder grazing the back of the sofa, her toenails clicking on the wood floor, the only things that kept her centered in this world. She kept moving forward, listening to sounds like the wind blowing outside, an owl hooting, and she had to investigate. She wanted to know what kind of owl it was in the worst way—her zoology psyche urged her on.

She reached an impenetrable barrier—a door—and felt a little outside air coming in nearby and checked it out. A panel in the wall. She poked it with her nose, and it moved. A wolf door, she thought. And she pushed all the way through. Her fur kept her warm in the chilly breeze as she breathed in the scents: pastureland, reindeer, and pine and fir trees. She saw the light snow falling and heard the owl hoot again, another from farther away answering its call.

She trotted toward the sound of the owl in a nearby tree. And then she saw him peering down at her from his perch on a branch high above. The stocky owl with his feather tufts above his large yellow eyes, dark-brown plumage, and white throat told her he was a great horned owl. He took flight with his large, powerful wings, and she watched him fly away. *Beautiful.*

———

Hearing a great horned owl hooting in the old tree near Josh and Brooke's house, Maverick stirred awake. The owls often nested there, but as soon as Maverick opened his eyes, he saw that Gina was gone.

He listened for a moment but didn't hear her in the bathroom or the kitchen or anywhere else in the house. He hurried out of bed. Her clothes were still on the floor where they had stripped. If it hadn't been that she'd been so newly turned, he wouldn't be worried in the least. But with her being a new wolf, that was a concern.

Naked, he headed down the hall and then peered out through the living room window and saw Gina, red wolf extraordinaire, watching the great horned owl take flight from the old oak next to Josh and Brooke's ranch house.

Maverick immediately raced back to the bedroom, grabbed his phone, and called his ranch manager, waking him. "Hey, Randall, Gina's out running as a wolf. I'm going with her, but if she changes back when we're out running—"

"I'll bring her clothes."

"I'm leaving them on the porch for you." Maverick raced back to the bedroom, grabbed her clothes, ran back to the coat closet to grab her parka, shoved them in a bag, unlocked the front door, and set the bag out on the porch.

Randall Anders was leaving the bunkhouse, pulling on his parka, and jumping in his Jeep while Maverick shifted into his wolf and raced out to join Gina.

Gina was watching Randall drive the Jeep to the ranch house, and then she saw Maverick running to greet her as a wolf.

She smiled at him in her wolf way and then lifted her chin and howled. He howled back, licked her face in greeting, and rubbed against her.

Now this was really nice. He was so glad he was able to run with her as a wolf finally. Then she and he loped off together, moving through the snow-covered, crispy grass while Randall followed them in the Jeep, the wheels crunching on the crust of snow. He was far enough back to give them some privacy but there for her with clothes and a ride home if she shifted again.

Maverick was so glad they were able to be wolves together and to hear her distinctive, melodic howl that he would remember forever. He was thankful his brother and sister-in-law were in town or the howling would have woken them, most likely waking the other ranch hands too.

They ran for a long time, and he wanted her to go as far as she wanted to, but he was worried that the farther from home she got, the higher the risk she would shift into her human form. But she wasn't stopping either. She seemed to want to explore the whole of the acreage all in one night.

Twice, he tried to steer her back home, and finally she turned around and trotted happily in the direction of the ranch house. She'd been having just too much fun with her newfound freedom as a wolf.

Randall dutifully waited as they passed him by and continued their trek to the house.

It would take them at least another half hour to get there, and when they finally reached the porch, Randall pulled up next to it and parked.

Gina pushed through the wolf door, and Maverick barked at Randall, thanking him. Then he went through the wolf door, shifted, opened it, and Randall was already at the door with the bag of Gina's clothes.

"Thanks," Maverick said again.

Randall smiled. "A newly turned wolf can be a handful, but I wouldn't mind her being *my* handful."

Maverick chuckled. "I hear you." Then they said good-night, and he shut and locked the front door. When he turned, he expected to see Gina as a wolf, waiting for him, but she'd left wet paw prints behind on her way to the bedroom.

He hoped she hadn't climbed into bed with wet paws and instead had turned into her human self. But when he reached the bedroom, he found her lying on top of the comforter sound asleep, a beautiful red wolf with a black-tipped tail like his, wet paw prints and a little dirt all over the bed where she had circled a few times before she had settled.

Later that morning, Gina woke in Maverick's arms under the comforter, feeling like she'd run for miles. Happily tired. Maverick leaned down and kissed the top of her head. "Are you hungry?"

"Starving. I felt like I went on a marathon run last night."

"We did run a long distance."

She frowned at him. "What?"

"Last night. When we ran as wolves. I loved hearing you howl."

"No way."

"Yeah, I loved your howl."

"No." She sighed and caressed his chest with her fingertips. "I didn't howl." Then she looked up at him. "Did I shift?"

"Uh, yeah." Maverick was looking really puzzled at her now.

"Oh, sorry about that." She figured she was probably kicking him with her wolf feet in her sleep as she ran through the snowy grass in her dream.

"Nothing to be sorry for. I was just glad we could run together as wolves."

She pulled back from him and stared at him. "We ran together? Outside?"

"Yeah." He frowned at her. "You don't remember it? I found you missing from bed, investigated, and discovered you in your wolf coat watching a great horned owl take flight near Josh and Brooke's house."

"Great horned owl." She tried to think, but, well, she vaguely remembered seeing a great horned owl in a dream and that was it.

"We ran, returned home, and you went straight to bed."

"As a human."

"No. As a wolf. You were lying on top of the comforter, dead to the world, and I had to wash your paws."

"Muddy paws?" She was horrified and looked down at the comforter.

"They were wet mostly. A little dirt. I cleaned the comforter before I lay down with you. You finally shifted about a half hour later, and I resettled the comforter over you, pulled you into my arms, and we slept the rest of the night. You don't remember any of that?" Maverick sounded a little shook up.

"I guess I need to warn you that I sometimes sleepwalk."

Maverick's lips parted, and then he smiled and kissed her forehead. "Okay, I heard your brother mention that when you were at the campfire. That you might have unzipped your tent and that's how I got out."

"You heard us? You were there spying on us?"

"Yeah, I was trying to catch wind of you to see if you smelled like a wolf. You didn't when I was lying next to your sleeping bag. I had to know if you were one or not, but I couldn't catch your scent. Okay, so if you sleepwalk, I mean, since you do, we'll need to lock the wolf door so you don't slip out on your own. In the summer, it wouldn't be so bad, though I would still worry about you getting lost. But in the winter, if you had shifted back into your human form somewhere far away from the ranch and I hadn't awakened and found you gone, you could have gotten frostbite."

She couldn't believe she'd sleepwalked as a wolf! That was a new one for the books. "I'm so sorry. This really adds to the trouble I'll be having with my control over shifting, doesn't it?"

He smiled again and tightened his arms around her. "No way. I had a lovely time running with you and enjoyed hearing your wolf howl. We'll just have to do it again when you're fully awake."

Grateful he didn't mind, she snuggled against his sexy, muscular chest, loving how protective he felt. She was glad he wasn't disturbed by her sleepwalking and amused he'd thought she'd been "all there" with him in the middle of the night. She kissed his chest. "I'm still hungry."

He chuckled. "I'll get us some breakfast."

"I'll help you."

And then they were both out of bed, grabbing fresh clothes, dressing, and heading down the hall where she saw telltale wolf prints on the wood floor, verifying what Maverick had told her was true. No matter how hard she tried to recall any of what had happened, she couldn't remember any of it, except vaguely seeing an owl fly off in her dreams.

She really hoped Maverick was being sincere about not minding her sleepwalking. One guy she'd dated had sworn she faked it to get attention—as if!

Maverick seemed in good spirits this morning, maybe because he'd finally gotten to run with her as a wolf. She sure wished she remembered running with him. And howling. She would love to know how her voice sounded as a wolf. And Maverick's.

Then she and Maverick broke eggs in a bowl, both of them having to fish eggshells out of the bowl and laughing about it. Even when they were washing up, he was getting her wet and she was splashing him, both of them smiling and chuckling. Once the baked eggs and Swiss chard with green olives were done, though Maverick added bacon, feta cheese, and chives to the dish too, they sat down to eat. She loved making meals with Maverick. She'd never dated a guy with whom she'd cooked before, and Maverick was just fun, playful. She really enjoyed being with him.

Then they ate their breakfast, and she figured that since she had shifted in the middle of the night, she would be all right to go with him while he did another reindeer program at a mall.

"I can go with you, can't I?" she asked, just to be sure.

"You sure can. You should be good. I was kind of worried about it until you shifted in the night."

She let out her breath with relief. "Good."

After they finished eating and cleaned up, they headed

out with the reindeer, and Randall came with them. "Did you have a good run last night?" he asked, climbing into the back seat of the pickup while she rode up front with Maverick.

Frowning, she glanced at Maverick. Had he told everyone on the ranch she was sleep-running as a wolf last night?

"He rode behind us in the Jeep, bringing your clothes with him in case you suddenly shifted out in the snow."

"Ohmigod, I never even thought of that. To answer your question, I have no idea if I had fun. I don't remember it at all." There, she said it. She guessed the whole pack would have to be aware of it in case she had trouble with this in the future.

"Oh, okay. My grandmother used to sleepwalk, so I totally understand. She was staying with me one time and walked, or I guess I should say sleepwalked, into my bedroom, confused as to where she was. Then my mother told me she sleepwalked when she was overly tired, had since she was a child, and being in new surroundings, she couldn't find her way to her guest room after she'd left it."

Gina was relieved at least Randall had experienced having known someone who had that trouble.

"Yeah, we'll keep the wolf door locked at night because of it," Maverick said.

"At least you should have gotten the wolf run out of your system for a while," Randall said.

For that, she was glad. But the next time she ran as a wolf out of doors, she wanted to know about it and experience it so she could remember it.

They finally arrived at the mall and the location they

were supposed to set up but saw Calypso's Reindeer Ranch was situated already nearby.

"Was that supposed to happen?" she asked, surprised to see two competing reindeer ranches in virtually the same area.

"Nope," Randall said before Maverick could. "They've been setting up at all the locations we have this season, knowing we're doing so well and trying to gain from our publicity and turnout."

"And setting up even earlier than us now to get a jump on the publicity. We want our reindeer to be more rested before the event." Maverick helped Randall carry out the corral fencing.

She could tell Maverick and the ranch hands were more interested in caring for the animals than being all about the money, the way they interacted with the reindeer, their horses, and the llama. All of the animals were treated like they were family, as if they were part of the wolf pack.

"I had hoped that Andy, the radio show host who shamed the Calypso Ranch owners for riding our coattails, might have convinced them to stop competing with us, but apparently that's not going to happen," Maverick said.

"Calypso must be making too much money off their shows." She grabbed some of the garland to decorate the corral.

Maverick moved another section of corral. "Yeah, exactly, and they feel no moral obligation to do what's right. Next year, our contracts are going to state that the businesses can't sign up to show their reindeer in the same vicinity if we already have an agreement."

"What if they don't agree?" Hauling out the battery-operated Christmas lights, she could just imagine Calypso getting all the contracts then.

"We've been doing this for years, and people are used to coming to see us. Hopefully that will make a difference," Maverick said. "We've never had any trouble before, but Calypso's ranch is under new management. They see our success and want to capitalize on it to promote their own."

"Do they go near Brooke's antiques store when you set up there?" Gina couldn't imagine they would be *that* brazen.

"No. Everyone there has Calypso's number. Brooke has been supporting the other businesses in her area, and they won't have anything to do with Calypso. We didn't even realize the other reindeer ranch was going to pull this until the first time they did it a couple of months ago. We hoped it was just a fluke, but it wasn't. We usually don't take reindeer calves," Maverick said as he and Randall began putting the sections of the corral together, "but after that first case, we've been bringing a few, and they're a real draw. Calypso doesn't have any this year, but betcha next year, they will."

"Maybe we should have brought the llama and her companion too," Gina said. "We could put a big Christmas collar on her. That would be something new and different."

Maverick smiled at her. "That's exactly what we'll do."

"Should we let Andy know that Calypso is at it again?" she asked.

"Nah, they're in a different radio listening area. I'm sure it wouldn't matter to his listening public." Maverick and Randall moved the adult reindeer into the corral while Gina was thrilled to bring the calves into a smaller corral where kids could come to pet the younger reindeer. She just loved being involved in all this. Though she was really irritated that the other ranch was pulling this. Then she helped decorate the corrals with the garland and Christmas lights. "One of us ought to turn wolf. Not me, though I'd love to, but I can't do it at will, and I'd be afraid if I did turn, I'd shift back at the most inopportune of times."

Randall looked at Maverick. "You want me to do it, boss?"

"Wouldn't we stand out if we had a tame wolf at our show that adored the reindeer?" she asked.

"The business owners might worry about liability issues," Maverick said. "But I'm sure it would be true if we had a wolf, we'd get some more interest."

"A wolf dog then?" Gina understood about liability issues, though their wolves wouldn't be a problem. But no one would know that but the *lupus garous*.

"Hold that thought." Maverick got a call. "Yeah, Josh?" He glanced over at the Calypso setup. "Yeah, they arrived even before we got here. Gina proposed that one of us should turn wolf. That could be a draw. No way could they beat that. She also had the idea about bringing the llama. I plan to when we go to the next show... All right. Talk later." He pocketed his phone. "Josh said we need to definitely bring the llama and her reindeer pal next time. Both seem to be used to crowds, and they're comfortable with the other reindeer."

"What about the wolf?" Gina asked.

Maverick smiled. "He said he could come as a wolf.

Brooke said in the background that she had the day off and she could too. If noncompete agreements don't work to deter these guys next year, maybe we'll add wolves to our show."

CHAPTER 13

MAVERICK AND GINA HAD BEEN SHOWING OFF THE REIN-deer and giving kids rides at the mall exhibit. "You might notice the reindeer have deep, rich blue eyes in the winter," he told a group of onlookers. "That's so they can see preda-tors more easily in the dark when the nights are longer, espe-cially up north where the days are dark. And in the summer, their eyes are golden or golden-brown because the days are much longer. Also, you'll notice they have fur covering their noses, all the way to the bottom of their hooves. That way their noses are protected from the cold, and they have a better grip on snow and ice with fur covering their hooves."

Which was the same thing for wolves with fur on the paws to protect them from the cold and to maneuver more easily on snow and ice, he was thinking. Unless the wolf broke through the ice on a lake.

"And reindeer travel in herds into the wind so they can smell scents. Their sense of smell is excellent for finding food under the snow."

"What do they eat besides carrots?" a young boy asked.

"Moss, ferns, grass, lichen—also called reindeer moss— the shoots and leaves of shrubs and trees. Their favorites are birch and willow trees. They also like apples and carrots."

"But they don't have red noses," a little girl said.

"Well, actually, some reindeer do have shiny red noses.

It's the, um, blood vessels in their nose that not only help keep their noses warm in the cold weather but help them find food in the snow. Here, let me show you. This is Mossycoat." Maverick brought the reindeer closer for the kids to see. "You see? It's redder than the other reindeer noses. You might even say it glows, in just the right light."

Some of the adults laughed.

Randall was taking pictures for families when Andy and April showed up. Maverick couldn't have been more surprised.

"We don't go on the air for several hours, but we thought we'd come and see if Calypso was trying to steal your audience away again," April said.

Maverick was thrilled to see them. "They are." To his irritation, but he was trying to keep a cheerful expression, and he was thoroughly enjoying spending this time with Gina. She was so expressive and sweet toward the kids, making them smile for the camera, convincing them to touch the reindeer calves for their pictures and telling them how soft and tame they really were.

Only two little ones were terrified, and it was a wash, but that was understandable. To them, even the reindeer calves were huge. Everyone else was enjoying their time with the reindeer, and when they weren't visiting with the Wilding Ranch reindeer, they were eating at food vendors, visiting the face-painting booth, or sitting on the mall Santa's lap. Calypso didn't have a Santa this time, though they still had the sexy elves, and Maverick noticed a couple of guys had their pictures taken with the elves.

But the kids were much more interested in the Wilding reindeer calves, and they were the real money draw.

Even Andy and April had their pictures taken with the reindeer, and when Maverick mentioned they'd bring the llama and her companion to the next showing, they said they'd be there. Then the couple headed for a pizza stand with promises to bring up the situation with Calypso Ranch with their listeners again.

Maverick smiled. He'd never expected to get continued support from a radio station before. But it seemed to him more people were boycotting the Calypso show this time. And that was good news.

"You didn't tell Andy and April about bringing any wolves," Gina said.

"That's only if we have issues with Calypso next year."

Then Maverick saw a pickup drive up and park next to their truck and trailer. "Josh and Brooke are here." But they didn't climb out of the cab of the truck. "Uh, I think I'm going to check on them."

Gina stayed with the calves and helped with the kids while Maverick approached the truck and saw Josh and Brooke in their wolf forms peering out the dark-tinted window at him. He chuckled and opened the cab door and let them out. Brooke barked at a handmade sign on the back seat, and when Maverick retrieved it, he realized she or Josh had made a sign stating: RARE RED WOLVES—$5 FOR A PHOTO WITH THE WOLVES. PROCEEDS GO TO RED WOLF PRESERVATION.

Hell, why hadn't he thought of that? Wolves were rare enough at exhibits, but red wolves? Unheard of at an exhibition like this, he imagined.

Gina quickly hugged Brooke and then Josh, looking like she fit right in with the pack already.

"Which corral do you want to go into?" Randall asked Josh and Brooke.

They went to the adult reindeer corral. Once Randall let them in, they greeted all the reindeer, who treated them like they were part of their herd.

Maverick quickly hung up the sign on the corral about the wolves, vowing to make his own special hand-carved one for future events. Then he took pictures while his brother and sister-in-law posed, sitting next to each other in front of a couple of the adult reindeer. He shared them with their social media sites: VISIT WITH TWO RED WOLVES AND OUR REINDEER, TODAY ONLY.

"Ohmigod, real red wolves?" a woman said.

Good news or bad? Maverick hoped she was just excited to see them.

"Can I get a picture with one?" the same woman asked.

"Sure, you can have a picture with one. We've raised them from pups, and they love the reindeer and people just as much," Maverick said.

And that was it. Suddenly, they were swarmed with people wanting to pet, hug, and take pictures with the wolves. Gina was their marketing genius.

Not only that, but Andy and April had to see what all the commotion was about and came to check it out.

"Real wolves?" Andy asked.

"Yep, they sure are. Rare red wolves," Maverick said. "We raised them from pups."

"As a zoologist, I can confirm they're truly red wolves," Gina said. "There are more than 200 captive-bred red wolves, known as *Canis rufus*, across the country. And these are two of them. But red wolves are currently critically endangered."

Maverick was glad Gina was well-versed in them already. "Red wolves had lived in the wild in Louisiana and Texas, and some have been reintroduced in the wild in North Carolina. Though they've also discovered some on Galveston Island in Texas more recently. They have a rangy, loping stride and are mostly tawny to even a rusty shade of red, silver-gray forehead, reddish snout, the underside more cream-colored, white or cream-colored legs, with cream-colored underbellies. And all of them vary in coloration and markings. So if you study them, you can see the difference between them. Besides personality. All wolves have their own personalities and temperaments—"

"Like dogs," someone said helpfully.

Maverick smiled. They didn't like to be compared to dogs because wolves took a mate for life; dogs did not. "Wolves mate for life, unlike dogs."

Then one of the Calypso elves came over to see why they no longer had any business at their display and ended up sitting between Brooke and Josh to get her picture taken with the wolves.

After about an hour of nonstop business, to Maverick's further surprise, a zoologist they affectionately called Zooman Thompson showed up. He knew about the red *lupus garou* pack, having years ago captured both Cassie and Leidolf and put them in the zoo. Until he learned they were not all wolf. Cassie had even become his wolf expert advisor to tell him when the wolf wasn't all wolf so he wouldn't make that mistake again. He even knew about jaguar shifters, but Maverick would explain that to Gina later.

Normally, they would have turned Thompson, since he loved wolves, but he had a wife and he had adopted her boy and girl, and Leidolf and Cassie hadn't wanted to turn all of them because they felt Thompson was an acceptable risk. Rarely did they allow a human to know about them like that and not either turn or eliminate him.

"Thompson," Gina said, sounding a little concerned.

Maverick realized then she must know him from working with him at the zoo, but she wouldn't know he knew about them being *lupus garous*. "I guess the two of you know each other."

"Uh, yeah," Thompson said, eyeing Gina as if he was trying to learn if she was a wolf shifter too.

"She's with us," Maverick said, and to Gina, "He knows."

Her eyes widened as much as Thompson's.

"It was on purpose?" Thompson asked. "Or has Gina always been one and I just didn't know it?"

"By accident," Maverick said and explained about falling through the ice. He didn't mention he was a wolf when it happened. He didn't need to.

"I'm happy about it," she quickly said. "I mean, I was shocked and am still getting used to some of it, but studying animals now is so much better. I can sense so many more details than before."

Thompson nodded. "I can imagine that. That would be

one reason I'd want to be one, except for my wife and kids. I just didn't want to uproot them from their friends. I just had to drop by and see the wolves. Looking healthy as ever. Do you mind if I get a picture with them?" He fished out his credit card. "Since this goes to a good cause."

"Sure," Maverick said.

And then Randall took pictures of Thompson and the wolves, the first time ever that Thompson had been able to have his picture taken with them. He looked thrilled.

Once Thompson was done, he rose to his feet and glanced at the Calypso setup. "Looks like you have some competition."

"They're trying to steal our customers again."

Thompson smiled. "So you upped the ante with red wolves."

"We had to do something," Maverick said. "Gina thought of it."

"You won't meet a better bunch of wolves," Thompson told her. "I've got to go. Keep in touch, Gina."

"I will."

Maverick was glad Gina could still consult with another zoologist, one whom she knew and who understood what she was and the trouble with being newly turned.

Then two different news media reporters showed up. Maverick hadn't expected that. He should have consulted Leidolf and Cassie about this first. They tried not to be in the limelight, well, mostly in the wild because there weren't any red wolves in Oregon in the wild. But he realized this could cause some blowback if people wanted to see the wolves at the reindeer ranch. Of course, he could always say they weren't on display there and they wanted to keep it that way.

Maverick texted a couple more ranch hands to help them pack things up. Normally, it would just take the two of them. But with so many people wanting to see the wolves still, they needed more help.

Before it was time to pack it up and leave, another pickup arrived with three more ranch hands to pitch in to help out.

So many people were hanging around to see the wolves that Gina took over picture taking while Randall and two other ranch hands secured the reindeer in the trailer. Maverick and the other ranch hand began taking down the Christmas decorations and packing them up. Everyone but Gina helped haul off the sections of the corral to the trailer.

The Calypso reindeer staff had already packed up and were just leaving the parking lot, but Gina was still happily taking photos of kids and families and adults with the wolves.

"Can you handle the rest?" Randall asked Maverick, once they'd packed up everything to do with the reindeer.

"Yeah, if you'll take the reindeer home and feed them, Gina and I will bring the wolves home in a bit in Josh's pickup."

"Okay, see you in a little while," Randall said, and then he and the other men headed for the two pickups.

The ranch hands left in the two trucks, one pulling the trailer, and Maverick finally thanked everyone who was still hanging around to get close to the wolves. "We really need to get the wolves home to feed them."

That convinced everyone that the wolves probably needed to be fed before they lost their cool.

Then everyone parted so he and Gina could leave with the wolves. He opened Josh's truck's door to the cab, let Brooke and Josh into the back seat, and then closed the door.

Gina climbed into the passenger seat in front, and Maverick drove back to the ranch. Once on the road, Josh and Brooke shifted and began to dress, the side windows darkly tinted just for that purpose.

"The two of you were so cute," Gina said. "I was so afraid the kids would maul you—I mean, some did a little. I bet their parents worried you'd be dangerous, but you both were the greatest ambassadors for red wolves of all time."

Before Brooke or Josh could respond, Maverick got a call on Bluetooth from Leidolf. "Sorry about not asking you and Cassie if it was okay for Brooke and Josh to be wolves at the reindeer exhibit."

"It was our fault," Josh said. "Brooke and I turned up in our wolf coats, and Maverick didn't have any choice."

As if they couldn't have just changed back into their human forms instead.

"What are you going to do if anyone ends up at the reindeer ranch to see the wolves? It's bound to happen, you know," Leidolf said.

"We'll tell them they're not on display," Maverick said.

"It's on the news."

"Uh, yeah," Maverick said. "And the radio talk show host came out to see us and will talk about it on his show tonight.

Zooman Thompson even dropped by, and he knows Gina, so we gave him a heads-up on that situation."

"Okay, well, I guess you are still having trouble with the Calypso Reindeer Ranch staff."

"We are," Maverick said.

"From seeing the crowds gathered around your exhibit, it looked like you were having a sellout show."

Maverick smiled. "We did, and the money we took in for sales of photos with the wolves will be donated to red wolf preservation."

"Good job. That's what we're all about. Preserving our own kind but also doing what we can to help our wild cousins. Carry on."

"Thanks, Leidolf."

"Oh, and Cassie wholeheartedly approved. She's taking one of our wolves on her next lecture tour. Seeing the wolves in person has more of an impact. I'll let you go."

Then they ended the call.

Brooke laughed. "I figured afterward we should have asked them if it was okay. But they're good pack leaders and fair-minded. We just got so caught up in the notion of upstaging the Calypso bunch, we didn't think of calling Leidolf or Cassie first."

"I guess you have to always do that?" Gina sounded a little concerned.

"Only if it could impact on our pack," Josh said, "and only if it's something we have some control over. When Maverick knew you were turned, he had to tell Leidolf and Cassie right away."

"Will you have lunch with us?" Maverick asked.

"Yes," Brooke said. "After all that, I'm ready to chill and have someone else prepare lunch."

Josh laughed. "I'll assist with anything you need help with."

When they arrived home, Maverick pulled out some steaks. "How about steaks, mashed potatoes, and green beans?"

"That sounds great," Brooke said. "You guys can grill the steaks, and Gina and I can make the veggies."

Maverick smiled, knowing Brooke had to always be helping out.

"You know this means you have to make a really cool sign for showing off the wolves if we do this in the future, Maverick," Brooke said as she and Gina got to work peeling potatoes.

"Yeah, that was my very thought when I hung up the sign you made. It was perfect for the situation at hand, but to match our branding, I'll make one."

"What about having people see the wolves at the ranch?" Josh said.

"I guess we could have a special showing, maybe like during Halloween," Maverick said.

"Oh, I would so go for that," Brooke said. "But we have our big pack Halloween party then."

"Then next year, the Saturday night before Halloween we could have a wolf viewing," Maverick said. "Let's go get the grill started."

Gina had already started the water boiling for the potatoes. "I'd love to be part of the Halloween fun at the ranch."

"Yeah, I think it could be a lot of fun. Dress up the reindeer stables in Halloween decorations, orange, black, and purple lights." Brooke placed the green beans in a frying pan and added a little olive oil and seasonings.

"And we could make hats and capes for the reindeer," Gina suggested.

"Oh, I like that idea. I'm so glad you are part of the pack. And Maverick adores you, if you didn't know it. He has dated before, but I've never seen him with a she-wolf he loves being with like he does you."

"I'm afraid he might have bitten off more than he could chew though. I went for a run as a wolf last night."

"Controlling the shifting is more difficult in the beginning, but Maverick is up for it," Brooke assured her.

"I shifted in my sleep."

Brooke finished sautéing the green beans and glanced sharply at Gina.

"I sometimes sleepwalk, though I didn't remember I had."

"Were you okay?"

"Yeah, Maverick was there every step of the way, and Randall came with my clothes in a Jeep in case I shifted back."

"At least Maverick knew what was going on and probably was afraid to wake you when you were sleepwalking."

Gina smiled at her as she drained water from the saucepan, added milk and butter to the potatoes, and mashed them. "He was clueless."

Brooke laughed. "Precious."

Gina really liked Brooke and thought she'd be a fun sister-in-law if she ended up mating Maverick. "Oh, and if Maverick hasn't mentioned it yet, he said all of us could have Christmas together, my parents and brother too, if that's okay with the two of you. I don't want to impose on any of you at all."

"Oh, no, that would be wonderful. We'll have a blast, and we always have so much food that it will work out great."

Gina was glad she'd asked, but then she got a call from her brother while Brooke finished up the vegetable dishes and put them on the table. "Yeah, Weston?"

"We have a problem."

CHAPTER 14

GINA KNEW FROM THE TONE OF WESTON'S VOICE THAT he was really concerned about something. She was going to get Maverick so he could listen in on the conversation, but he and Josh walked inside carrying the steaks on a platter just then. "Weston's on the phone." She was frowning, and Maverick looked like he understood at once there was a problem.

"Can you put it on speakerphone?" Maverick asked as he set the platter of steaks on the table.

Gina nodded. "I'm putting this on speakerphone, Weston. Go ahead."

"They saw the news about the red wolves at the reindeer exhibit. Bromley and Patterson. They called me and said that either Maverick and you were lying to the news reporters about the wolves being real wolves or Maverick had lied to us about them being wolf dogs on the hike. In any case, when they watched how the wolves were so doglike while they interacted with the visitors to your exhibit, they were sure they truly were wolf dogs, or werewolves, like we had suspected," Weston said.

"Okay, um," Gina said, not sure how to handle this.

"How about you have them meet you at your place tonight?" Maverick said to Weston. "They shouldn't feel threatened there."

"All right, then what?"

"We'll be there for you," Brooke said. "This is Brooke speaking."

"Yeah, this is Josh. Both of us will."

"Me too," Gina said.

"I will also," Maverick said.

Weston didn't say anything for a moment.

"What, Weston? Are you afraid of having them turned?" Gina asked.

"Of how they might react. You and I didn't go ballistic over it. At least I was at Maverick's ranch when he turned me. What if the guys scream out in terror, try to flee, or do flee my apartment? What if the neighbors overhear the screams? What if they tell others that wolves bit them? That werewolves bit them?"

"No one will believe werewolves bit them," Gina said. "Well, except for Thompson, the zoologist I know."

"He's one too?"

"No, he isn't. But he's a rare exception to knowing and not telling," Maverick said.

Weston cleared his throat. "Okay, yeah, Bromley and Patterson wouldn't keep quiet about it. Not at first, I don't think. Not until they figured out what was at stake."

"How do you think Patterson and Bromley would feel about being turned?" Gina asked her brother.

"Cheated," Weston said.

"Cheated?"

"Yeah. They wanted to be famous for finding the werewolves. I don't think they'd like the idea of becoming one of them and having to keep the secret," Weston said.

"Okay. I can see that, but can you end your friendship with them like Sarge had done with us?" Gina asked.

"No. We thought he was dead. They'd know I'm here, and they'll know something is wrong with this whole situation."

"So we have to turn them," Gina said.

"Maverick will," Weston said.

"Others are royals." Gina didn't want Maverick to have to turn the whole lot of them. Especially if it caused so many issues and he felt responsible for it, more than he already did because he'd turned her.

"Okay, others can. Leidolf maybe. He turned Sarge, though Sarge told me Leidolf scared the crap out of him, but that was because Sarge's friends had taken werewolves hostage," Weston said.

She noted for the first time Weston hadn't called the other Dark Angels his own friends. After she had learned they had killed a couple of supposed werewolves, she had wanted to distance herself from them too.

"Maybe at the New Year's Eve party," Weston said.

"No. They might bring dates," Gina said. "And if you said no dates, they'd probably be suspicious."

"Oh, yeah, you're right."

"Do you think they would come to our reindeer ranch?" Maverick asked.

"I don't know, but I think it would be safer there than at my place."

"If you want, we could make dinner for all of us and tell them I'll show them the wolves. Since they saw the wolves in the news, they could see they were perfectly harmless or they wouldn't be out in public, serving as ambassador wolves. We could tell them there's no way we would expose some of the red wolves if they were werewolves," Maverick said. "At least they might consider that notion."

"I don't know if they'll buy it, but we can try," Weston said. "The only problem I see is that they might think I've been turned, and they won't trust me. If they did spread the word about us being werewolves, some others who believe in them might come to call."

"Okay, try that and see what happens," Maverick said. "Tell them we can have them over at seven. We're having steaks for lunch, so we could fix brisket. Would that work for all of you? Our last tour group is out of here by seven."

"Yeah. We all like brisket. I'll tell them. Don't be surprised if they drop in a lot earlier than that, when the tour group is still there, or if they make some lame excuse about not being able to come in the event they think it's a setup."

"All right. We'll be ready."

"We're sitting down to eat lunch," Gina said. "Oh, have you seen the wolf you had danced with at the Christmas party yet?"

"Dorinda? No. I swear the pack is conspiring against me and making sure I can't see her."

Gina chuckled. "Ask Cassie for Dorinda's phone number and ask her to go with you to the New Year's Eve party if she doesn't have a date already, since you're a wolf now."

"I'll try that. I'll call you back to let you know what's up."

"Talk soon," Maverick said.

When they ended the call, everyone sat down to eat.

"Okay, I know what we'll be doing," Brooke said. "Hanging around the ranch for the rest of the day."

"You could return to the store if you want," Josh said.

"And miss out on all the news? No way. I'm here to help in any way I can." Brooke started slicing into her steak.

A short while later, Weston called back, and Gina answered, putting it on speakerphone. "You're on speakerphone, Weston. What did they say?"

"They can't make it tonight because they have other plans, but they could do it tomorrow night, if Maverick is agreeable."

"What do you suspect is truly going on?" Maverick asked.

Gina realized what a wary wolf he was, and he wasn't buying their story. But she wasn't sure. What if they did have commitments? It was really short notice. Still, she could see where Maverick was coming from. She wanted to think best of the plan, but they probably needed to plan for the worst.

———

Maverick figured that if anyone knew his friends well, it was Weston, and he would have a better feel for what his friends' reaction to having dinner at the reindeer ranch would be, good or bad—which was why he had posed the question to him.

"I'm not sure. Both of my friends hesitated to answer. They covered the mouthpiece to discuss options. I could hear their muffled voices but couldn't make out what they said exactly. I heard Bromley say, 'No, too soon.' It took them too long to tell me they had other plans, and they didn't tell me what they were, like they normally would have."

"As if you were in the enemy's camp already," Maverick said. Brooke, Gina, and Josh listened in while continuing to eat lunch.

"Yeah, because Gina's working with you, Maverick, and they're not sure about me. I'm not telling them I'm staying at Leidolf and Cassie's ranch, but if they drop by my apartment, I won't be there, unless it's a case of me grabbing some more of my stuff. Some of Leidolf's men helped me gather a lot of my clothes already. But I still have a lot of stuff there."

"Okay, tell them tomorrow night is fine. We have another tour group here—which may be why they want to be here at that time. It's one of our late-night tour group shows. And they can be part of the group to see all the reindeer and the llama. And the two wolves."

"Three, because you had two males before. Now you have two males and a female. I'll tell them. Maybe they'll figure it will be safe with others there. I'll let you know."

"We'll be waiting to hear from you," Maverick said.

When they ended the call, Josh shook his head. "Sounds like these guys are wary."

"Wouldn't you be if you already believed Maverick and his friends could be werewolves and the story keeps changing about having wolf dogs and now red wolves? Even I verified you two were red wolves in front of all the people there today at the show. So I knew and never told Weston's friends. And he didn't either, though he could have let on he hadn't known and hadn't even seen the show. For all they know, he's back at work and not having to do with any of the people at this ranch or Leidolf's."

"Well, I'm all for staying at the house for the next few nights then," Brooke said, "just in case we have some unwelcome visitors pop in just any old time."

"Do you want to return to the shop and do any more markdowns or label anything this afternoon in the meantime?" Josh asked.

Brooke nodded. "I might as well go to the shop since they're not coming this evening."

"Plan to have dinner with us at our place then," Josh said to Maverick and Brooke. "Your brother can come too, Gina, if he'd like."

"That sounds great," Gina said.

Then they cleared the dishes, and Josh and Brooke took off for town.

Weston called Gina back while she and Maverick were cleaning up the kitchen. "It's a go for tomorrow night. They were eager to see the reindeer and the wolves, of course."

"Okay, that sounds good," Maverick said. "And we'd love to have you come and have dinner with us tonight. Josh and Brooke's treat. Bring Sarge, if you'd like, since you're staying with him."

"Right. He can be my designated driver."

"I guess we both have to have one now," Gina said.

"Yeah. It's a bit of a bother, but lots of people are willing to help me out," Weston said.

"Did you ask Dorinda if she'd go with you to the New Year's Eve party?"

"Uh, yeah, and Dorinda said she would—because she feels sorry for me."

Maverick chuckled. "Believe me, she's dating everyone, not taking chances on mating the wrong wolf. So if she said she will go with you to the New Year's Eve party, she's interested in you."

Gina smiled. "Great! See you tonight then."

"See you." Weston ended the call.

"When's your next show someplace else?" Gina sounded hopeful she could attend while she put the last of the dishes in the dishwasher.

"Tomorrow afternoon." Maverick finished washing the saucepan and frying pan. He hoped she could come too. But if she couldn't, he'd stay at the ranch with her and do the show for the tour group visits instead. That way if she had to shift, he'd be there for her.

"Okay, maybe I can sleepwalk as a wolf again tonight."

Smiling, he rubbed her back. "Or just go running with me as a wolf while you're awake."

"Oh, sure, even better."

Then they pulled on their parkas and headed outside. She was documenting things, and he worked with the ranch hands getting things ready for the afternoon show here. But he also told Leidolf of the situation with Weston's friends and the dinner date with them tomorrow.

"I'll be there," Leidolf said.

"You're coming to dinner?" Maverick was surprised. He was afraid that would make the men warier.

"No. But I'll be there to help turn the men."

"In the shadows?"

"I'll stay at Josh and Brooke's house. When you need me, one of you can text me and I'll be there."

"Will do, Leidolf." Maverick wondered if any of the men, Weston included, had figured out that Leidolf's name was old Norse for "descendent of the wolf".

Gina was out in the field taking pictures of some deer, and he watched her for a moment. Then she turned to see him observing her, and she headed toward him. The deer scattered. He was about to walk toward her to join her when Randall intercepted him. "Hey, boss, I thought you told Gina about jaguar shifters."

Ah, hell, he had meant to. "Uh, no, I guess you told her. I hope she's all right with it."

Randall smiled. "Shocked is more like it."

"I suspect so. I'll go talk to her." Maverick headed in her direction again and soon joined her.

She shouldered her camera and wrapped her arms around his neck. "Is there anything *else* you want to tell me about?"

He smiled and kissed her cold lips and her cold nose. "Okay, so, yeah, jaguar shifters exist, and we've heard rumors bear shifters and cougars do too. Which makes me think that others might also. It's just hard to believe they exist until we've seen it for ourselves. We've actually dealt with a policing force called the United Shifter Force that was started by jaguars. Wolves have joined their ranks. So you never know when their staff might expand to include different kinds of shifters. I meant to tell you after you got over the shock that you're a wolf and that our kind exist."

"Wow, that would be amazing to see."

"Yeah, I missed out on all the drama when they were at Leidolf's ranch, too busy with the reindeer activities at the time."

"So they don't live here," she said.

"No, they're located in Dallas and the Houston, Texas, area. They might need to expand their network, but that's all I know of for now."

"Okay, so if I see a bear or a cougar on your acreage, it might be a shifter?"

He frowned. "If you see either, you treat them like they are wild animals."

She laughed. "Of course. I'm a pragmatist. I wouldn't be foolish enough to think any wild predator was a shifter. But you better believe I'll be watching them for unusual behavior if I see one."

He smiled and kissed her again. "Okay, that sounds good."

"No other secrets?"

"Not that I know of."

They heard the sound of a tour bus driving up, and he glanced back at it. "It's showtime. Are you going to help with it, or do you want to continue your work with the wildlife out here?"

She slipped her gloved hand in his. "I want to do this with you."

"I'm glad." He kissed the top of her head and walked her back to the stables where Randall was starting to talk to the tour group. "Do you want to work with the kids and the reindeer calves?"

"I certainly do." Gina looked eager to greet the kids.

Early that evening, they saw Brooke and Josh arrive at their own home and waved at them.

After the group tour was done, Maverick and Gina walked inside his house to warm up and have some hot cocoa before they went over to have dinner with Brooke, Josh, and her brother.

They pulled off their parkas and gloves and washed up.

"Do you ever wish you were just human?" Gina asked as they sat down in the living room and enjoyed their cocoa by the Christmas tree and the fire.

"No. I've never known anything other than being a shifter, but with the faster healing, all our enhanced senses, our increased longevity, and the freedom we have as wolves, I wouldn't want it any other way." But he was worried about Gina changing her mind, especially with the situation of having to turn their friends and her parents. "What about you?"

"Oh, I love being a wolf. I could smell the deer, their different scents distinguishing each of them, heard some of the sounds they made that I wouldn't have as a human. Plus I feel more like them, wilder, on a par with them, not as a human looking down on them, feeling more superior. It's proving to be a wonderful gift for my research."

"That's great," he said, leaning over to kiss her, when they heard a truck park outside.

"That's probably Weston and Sarge." She kissed Maverick, and he kissed her deeply, and then they reluctantly separated.

He wanted to kiss her right into his bed. "Yeah, that's

Sarge's truck. I can tell by the roar of his engine." Maverick's doorbell rang.

"I'll be able to recognize it from now on."

"Exactly. It's a great ability to know if someone new has arrived unfamiliar to you or it's someone you know." Maverick answered the door. "Hey, Weston, Sarge." He shook their hands and told them to come in.

"Are the two of you mated yet?" Weston asked.

"No," Gina said. "And don't ask. If it happens, we'll let you know."

"If you're not going to mate her, let me date her," Sarge said.

Maverick gave him a look like he couldn't be serious.

"Okay, I know that look, and that means a big fat no," Sarge said.

Maverick pulled on his parka, and she took his hand, telling everyone there she truly was with him. He liked the intimacy they shared. He couldn't wait to run with her as a wolf again and really play with her if she was up for it.

They all headed over to Josh and Brooke's house, all lit up just like everything else. Maverick loved this time of year when everything was brightly illuminated. It was so cheery and welcoming.

When they reached Josh and Brooke's house, Brooke opened the door and greeted them. "Come in, come in. We'll have drinks first, and then we'll have dinner. We're so glad you joined us too," she said to Weston and Sarge.

"Thanks for inviting us. Everything smells great," Weston said. "With our sensitive sense of smell, I can't believe how the aroma of food seems even more mouthwatering." His stomach grumbled.

They all smiled.

"Okay, special Christmas cocktails all around. This is a combination of Irish cream, coffee liqueur, vodka, and double cream," Brooke said.

They took their drinks and said "Merry Christmas" to each other, clinking their glasses together.

"Okay, what about battle plans?" Josh asked as they sat down in the living room, a crackling fire going, the Christmas tree all lit up.

"Tomorrow night we'll have dinner at our place," Maverick said. "Leidolf plans to be at your house during dinner, if he didn't already tell you, and will wait for us until one of us texts him. He'll help turn one of the men. I guess it's up to you or me to turn one or the other, however it works best."

"I can do it," Brooke said.

Josh ran his hand over her shoulder. "I'd prefer one of us to do it. I don't want either of the men injuring you."

"I'll still be backup," she insisted.

"I guess Weston and I can't be backup," Gina said.

"No. Even if you could call on the shifting at will," Maverick said, "it would be better if a royal turned the men."

"How are things going between the two of you?" Gina asked Weston and Sarge.

"Good. He's usually at work during the day, and I work at his place. We have dinner together, watch shows, and when I shift, we can go running together."

Gina reached over and squeezed Maverick's hand. "I hope we can too again soon."

"I do too."

They finally ate dinner, and then Sarge and Weston left for the night. Maverick and Gina said goodnight after that and then left.

"Are you ready for bed?" Maverick was ready for much more than that with Gina. He just hoped she wouldn't get the urge to shift at the wrong time, not because he would be upset about it, but he was afraid she would be.

CHAPTER 15

GINA WAS SURE READY FOR BED AND LOTS MORE HOT wolf loving from Maverick. They began getting ready for bed play, pulling off their clothes, and her blood was heating. But then she realized it wasn't because they were getting ready to have sex. She was shifting!

"No, no, the shift is coming on." She was happy and disappointed at the same time. She really wanted to make love to Maverick, and she hoped he wasn't frustrated with her. She could see where this could be a problem, especially if they were mated and they couldn't just make love whenever they were ready and willing if the shifting issues came up at the same time.

"Oh, ready for a run instead," Maverick said, hurrying to help her out of the rest of her clothes. He sounded fine with switching gears so all of a sudden.

She was so glad he was helping her pull off her clothes in a rush. She didn't think she would have made it in time otherwise. Once she was naked, she couldn't hold back the shift, but she still got in a super-quick kiss, and then she dropped to all fours and was a wolf. She howled, telling the world she'd mastered another shift one more time. It was the first time she had actually heard her own wolf howl.

Quickly ditching the rest of his clothes, Maverick smiled, grabbed his phone, texted Randall, and shifted. Maverick and

Gina raced each other to the wolf door, their nails clicking on the floor, their bodies bumping each other in playful fun.

Now this was great. She figured he would have gotten to the wolf door first with his longer legs, but he was being a wolf gentleman and let her go first. She was glad he hadn't locked the wolf door already as she barged through it. They would have to do it after they returned for the night, just in case she shifted and went sleepwalking again.

Then he bolted after her through the wolf door and out of the house. She woofed, he howled, and they tore off together. Randall was running out of his house, waved at them, thumbs up to Gina, and headed to Maverick's house to get her clothes for her, she figured.

She was glad Randall would bring her clothes in the event she shifted back while they were on their snowy run. Small snowflakes fluttered in the air, catching on their wolf whiskers and eyebrows. She felt alive, free, wonderful as she chased around Maverick in circles, and he tried to catch her tail. She swore he was smiling while he did it.

They played chase back and forth, and she heard the Jeep coming for them—Randall to the rescue, in case she needed it. But she sure hoped she wouldn't because being with Maverick as wolves was so entertaining. She tried to stay on more of a beaten path so that Randall could follow them in the Jeep. Then she realized she was on the same trail as she'd been on last night. She'd left her scent from her paw pads. Oh, this was so cool!

Okay, so if she went this far last night and didn't shift all the way home, she should be able to this evening, she assumed. She paused and looked back at the ranch houses off in the distance, the Christmas lights all turned off for the night, yet she could still see the homes with her wolf's night vision and the security lights illuminating certain key places on the ranch.

Maverick was waiting with her, watching to see what she wanted to do, maybe worried she felt the urge to shift and was thinking of running back to the house. But she wanted to run all night long, explore as much as she could as a wolf, leave her scent trail to say she belonged here. She wanted to see everything she could with her night vision, smell all the smells, hear all the sounds, and taste the snow falling from the clouds, all as a wolf.

She trotted off again, not in as much of a hurry now, and saw a rabbit dart into a hole. She heard an owl hooting off in the distance, another responding. She sat then and lifted her chin and howled again. Hearing her own howl sounded so hauntingly beautiful and strange, but outside where it could carry farther, it was even more wondrous. Maverick stood beside her and lifted his chin and howled with her, as if singing his love for her. It was such a beautifully romantic moment.

Then from the direction of the bunkhouse and Josh and Brooke's house, she heard more howls, the wolves telling them they heard, they were united, they were pack mates.

She loved hearing the camaraderie of the wolves. Of course, it made her think of documenting wolf behavior— tame, not wild, because they weren't all wild. And they weren't all wolf.

She and Maverick continued on until she reached the end of her scent trail and she smelled something else. She wasn't sure what it was.

To her surprise, Maverick shifted. "Coyote. We can chase him off or head home. How do you feel?" He shifted back into his wolf.

She'd had a ball. She felt that when she had turned into her wolf, she might not be able to do it again, though she also had the worry that she might not be able to change back to her human form after she was a wolf. All newly turned wolves probably felt the same way.

She wanted to make love to Maverick, but she might not shift back right away. She sighed. She would rather run all the way back home with him as a wolf than have to shift and get a lift back home while hurrying to dress in the Jeep, freezing her butt off.

She licked Maverick's face, and he kissed her back in his wolf way. Her sensitive whiskers felt his whiskers, which heightened the experience, making them tingle with pleasure. Determined to get back on her own as a wolf, she loped toward the ranch house. He quickly joined her.

Randall waited for them to pass his Jeep, and he turned around to follow them home.

But suddenly, there was a commotion at the stables, then reindeer grunts, the pounding of hooves, the jingling of sleigh bells on their collars as they raced in their direction. The reindeer and llama had been released from the stables and spooked.

Gina didn't know what to do. She wanted to round them up, but she was afraid they'd run over her while they were stampeding from some unknown threat. And she wasn't sure she had the wolf roundup ability in her repertoire yet.

Maverick started to turn the reindeer back to their stable, and she watched him for a moment and then figured it had to be a natural wolf-hunting ability and she had to have been gifted with it as well. She began to steer the reindeer back to the ranch, and the next thing she knew, ranch hands on horseback were riding out to help them.

Though she noted Randall was staying nearby her in his Jeep, just in case she suddenly shifted, and she sure hoped she wouldn't! It would be bad enough if he saw her do that, but the other ranch hands too?

As the ranch hands got the herd under control, Maverick dashed for her and urged her back to the house.

She guessed he was worried about her shifting, but then Josh pulled a truck up next to them and opened the door. Maverick jumped in and shifted. "I'll meet you at home, Gina."

She *wasn't* staying behind, and she jumped into the back of the cab with him. Randall roared up next to them in his Jeep and threw his door open, and with the bag of her clothes, he raced out of it. He tossed the bag into the back seat. "Be right behind you guys."

Then he slammed the door shut and ran back to his Jeep. He jumped in, yanked his door closed, and tore after Josh's truck as he drove through the gate.

She realized then that someone hadn't left the stable

doors open and somehow all the reindeer got out on their own. They had to have had help.

Maverick had shifted, pulled clothes out of a bag in the backseat, and was yanking them on. "We have clothes in the vehicles for ourselves, just in case of an emergency," he told her. "We'll have to do the same for you."

"They were Calypso's men," Josh said. "When everyone else was herding the reindeer back to safety, Brooke and I checked the scents in the stable, and it was the same men we saw at the setup earlier."

"We saw a coyote on our run. I was worried about the reindeer coming upon a pack of coyotes, especially the little ones. Though reindeer calves can outrun bears and wolves even." Maverick pulled his shirt over his head and gave Gina a hug.

She hoped he wasn't annoyed with her for coming with them, maybe worried she would shift at the wrong time. But if she stayed in the truck, she should be all right. And no way had she wanted to wait at home for him. She was one of the pack members now, and she wanted to do what she could to help out.

She wished she could turn back into her human form and ask them what they planned to do. With only three men here, they wouldn't be able to do a whole lot if the Calypso staff outnumbered them or were armed.

She glanced out the window and realized Josh was driving in the direction of Leidolf and Cassie's ranch.

"They're not headed in the direction of the Calypso Ranch," Maverick said.

"They want to throw us off. They wouldn't want to lead

us straight back to their ranch. But the men were driving a pickup with the Calypso Reindeer Ranch logo on it. I called Leidolf. He's got men headed this way. They'll intercept them," Josh said.

Oh, good, more men. She had worried about that. She loved how the pack worked together.

"If they don't slow down when we get to that curve up ahead, they won't make it," Maverick said.

"That will serve them right." Josh got a call on Bluetooth from one of their ranch hands. "Yeah, go ahead."

"All the reindeer are accounted for, no injuries, and everyone's back to bed. Did you catch the bastards yet?"

Just then, they saw a truck overturned down the hill, the headlights sending light into a snowy fog bank, right where Maverick said they'd have trouble if they didn't slow down.

"Yeah, we found them in an upside-down truck," Josh said.

"At Deadman's Curve," the ranch hand said.

"Yep."

"It isn't really named that," Maverick said to Gina. "No one's died there that we know of, but the pack members all know about it because there have been tons of vehicular accidents at that point in the road. We've warned our people to heed the posted speed limit signs."

Josh pulled off the road and parked, Randall parking right behind him next in line on the shoulder, both of them leaving their headlights and flashers on to warn of an accident.

Josh quickly called the others who were joining them

from Leidolf's ranch. "Hey, we're at Deadman's Curve. The Calypso truck is overturned here. Checking on them now."

"Do you want to stay in the truck?" Maverick asked Gina, giving her the choice this time.

She shook her head, and when he got out, she bounded after him and was down the incline before any of the men were.

"Holy shit, it's one of their wolves," one of the Calypso men said.

She didn't need to growl at them, they were terrified enough. Good. See? She knew she had a part to play.

Maverick and Josh quickly joined her; Randall arrived right after that.

"Do you have any broken bones or internal injuries?" Josh asked.

The two men were still seat-belted in their truck and were upside-down.

"Just get us out of here," the blond snarled.

Maverick checked the truck's engine. "I smell gas. Let's get them out of there in case the engine blows."

The men's eyes widened, and they tried frantically to unbuckle their seat belts.

"If we move you and you have internal injuries, it could make them graver," Maverick said.

"Yeah, but a fireball would make their injuries even worse," Josh said as he and Maverick cut the seat belt for one man and hurried to move him away from the truck.

Gina paced, wanting to help but unable to do anything

for the moment. Randall was cutting at the other man's strap, and then another truck arrived. Maverick helped Randall move the driver from his truck. The driver cried out, and Gina suspected he might have a broken limb. Leidolf and some of his men piled out of their vehicle and ran down the hillside. Leidolf raised his brows to see Gina in her wolf coat, though he'd never actually seen her as a wolf, but she suspected he smelled her.

She wagged her tail at him, hoping he wasn't irritated with her for being there. Leidolf smiled, and that little smile made her feel good.

Then he said to everyone there, "An ambulance and tow truck are on the way. Also the police are coming. How are the injured men doing?"

"They seem to be okay, except this guy might have a dislocated shoulder and a broken arm, the other might need some stitches for the cut on his forehead and a nose job to straighten out the crooked nose," Maverick said. "So why were you at the Wilding Reindeer Ranch releasing our reindeer and causing a stampede?" He practically growled the words at the injured men.

Neither of the men would say anything. Then one said, "We want a lawyer."

"I can't imagine why in the world you would release the reindeer unless you thought they'd be injured and we couldn't do our shows for the rest of the season," Maverick said. "You couldn't believe this would stop us."

They heard the ambulance and two police car sirens en route.

She thought Maverick would put her in the truck so that

no one would be afraid of the wolf, but he didn't. He just took pictures of the upside-down truck and of the men. They were wearing gloves so she knew the Calypso men wouldn't have left any fingerprints behind at the Wilding Ranch.

Another ambulance sounded in the distance, and the first one and the two police cars arrived. She kept looking back up the hill at Josh's truck, and finally Maverick said, "Do you want to get in the truck?"

He probably worried then that she was feeling like she was going to shift.

He trudged up the hill while she ran up it as the police officers—who blessedly smelled like wolves and she wanted to laugh, she was so thankful—glanced at her, smiled, nodded in greeting, and hurried down the slope to document the accident. The EMTs were on their way down right behind them. They weren't wolves, but she suspected the police officers were part of Leidolf's pack so they would find everything in favor of the Wilding brothers no matter what the circumstances had been.

It paid to have wolves working in various occupations, she realized. Maverick opened the truck door for her. "Do you have to shift?" he asked for her ears only.

She shook her head. She'd been more worried about the emergency crews and the police arriving and seeing a wolf on the scene.

"Okay, good. We're just going to give our version of the story, and then we can leave. If it takes too long, I can drive you home. The police won't keep me."

She nodded, though she wanted to tell him to stay as

long as he needed. They had to stop Calypso from doing anything further to the Wildings' business. That's when she heard another vehicle coming, and she peered out of the window to see a news van pull up behind Randall's Jeep. She smiled. That's just what they needed—a news report putting the Calypso Ranch in a bad light—and she was glad she'd returned to the truck, not wanting a wolf to garner any attention. All of the heat should be on the bad guys.

Maverick had worried that Gina had suddenly needed to shift, but it appeared that the only trouble was she was anxious about the arrival of the emergency crews and them seeing her as a wolf. He couldn't wait to get this business taken care of and go home to make love to her. If she was even in the mood now.

After seeing how much she loved the reindeer and loved to be part of the shows with the calves and the kids, he had been searching for just the right reindeer calf to give her for Christmas. It would be hers to raise and love. But he was buying her a special one—a leucistic calf so she would have something even more special to study. He would do everything to make her happy to be staying with them. With *him*. Some leucistic reindeer calves were often deaf. Her eyesight wouldn't be as good as the reindeer without leucism, but in a setting like they had, she would always be safe, as long as they didn't have problems with thugs like the Calypso Ranch hands trying to run off the reindeer into the wilderness.

Because of Gina's propensity to study wildlife, he assumed she'd love the opportunity, though he even thought having a rare white reindeer would add to their exhibits' uniqueness.

He left Gina in the truck and returned to the accident site to see if anyone needed his help. Josh, Randall, and Maverick gave their statements to the police. The EMTs finally got the men into the ambulances, and when they left, the media vans took off.

Leidolf said, "Okay, good job, men. They'll be charged with a number of crimes on your property and off."

"They should be," Maverick said, furious that anyone could have so little disregard for the animals when they cared for reindeer of their own.

"And the news is reporting on it, so Calypso is getting a black eye over all this," Josh said.

"Their new management deserves it," Maverick said. "Maybe something good will come of this."

"Why don't you two take Gina home?" Leidolf asked.

"Yeah, we sure will," Josh said.

Maverick agreed that they should go. Then he and Josh climbed back up the hill to the truck.

"Are you okay?" Maverick asked Gina, settling into the back seat with her, and then Josh drove them back to the ranch.

She licked his cheek and laid her head on his lap. He took that as a yes. He wondered if she would shift soon. And then she raised her head quickly, and he had his answer. She shifted in a beautiful blur of forms and was instantly in her human body. He helped her dress, and Josh turned up the heat so she wouldn't get chilled.

"Oh, I hope the news media rakes Calypso's management over the coals," she said.

"Yeah, how much do you want to bet that the management refutes that they had any part in any of this?" Maverick said.

"They would, to avoid repercussions," Josh said.

But with some of the radio show host flak they'd been getting and now this, really endangering the reindeer? Maverick suspected they would be in trouble.

Gina finished dressing and gave Maverick a hug. He kissed her mouth, deepening the kiss, promising her much more when they got home.

CHAPTER 16

As soon as they reached the reindeer ranch and Maverick's home, Josh dropped Maverick and Gina off. She was so eager to take this all the way with Maverick. She just hoped he would feel the same way as her.

"See you tomorrow," Josh said.

"Yeah, 'night, Josh," Maverick said.

"'Night," Gina added.

Then Maverick and Gina went inside, and she locked the wolf door, just in case she had to sleepwalk as a wolf tonight, though she figured she should be okay for some hours now.

She kissed Maverick, and they dumped their parkas on the back of the couch. He picked her up and set her on the couch and then pulled off her boots. She pulled him down onto the couch and then got up to pull his boots off, removing each of his socks and tossing them. He smiled and got up from the couch and took her hand and headed back to the bedroom. If she could have, she would have stayed in her wolf form before they arrived home. Then she could have just shifted, been naked, and not had to remove her clothes again. Not that she'd had any choice.

But once they were in the bedroom and Maverick started removing her shirt and she pulled off his, she realized this was nice too, working up the heat, their hearts thumping harder, their breaths quickening. Then they began unfastening belts, their mouths fused together in a never-ending kiss.

"How long do we need to date before we can mate?" she whispered against his mouth.

He pulled his face away from hers and smiled down at her, raising his dark brows expectantly. "It's for life, and we live long lives."

"Yeah, so is that a problem?" Tension knotted her stomach as she stroked his muscular arms. She had decided she wanted this, and she didn't want him to talk her out of it unless he really wasn't ready for it.

He chuckled.

"You turned me." She ran her hands up his glorious abs. "I wasn't going to say you were stuck with me because of it. I don't want you to feel that way." She sighed. "I don't know if it's the wolf instincts or what, but I want you all for myself. I don't want to dance with other wolves at dances. I don't want anyone else to think they have a chance at dating me if you feel the same way about me as I do about you. I've fallen hopelessly in love with you. Is that possible?"

She really was hooked on him, and she kept thinking she was nuts, that she couldn't possibly know him well enough to feel he was the only wolf for her. But she felt the pull so strongly that she couldn't think of anything else. She wondered if she really understood the way it was with the wolf kind or she was wrong about all this. Maybe if she gave other wolves the chance to date her, she wouldn't feel so strongly about Maverick, but she didn't think so.

He smiled down at her and put his hands on her shoulders

and gently caressed them. "For wolves, like other wild animals that mate for life, the need is instinctual. It's just something we recognize when we meet the right wolf. It's undeniable. We can keep seeing each other, and we can see others, but we're going to continue to want to be together. It's a stronger need than humans have. It's a biological need that goes so much deeper. And, yeah, I feel the same for you. I was going to wait until we had more time to be with each other so you would be certain, but I'm totally into you. Turning you certainly made me feel the need to be protective and take care of you, but it goes *way* beyond that. I'm ready to be your mate if you are ready to be mine. I couldn't be any luckier or gladder for it." He kissed her upturned lips and smiled against them. "I love you."

"Oh, good, I'm not being too impulsive then."

He gave a lusty laugh. "No. I've wanted to do this since I learned you were one of us."

That made her heart sing. "I love you right back. Then we're good to go." And she kissed him again, her tongue plunging between his parted lips. He tasted so good, and she wanted to drink every bit of him in.

He wrapped his arms around her and rubbed his aroused body against hers. Hot, hard, sexy. He knew just how to trigger her need to want him deep inside her, their raw pheromones playing to each other.

She pressed her body harder against his, moving in a way that encouraged the contact and intimacy, feeling emboldened by his wolfish hotness. He moved his mouth from hers to press kisses to her jawline, her throat, making her tingle with need, her stomach muscles tightening.

She lost all perspective when she was with him. He was her world, and nothing else mattered. She leaned down to kiss his pecs and lick his nipples, pebbled delight. Sucking in his breath, he kissed the top of her head.

He had such a rugged charm about him, his shadow of a beard making him look roguish, his dark eyes smiling down at her before she unfastened his jeans. Then she unzipped his jeans and pulled them down his legs. He pulled off her pants too, and then they were kissing again.

His hands shifted down to her buttocks, and he pulled her firm against his erection. She was feeling so hot, and she hoped it was only because of the lovemaking and *not* because she was shifting again.

He reached behind her and unfastened her bra and pulled it off her, and then he took hold of her breasts, rubbing his thumbs over her sensitive and taut nipples, making her feel heavenly. Then their mouths fused together in a long, lingering, lascivious kiss.

They turned their attention to her panties and his boxer briefs, pulling them off each other at the same time. They crouched together, kissed, and then kicked off their underwear. Then he scooped her up and set her on the bed, joining her.

This was it, she thought. The mating.

But he didn't press his stiff erection between her legs like she believed he would to mate with her. Instead, he began stroking her clit, arousing her already-stimulated feminine nub to the nth degree. At the same time, he began kissing her breast, suckling her nipple, and she moaned with pure pleasure. He was a master at the art of making love to her. And she was so glad they weren't waiting to do this.

She ran her hands through his hair as he kissed the valley between her breasts and licked and suckled her other nipple, but he wasn't giving up his stroking her bud either. She was getting close to the end, the feeling overwhelming her. Holding on with everything she had, she wanted to reach the top. She was climbing, climbing. The climax suddenly hit, and she shattered into a thousand blissful pieces. She felt so good and let out the breath she'd been holding in anticipation of the end.

"Gina," he whispered. "Love you."

And she smiled. "Love you too."

Then he quickly moved her legs farther apart and inserted his penis between her feminine lips and pushed until he had filled her to the max. He began to push and then pull out. He deepened his thrusts, and she was totally in heaven, wrapping her legs around him, giving him deeper access, one of her sock-covered feet stroking the back of his leg.

He continued to press his advantage, so beautiful, his muscles rippling, his mouth connecting with hers, kissing her, and thrusting his erection deep.

Her hands caressed his face, her body open to him, her lips parted and encouraging their tongues to explore and tangle with each other. And then he was slowing his thrusts, speeding up again, and then coming home.

Yeah, he was home. They were mated wolves as he exploded inside her. "Oh, ahh, yeah."

She felt so hot, so complete, and then he settled down on

top of her, spent, smiling, kissing her. "I love you, but…" she started to say.

"I love you too. But?"

She pushed him off her. "I need to shift."

He laughed. "Let's go for a run, my beautiful she-wolf."

She thought it wouldn't happen again so soon, but that's what Maverick had warned her about—shifting was totally unpredictable in newly turned wolves.

She shifted, only she was still wearing her socks. He pulled them off and then shifted too. She leapt off the bed as a wolf, and he joined her on the floor and then chased her down the hall, gaining on her. She turned and woofed at him. He ran into her, not meaning too. She knew he just hadn't expected her to turn on him like that. She wanted to laugh at his surprised expression as they fell in a tumble of wolf fur and legs. Then he licked her, and they untangled themselves from each other and ran off again, her in the lead, him nipping at her tail. He suddenly woofed at her before she hit the wolf door, but she didn't heed his warning and smacked into it with her nose, realizing too late she'd locked it. He shifted, unlocked it, and she barged through it, tearing off into the night, wanting to run as a wolf, as newly mated wolves together. He burst through the wolf door and caught up to her, pausing only to howl, and she saw Randall's lights go on in his house.

Aww, Maverick was worried about her shifting on the run. She had to remember that always. She ran over to Randall's house and howled too; then she rubbed up against Maverick. He was such a dream boyfriend, lover, wolf mate.

Maverick was surprised that Gina had to shift again so soon when he'd expected to be cuddled against her and sleeping and making love again. But he was glad she hadn't shifted in the middle of making love to each other. She was beautiful, and he loved her. And he was thrilled she wanted to run with him as wolves tonight—their mated-wolf lap.

Randall waved at them and got into his Jeep and then followed them. Maverick appreciated him. He'd never thought that turning a woman would put so many demands on his ranch manager. But Randall was good-natured, and he didn't seem to mind at all.

Maverick smiled at his mate, still amused at the way she had suddenly stopped in the hallway and he'd collided with her. That was a newbie mistake on her part, but he should have anticipated it. When she'd run into the locked wolf door with her nose, he had felt for her—hoping she hadn't hurt it, but she had just barged right through as if she were fine. He loved her for that.

She kept rubbing her body against him, bumping him, nipping at his cheek and ear, playful and having fun. He likewise matched her moves, playing with her and rubbing against her in a way that said he truly loved her, sharing his scent with her, taking her scent back with him. They startled some deer and stopped for a moment, watching them bound off.

They continued to run, and then finally she sat down on her rump and just looked up at the moon. He observed the moon, waning gibbous, 96 percent visible, so it was mostly a full moon still and had a strong pull on newly turned wolves. It was beautiful out here, the sky filled with wispy clouds and stars glittering against the dark night.

She nuzzled him and nipped at him, and he licked her face. Then they turned and ran back to the house, woofing at Randall. He followed them back until they ran through the wolf door at home and raced each other down the hall. But she couldn't shift back right away, so Maverick turned on the gas fireplace, and they sat by the Christmas tree and the fireplace, lying there together on a braided rug, curled up together as wolves. He was just as happy to be with her like this.

He actually fell asleep and felt her stir and realized she had shifted and was trying to keep warm. He shifted then and turned off the gas fireplace, lifted her in his arms, and carried her to bed and pulled the covers over her. Then he walked over to the bedroom door and shut and locked it, just in case Gina shifted again; he didn't want her somehow leaving the room.

Then he climbed into bed and pulled her into his arms, thinking that his falling into the lake had been the best thing that had ever happened to him because Gina was in his life now. He loved her. But they still had to deal with the other fallout—turning her and Weston's friends and her parents without too much drama.

Gina finally woke and was back to her human form cuddling with Maverick. She remembered falling asleep next to him as wolves next to the fireplace and the Christmas tree, so lovely and such a fun thing to do because she couldn't shift back right away. She had been so tired, she couldn't stay awake with the warmth of the fire and Maverick surrounding her. She kissed his chest and licked his nipple. "What happened last night?"

"You remember we returned to the house, right?"

"Yeah, and we curled up next to the fireplace and the Christmas tree all lit up. Really pretty."

"Exactly. Then you finally shifted, I shifted, and I carried you to bed."

"Hmm. Thanks for staying with me as a wolf then."

"I would have slept with you as a wolf for the rest of the night if you hadn't changed back for most of the evening. I love you, honey. We're in this together."

"I love you too. I just had a wonderful time. I hoped you weren't disappointed that I had to shift and run instead of just cuddling last night after we mated each other."

"Are you kidding? That's part of the fun of being mated wolves. It was our first mated run."

"That's true. I forgot poor Randall would have to follow us in case I shifted."

"He's glad I've found a she-wolf to adore. And he's understanding about newly turned wolves. We all help out when we can."

She kissed his mouth and then sighed. "Okay, well, I'm starving."

"Me too. Let's go get some breakfast."

They decided on cinnamon pancakes for breakfast and had a lot of activities planned, but first, both of them had to call their brothers to tell them they were mated. "Let's call your brother first." She figured he would be the most thrilled. Her brother might be worried she had done this too quickly.

When Maverick called Josh and told him the news, his brother asked, "What took you so long?"

"Hey, I had to be sure Gina was ready for this after all the other changes in her life," Maverick said.

"Oh, you better believe I'm ready for this. I wouldn't have it any other way," Gina said, so glad they hadn't waited any longer.

"Brooke and I are really happy for you. She's with a customer, but she's waving at me and saying she's thrilled," Josh said. "After we take care of things with Weston's friends, we'll have to have a celebration dinner. Maybe some time next week."

"That sounds good," Maverick said, Gina agreeing.

They ended the call and got hold of Weston and put it on speakerphone. "Hey, brother, Maverick and I are calling to tell you we're—"

"Hold that thought. I'll talk to you later. Got to go." Weston hung up on her. His voice had been tense, anxious.

Frowning, she stared at the phone and then looked up at Maverick.

Maverick rubbed her arm in a comforting way. "Maybe he suddenly had to shift."

"Possibly, but wouldn't he have said so? It was more like

he had the phone on speaker, and he didn't want someone to hear what I was going to say."

———————————

Concerned that Weston was in trouble, Maverick wasn't going to delay looking into the issue. "Likely his friends Bromley and or Patterson are there with him." He immediately got on his phone and called Sarge and put it on speaker so Gina could judge his response too. "Hey, Sarge, is Weston with you?"

"Can't talk right now." Sarge ended the call.

"Okay, I really don't like the sound of this." Maverick called Leidolf as Gina listened in. "I think we've got a situation. You put a tracker on Sarge's truck, right?"

"Yeah, after he and Cassie stole away before she and I became mates, though he has never run again. What's wrong?"

"I think Sarge and Weston are in trouble. Can you locate where they are?" Maverick asked.

"Let me have one of my men check."

Maverick pulled Gina into his arms. "Okay, we're waiting to hear. Oh, and we mated each other."

"Hot damn, I'll let the pack know." Leidolf sounded thrilled.

"That's what we were calling Weston about, but his phone was on speaker, and he wouldn't let us tell him what was up, like someone was listening in on the conversation and he was afraid of what we might say. When I called Sarge, he reacted the same way."

"You've got good instincts, Maverick. Hold on… Okay, yeah? All right." Leidolf said to Maverick and Gina, "Weston and Sarge said they were going to Weston's apartment. He needed some more stuff for work. That's what the tracker shows. He's at his apartment."

"I know where it is," Gina said, pulling away from Maverick and grabbing their parkas.

"Okay, we're on our way there now," Maverick said.

"I'll be there as soon as I can get there. So much for the best-laid plans," Leidolf said.

"Don't you know it. See you soon." Maverick figured he'd have to turn both men, and this was going to be a messy situation. Instead of turning them at dinner at the ranch, where they would have privacy, this was going to be a rescue mission and then a wolf fight, he was afraid.

He called Randall next as he and Gina headed outside for the pickup. "Hey, we've got a situation with Weston's friends, we believe. We're not positive, but we're headed to his apartment now."

"I'll go with you."

"I need some men to take care of the tour group and some to take the reindeer to another venue," Maverick said.

"Who else is going with you?" Randall asked, stubbornly resisting the idea Maverick should do this on his own.

Maverick got a call from his brother then and answered the call and explained the situation and where they were going.

"I'm on my way," Josh said.

"Okay, Josh is on his way to Weston's apartment also," Maverick told Randall. "You take another man and the reindeer to the other venue. We'll be there when we can. Leidolf's joining us at Weston's apartment, but it'll take him longer to get there." Maverick was afraid Josh would get there before he did and try to rescue Weston and Sarge on his own.

"All right," Randall said, sounding reluctant to let his boss take all the heat. "We've got this. Don't worry about it."

"Thanks. I know I can always count on you." Then Maverick and Gina drove off and Maverick said to his brother, "You wait for me until I can get there."

"Leidolf called Adam, and he's on his way. Also Masterson."

"Okay, good." Maverick had thought of Adam, since he was a police detective and Josh's partner before Josh retired. And Masterson was a wolf DEA agent.

"Park farther away from the complex. We'll have to make our way there individually so we don't look like we're a SWAT team," Josh told him.

"Gotcha." Though Maverick hadn't been trained in police procedures like the rest of them, his wolf instincts gave him some of the same intuition.

"Is Gina with you?" Josh asked.

"Yes. My brother's involved. I had to come," Gina said.

"I recommend you stay in the truck then when you arrive. If Bromley and Patterson have taken your brother and Sarge hostage, we don't want you to become a hostage too," Josh said.

Maverick hoped she would listen to his brother since he was trained in tactics like this.

"All right. I will."

Maverick sighed with relief.

She smiled at him and ran her hand over his leg.

"We're here," Josh said. "Adam and Masterson too."

"We'll be there in another ten minutes." Then Maverick saw the police vehicles that had come to the scene of the accident last night pass them by and honk their horns in greeting.

"Are those the police officers we saw at the accident last night?"

"Yep, they sure are. The wolves are in force."

She sighed with relief. "What if Bromley and Patterson are armed?"

"That's why Josh doesn't want you there either." Maverick smelled her nervousness. He didn't blame her. She could probably smell his too. Anything and everything could go wrong.

They finally reached the apartment complex, and he saw the various vehicles parked along the way. The police cars, Josh's truck, Adam's Hummer, Masterson's SUV.

"They're all here," Maverick said, pulling over to park.

"What if we're mistaken that my brother and Sarge are in trouble?"

"Then we'll all have a good laugh over it. We'd rather be overcautious than ignore the possibility they're in danger. Okay, stay here. I'm going to join the others so we can make plans." Maverick didn't really want to leave Gina alone in the truck, but he knew she'd had to come. He would have felt the same as her if his brother was in trouble. He leaned over the console and gave her a quick kiss, and she kissed him back.

"I will. Be safe."

Then Maverick joined the others, and Adam said, "Okay, all of us were at the Christmas party, so they might have seen us briefly. The police officers were on duty and not at the party, but both are in uniform, so that may make the men suspicious."

"But if Gina was worried about her brother, she might have called the police to do a health and welfare check on him," Maverick said.

"That's what I was thinking. What would be the likelihood that they would think the officers were wolves?" Adam asked.

"Slim chance," Maverick said.

"And Weston's never met us," one of the officers said. "Sarge will know us, but he'll guard against his reaction."

"Okay, so let's go with that." Adam turned to the officers. "You check and see if everyone seems okay. I'll be in the hallway where they can't see me. Everyone else will be nearby in case one of the men escapes."

"Should we arrest them?" one of the officers asked.

Maverick smiled. "Yeah, now that would be the way to go. You could arrest them and take them to Leidolf's ranch."

Leidolf arrived then and said, "Okay, do you have a plan in place yet?"

———————

Gina hated sitting in the truck waiting to get word. She wanted to see for herself that her brother was safe. Then she got a call from Maverick, and she hoped everything was okay.

"Hey, honey, the officers are going to make first contact. The rest of us will be waiting in the wings. If this goes as planned, they'll arrest them and take them down to Leidolf's ranch."

"Oh, that would work." If nothing went wrong.

"Got to go. Will update you as soon as I can."

"I love you."

"Love you too." Then Maverick ended the call, and she saw the rest of the men moving in different directions toward the apartment.

She got out of the truck and folded her arms and watched. She had wondered how they were going to shift into wolves and bite the men without announcing what they were going to do at the apartment. But no one was wearing a wolf coat as they moved around the building and waited. She hoped this was all a fluke, that her brother and Sarge couldn't talk to them for some perfectly legitimate reason, but she suspected that wasn't the case.

CHAPTER 17

MAVERICK WANTED TO BE AT THE DOOR WHEN THE police officers knocked. But since he couldn't, both officers had their body cameras on to capture the conversation while Maverick, Josh, Adam, and Masterson listened in. Adam went with the police officers and planned to wait in the hallway, not visible to the occupants of the apartment, since he officially was a police detective, but they might know him by sight. Leidolf was waiting at his vehicle for word to advance. Maverick knew he wanted to turn one of the men since he was their pack leader, and it would be on him.

They heard a knock at the apartment door. Then the door opened, and Officer Smith said, "Hi, I'm Officer Smith, and we're here doing a health and welfare check on a Weston Hutton. Would either of you men be him?"

Either. Which meant just two men were visible to the officers.

"I'm Weston Hutton," one of the men said.

Maverick recognized Weston's voice. Josh nodded, indicating he thought it was Weston too.

"Can I see some ID?" Smith asked.

"Yeah, sure, Officer. Who called this in?" Weston asked.

"Gina... Your sister, right?"

"Uh, yeah, I had a break-in last year, and she had to

call the police when I was injured, so she must have been worried something was wrong. In truth, I had eaten something that hadn't agreed with me and have been having some stomach issues ever since. I had to suddenly end the call with her. And I've been in the bathroom several times since then."

"That's understandable. And who are you, and can we see some ID?" the officer asked the other man.

Either the officer didn't know the man or it was Sarge and he didn't want to give away the fact they knew him if someone else was hiding in the apartment.

"Walter Bromley," the man said.

That confirmed one of the friends was in the apartment. But where was Sarge? Were Bromley and Patterson holding the men hostage?

"Is there anyone else in the apartment?" the officer asked.

"No," Bromley quickly said.

From the tone of his voice and the way he answered so abruptly, Maverick was sure he was lying and he was holding Weston hostage, at the very least.

"We'll need to check out the rest of the apartment," Smith said.

"You have to have a search warrant," Bromley said.

"It's up to the renter, Mr. Hutton. He's the only one listed on the lease agreement," Officer Smith said, quick thinking on his part. "So, Mr. Hutton, do we have your permission?"

"Hey, Officers, I've got to go to the bathroom really quick." Weston sounded like he was in pain, hopefully making a story up as he went along. He would have known right away that the police officers were both wolves once he'd smelled their scent, and he might have been trying to give them a chance to grab Bromley at least and take him into custody. But only if they could do it quietly enough if Patterson was holding Sarge hostage in another room.

"Do you mind if I check the bathroom out for you first?" the officer asked.

Good move, Maverick was thinking.

"No. Go ahead, but make it quick, please," Weston said, which made Maverick believe no one was hiding in there.

Then the officer said, "It checks out. Go ahead, it's clear. We'll just wait on you."

The next thing Maverick and the others heard was the door to the apartment quietly opening and closing and Adam whispering, "Got Bromley. He was armed with a 9mm gun. We knocked him out before he knew what hit him, disarmed him, zip-tied him, and I'm taking him out to Leidolf's truck. Leidolf has got a couple of other men with him who will watch Bromley. The two officers are still in the apartment with Weston."

Then everything was quiet.

The apartment door opened quietly and shut again. The toilet flushed, and then the door to the bathroom opened.

"Okay, so will you let us check the other rooms in the apartment?" the officer asked Weston again.

"No, I'm fine. I'll call my sister and let her know I've just got a case of food poisoning. Thanks for checking on me."

"Okay, sir, goodbye."

Then the door shut with a loud thunk, and they heard

someone lock it. Maverick hoped the police officers were still there.

"Hey, the police officers are gone," Weston called out. "Hell, I can't believe you think Sarge and I are werewolves. If we were, wouldn't we have just turned into a wolf monster and come after you?"

The door to another room opened, and Sarge said, "Patterson escaped through the side window."

Maverick and the others leapt into action. He saw Patterson first racing around a bunch of evergreen hollies, recognizing him from the camp and hike in the woods. Patterson was looking back over his shoulder. Total mistake on his part. Don't look back, just get away. Maverick rushed forward and took him down to the snow-covered grassy area, and Josh and Masterson were there right after that. Masterson quickly used a zip tie on him to confine him.

"You're all werewolves," Patterson said, his voice shaky, his eyes wide.

Maverick and the others laughed like he was making a joke. Then they hauled him off to one of the police cars, and the two vehicles drove off.

Adam said, "Weston's apartment is clear. Both Weston and Sarge are safe, a little shook-up but that's all."

Maverick called Gina. "Weston and Sarge are safe. Bromley and Patterson are in custody and on their way to Leidolf's ranch."

"Oh, good. I'm on my way."

"No, I'm coming for you." Maverick figured *she* had to be shook up, and he wanted to be there for her. As soon as he reached her, he took her into his arms, squeezed her tight, and kissed her. "He's okay."

She kissed him back, all her worry diminishing in that searing kiss. "Thank you and the others for coming to my brother and Sarge's rescue. I figured they had to be in trouble."

"Yeah, I did too."

When they reached Weston's apartment, they headed inside. Adam was just leaving but paused to tell Gina she'd made a good call and all was well. She thanked him, and he said, "I've got a case to work and have to get back to the bureau, but I'm glad everything worked out." He smiled at her; then he and Masterson left.

Gina hurried to hug her brother. "God, I'm so glad you're all right."

"Yeah, I hoped you'd figure out that something was wrong. As soon as the cops were at the door, Bromley looked through the peephole; then he told Patterson to take Sarge back into the bedroom and wait until he got rid of the cops."

"What were they going to do with you?" Gina asked, taking a seat in the living room with the others.

"They wanted us to shift, and then they were going to record it and share the news with the public. But of course I don't have any control over shifting, and Sarge wasn't about to. We just kept trying to convince them they were wrong. That at first Maverick had said he had wolf dogs when we were hiking because he was afraid someone would report him for having wolves with him on the hike through the state park. Then he was having difficulty with the Calypso

Ranch staff trying to steal his sales and so he had a couple of his wolves on display," Weston said, bringing bottles of water out for everyone. "They knew you wouldn't verify the wolves were real wolves, Gina, unless they truly were, or you'd lose your credibility with your peers."

"Yeah," Sarge said. "When they realized Weston knew I was alive and had said nothing about it to them, they were certain we were both werewolves."

"Why did you even open the door to them?" Maverick would have been warier of that and called for wolf backup right away.

"We were just going inside the apartment when they rushed us, shoving us inside, and locked the door. Before that, they had been watching Leidolf's ranch, saw us leaving, and followed us to Weston's apartment," Sarge said. "We didn't know how to deal with the situation. We hoped Leidolf would realize something was wrong when we didn't return to the ranch after a few hours."

"But when Gina called, we had our chance to warn her we were in trouble. We had to be careful that we didn't spook them, any more than they were already. Both were armed, and they were scared of us," Weston said.

"Not to mention we were scared of them," Sarge said.

"Did they tell anyone else about us?" Maverick asked.

"No," Weston said. "They wanted to prove we were werewolves before they brought anyone else in on this."

"Okay, good," Josh said.

"Well, I just needed to get some of my work stuff and take it back to the ranch. I never expected this to happen. Oh, and they were sure the reindeer ranch dinner was a setup. That as soon as they arrived at the ranch, wolves would come out and bite them."

"Well, they were right about that and everything else." Maverick smiled. "I'm just glad everyone's fine."

"Is it okay if we return to the ranch now?" Weston asked.

"Yeah, we can do that," Maverick said. "I'm sure you want to see your friends and talk to them about us."

"I do," Weston said.

"I want to go too," Gina said. "Just for a short while. I just want to see them, talk to them, tell them how wonderful being a *lupus garou* is."

"Yeah, sure." Maverick understood.

But first, they helped Sarge and Weston fill up the truck with stuff that Weston had wanted to remove from his apartment and take to Sarge's house.

"We'll see the guys and hopefully everyone will be okay." Maverick called Leidolf to tell them they were going to his ranch. "How are things there?"

"We're talking to Bromley and Patterson all about the world of *lupus garous*. I'm sure they would love to see all of you."

"We're on our way down." Then Maverick ended the call. "Who all is going to the ranch?"

"We are," Weston said.

"I'm returning to the shop to help Brooke," Josh said. "Tell us what happens."

"You know we will. Oh, and maybe we can still have our brisket dinner with them, except we won't have to turn them this time, they'll be wolves too." Maverick took hold of Gina's hand.

"By the way, what *were* you calling me about?" Weston asked Gina.

"We're mated."

Weston laughed, hugged her, and then shook Maverick's hand. "I guess I just gained a brother or two. Congratulations, you two."

"Thanks," both Gina and Maverick said at the same time.

Weston locked up his apartment and got into Sarge's truck, the two of them heading out. Maverick and Gina did the same thing while the others went on their way.

"Leidolf can give them a choice now," Gina said, settling back against the seat.

"What do you mean?"

"They can be turned by a bite or the saliva in the bloodstream method, since they know what we are, and they have that choice."

"Oh, yeah, I thought maybe you were thinking they had a choice about being turned or just being released."

"No, I know that's not an option for them."

"Okay, good. How do you feel about it?"

She smiled. "Relieved. Now it will be done, and we don't have to worry about them reporting what we are. I hope they're okay with it. If they hadn't persisted in trying to learn the truth, it would have been okay. But maybe they can enjoy the irony of it. They found a whole werewolf pack. Except they can't share the truth about it with non-werewolf types."

"And they can still search for Bigfoot during the new moon."

She chuckled. "Exactly. What if they exist and are shifters too? That's why they've never been spotted."

"Then Patterson has got my vote as being one of them."

"Ohmigod, yes, I've always told him that! That he was a descendent of one."

Maverick smiled.

When they reached Leidolf's ranch, the gate guard said, "They're up at Leidolf's house."

"Thanks," Maverick said.

They drove up to the house, and Cassie came out and greeted them just as Sarge and Weston parked as well.

"Come in. We're having grilled cheese sandwiches, hot cocoa, and chocolate cheesecake," Cassie said, motioning for them all to go inside.

"We had a late breakfast," Gina said. "But the hot cocoa and chocolate cheesecake sound great."

"Okay." Cassie smiled and served them some slices of cheesecake and fixed some Santa mugs of cocoa. "Congratulations are in order. Leidolf told me you are mated."

"Thanks. Neither of us could wait." Gina heard laughter inside and frowned. "That's the guys. They're not upset?"

"When we told them all the benefits of being wolf shifters, they were relieved," Cassie said.

"Oh, I'm so glad they're good with it," Gina said.

"Well, except they are peeved with Weston and Sarge for not telling them the truth in the first place." Cassie led them into the sunroom where the men were laughing and drinking their cocoa and eating their cheesecake.

"Oh, hell, here they are," Bromley said, standing.

Patterson stood too. He and Bromley hugged Weston and then Sarge.

"Leidolf told us about the other guys," Bromley said.

"Are you okay with it?" Gina set her cocoa and cheese-cake on a coffee table and hugged each of the guys.

Maverick set his plate and mug down next to hers so he could strip out of his clothes, shift, and bite one of the men if that was the option they agreed to.

"Yeah, Gina. Leidolf told us how Maverick accidentally turned you and then all the rest of the story."

"Have you been turned yet?" Gina asked.

"No, when Leidolf said you were on the way, we told him to wait," Patterson said. "We were offered a bite or the saliva method."

Bromley shook his head. "How could we ever tell our story of how we became one of you to generations to come if all we did was got an injection of werewolfism? We're opting for a bite."

"Ready?" Leidolf asked, stripping out of his clothes.

Gina squeezed Maverick's hand, cuing him to be the other one to turn one of their friends, and he began to strip.

"Yeah, bring it on," Bromley said, pulling up his sleeve.

Patterson did the same thing as if that was the protocol.

And then Leidolf shifted, and the men's jaws dropped. Weston was standing there smiling, arms folded across his chest. "Yeah, I felt the same way when I saw Maverick shift."

Maverick pulled off the rest of his clothes and shifted. Both he and Leidolf targeted one of the men, Leidolf going for Bromley, Maverick biting Patterson, but both men jumped back, a natural reaction to the wolf attack.

Neither Maverick nor Leidolf bit them hard, just enough to break the skin and lick the wounds, to make sure they turned the men.

Then he and Leidolf returned to their discarded clothes, shifted, and dressed.

"Where are you staying?" Gina asked as everyone sat down to eat the rest of their lunch and for Gina and Maverick to enjoy the cheesecake and cocoa.

"With me," Sarge said. "We have a lot of catching up to do."

"What about the brisket dinner tonight?" Bromley asked. "We were afraid you'd ambush us at the reindeer ranch, but now that we're wolves, we want to join you for dinner if it's still all right with you."

"Absolutely. You're part of the pack, like family now. So, sure," Maverick said, once they'd both finished their dessert and cocoa. "If you're all set to go, Gina, I'm ready to return home."

"Uh, yeah, I sure am." She gave her brother a hug again. "We'll see you all tonight at seven then." And then she said goodbye. They left and she said to Maverick as they got into his truck, "I hadn't expected them to want to be turned."

"They probably figured they wouldn't ever get to see werewolves shifting unless they became one like us." Maverick was just glad it had all worked out.

"True. Are we going to the reindeer exhibit that Randall was handling?"

"I texted him, and he said he's got enough help. And the ranch tours are covered. So if you want, we could just go home and—"

"Yes! I'm ready."

He smiled. "I have a proposal to make. We have 4,000 acres of land, and I'd like to give a parcel to your parents so they can build a home on it. They would be close to us and my ranch hands, brother, sister-in-law, and we can all keep an eye on them, giving them assistance anytime they need it. I want to make the same offer to your brother so he could have a home of his own, and when he finds a mate, they'll be all set. It would be their Christmas presents from us."

"Ohmigod, yes, that's a splendid idea. You are such a wonderful mate."

"We have plenty of land, and we're all family now. I'm glad to do it."

"I'm sure they will be thrilled. Weston can't stay with Sarge forever. And now with Bromley and Patterson staying there, I know Weston will be grateful."

"Family takes care of family. Josh and Brooke and I haven't had any in so long, we are all in agreement."

"Oh, of course, yes."

"That means when we have little ones—"

Gina smiled. "My parents will be glad to help out and love on the grandkids. And when Weston settles down, the same thing. Oh, and when Josh and Brooke have some, they'll dote on them too, believe me. I can't believe how much my life has changed with you in it and all for the good."

"I feel the same way about you."

When they got home, they made love, Maverick not wanting to wait just in case Gina had to shift all of a sudden again.

CHAPTER 18

WHEN THE GUYS ARRIVED FOR DINNER THAT NIGHT, BOTH Bromley and Patterson were wolves, amusing Gina and Maverick. She really hadn't expected that. But in the world of wolf shifters, she realized nothing would ever be the same as far as expectations went. Weston carried a bag she suspected contained their clothes.

Bromley and Patterson were bouncing around in the snow like two wolf pups who couldn't have been happier.

"Well, one good thing about being wolves, they can still enjoy the brisket." Brooke motioned for them all to come inside.

"And we can go running with them," Josh added. "If anyone else can and wants to, we'll go as a pack."

The guys woofed, and Brooke gave Bromley and Patterson dinner plates of food on the floor so they could eat, while everyone else sat up at the dining room table and enjoyed the meal and the conversation.

"So the guys are fine with Maverick and Leidolf turning them?" Gina asked.

"Man, are they," Weston said. "They've been itching to shift into their wolves ever since they were turned. Just as though it was Christmas. Of course, then I wanted to shift too but couldn't. Sarge could, but we needed someone to drive us here."

"Well, I'm glad it all worked out for you," Maverick said. "And you have the war wounds to prove it."

"All gone. They were amazed how fast the bite marks healed," Sarge said.

"Oh, but not everyone is enthusiastic that we joined the pack, by the way," Weston said, though he didn't seem bothered by it.

"Oh?" Gina asked, surprised.

"Female wolves are at a premium," Maverick said.

"Now I know why you turned me," Gina said, chuckling.

Everyone laughed.

"Yeah, you found me out." Maverick leaned over and kissed her cheek.

"So they're annoyed with you for asking Dorinda to the New Year's Eve party?" Gina forked up some of her mashed potatoes and gravy.

"Yeah, a couple of bachelor males are not really happy about it."

Maverick nodded. "That's the way it is when you're a wolf like us."

"I for one am glad you all were turned," Sarge said. "I hated not being able to tell you what had happened to me, afraid I might run into you someday. I worried no one would believe any story I tried to come up with and I'd get tripped up."

Maverick got a call on his phone. "It's Leidolf. Putting you on speakerphone. Go ahead."

"The management of the Calypso Reindeer Ranch denied any involvement of their ranch hands in releasing

your reindeer, endangering the animals, breaking and enter-
ing, and more. It's on the news. The owners have been contacted in the South of France where they've been living.
They're horrified at all the news they've been receiving
about the management. The owners fired them and hired
new management. Hopefully, that will be the end of all the
business with them trying to usurp your sales and pulling
any other shenanigans."

"That's good news. What about the men who actually
came to the ranch and freed the reindeer and chased them
off?" Maverick asked.

"They're spilling their guts to law enforcement, but
they're still being charged with endangerment to the animals
and more."

Maverick and Brooke smiled. "Good," Brooke said. "We'll
have to see what happens at the activities tomorrow."

"Yeah, hopefully their new management will have been
told to not cause any trouble for us so the Calypso Ranch
doesn't get any more bad publicity after this," Maverick said.
"Thanks, Leidolf, for updating us on the news."

"You're welcome. I knew you'd want to know soonest."

They said goodnight, and then Weston was jumping off
his chair and yanking his shirt over his head. Everyone sat in
stunned silence. Then they realized he was shifting!

Everyone else continued to eat. Brooke set out some
more brisket for Bromley and Patterson. They wolfed it
all up.

"Did you want to go for a run then?" Josh asked as everyone was finishing their dinner.

"I do." Sarge quickly finished his last bite of brisket. And then he rose from the table and began clearing dishes.

"Don't worry about the dishes." Brooke packed up the leftover food and put it in the fridge while Josh helped her.

Gina, Maverick, and Sarge cleaned up the dishes and pots and pans anyway.

"That's a really good way to get out of cleaning up after dinner," Gina told her brother, teasing him.

He woofed at her.

"I guess we'll take the Jeep and follow them with their clothes, just in case," Maverick said.

"You can run with them. I'll drive the Jeep." Gina didn't want Maverick to feel he couldn't run just because she couldn't.

He took the reindeer-decorated dish towel from her and wrapped his arms around her and kissed her soundly on the mouth.

"Unless you want Randall to follow them, and we can return home and occupy ourselves in our own way." She smiled up at him.

"Afterward for sure. We'll do the driving this time."

She was actually glad they could help out too and give Randall a break.

Not long after that, everyone but Maverick and Gina took off to run as wolves, all their clothes gathered in Josh's truck as Maverick and Gina followed behind the wolves.

Josh had to keep Bromley and Patterson from straying in the direction of the woods. Gina guessed they should have given them some rules—no getting so far from the beaten path where they couldn't follow in a vehicle if either of them shifted.

But the guys were having just too much fun running as wolves, nipping, biting, tackling each other, and she was dying to run with them.

"That was such great news about the management at the Calypso Ranch," Gina said.

"I agree. But we're still taking the llama with us to give us additional interest just in case. Randall said when he took her this afternoon, crowds were delighted. Oh, and people who had heard about the men's arrest for hassling our reindeer boycotted their reindeer exhibit."

She stretched out her arms. "Oh, good. So then that should be the end of their tyranny."

"Hopefully."

She sighed. "Okay, exactly when are we going to turn my parents? They're coming for Christmas Eve tomorrow night and then Christmas Day, and I'm delighted, but I'm still not sure about turning them then."

"They won't feel the same way about being turned as Bromley, Patterson, and your brother?" Maverick asked.

"I doubt it."

"We could have trouble with them shifting in the middle of all the festivities. Why don't we do it after the Christmas Day meal? That way they can enjoy all the festivities, opening presents, eating the meal, and if they shift later, we'll run together as wolves, as much as any of us can," Maverick said.

"Their final Christmas present," she said.

"Well, we can tell them about the gift of the land then too, and hopefully they'll be able to live with it."

"True." She got an email saying she'd had a package delivered at Josh and Brooke's house. She loved ordering online, especially since she'd had to order Maverick's presents that way so he didn't see them.

She'd seen packages coming in that Maverick had been storing in a back bedroom too. When he wasn't around, she was hiding her packages for him in another guest room with a sign tacked on: DO NOT OPEN UNTIL CHRISTMAS DAY.

She still needed to wrap them, which she planned to do tomorrow in the morning when they had their last show. Maverick was going to help with a tour group to give some of his men some time off to do some last-minute Christmas shopping.

She couldn't believe she was mated to a wolf for Christmas.

"Do you want to get married, and if so, when?" Maverick asked her. "Not all wolf couples do it, because mating is for life and we don't need to prove to anyone we've made a commitment to each other. But some do it for tax purposes and for other reasons."

"Let's do it when we have a lighter season for reindeer tours and such."

"That's in the summer normally. In January, we still have a lot of groups visit. In February, we have a Valentine's Day special. We could do it in March."

"Let's do it in the summer, if that's your quiet time. We could have it at the ranch, right?"

"Absolutely. And that will give us time to make all the arrangements."

She pulled up the moon phases calendar on her phone. "Okay, let's make it June 28. That's when the new moon will be out. All the wolves, the reindeer, and the llama will be in attendance. Tomorrow, I'll let my parents know we're engaged. They'll expect to see a ring though."

"I can get you one, but you'll only be able to wear it during the new moon."

"Well, it's not going to be too long before they're turned anyway, and we can tell them about the jewelry issues as far as wearing jewelry and shifting after we've turned them."

"That's really the best idea," Maverick said.

Gina frowned. "You have the heater turned up way too high in the truck."

Maverick glanced at her. "I haven't changed it."

"Oh, no. Okay." Gina started yanking off her clothes in a hurry.

Maverick called Randall on Bluetooth. "Hey, I'm going to need your help. Gina's shifting. Uh, shifted." He gave him their location.

"Okay, I'm on my way," Randall said over the Bluetooth.

"Thanks." Then Maverick parked the truck and opened the doors. "I'm coming with you. If anyone shifts back before Randall gets here, they can return to my truck."

She had shifted before she could even respond. She couldn't believe it happened so quickly, but she was thrilled she could run with all the other wolves.

She licked Maverick's naked chest. He smiled and kissed the top of her nose; then he shifted, and they left the truck, bounding off into the night after the other wolves, barking and howling. The other wolves stopped and howled for them to join them. New howls filled the air, some that she hadn't heard before. She recognized Josh's and Brooke's.

She and Maverick howled back, and they headed for the others and finally joined them. In the distance, they heard Randall driving his Jeep to follow them. She'd never even considered they'd need to call poor Randall to help them out. Not that she could help it. She had to shift, and she was glad that Maverick had come with her. They were meant to run as wolves together.

They finally reached the others, and all greeted each other as if they had always been wolves and understood the way it was. She loved that her brother was a wolf and that their friends were too.

Weston and his friends were playing and growling, biting each other, rolling in the snow, having a ball. Maverick stayed with Gina, showing he'd rather run with her. Likewise, Josh and Brooke hung out together, and Gina suspected the friends needed to work out their aggressions by playfighting and would learn from their mistakes and maneuvers on their own without the royals showing them how it was done.

But then Josh and Brooke were corralling them again, ensuring they didn't chase each other through the river or into the woods where they couldn't easily reach them with a vehicle and their clothes if they suddenly shifted.

Gina was so happy to be out here with everyone as a wolf, breathing in the scents of snow and pines and fir trees and a rabbit somewhere nearby. When her brother and friends finally wound down from fighting and playing, they headed back to Brooke and Josh's home. At first, they were loping, and then both Bromley and Patterson were racing each other as if their lives depended on it. Suddenly, Bromley stopped and shifted.

Randall drove to where he was located, and Bromley climbed into the Jeep and began to get dressed. Gina didn't think she'd ever get used to seeing people shift and be naked in front of her. She thought of that happening to her parents. Oh, no way did she want to see them like that, nor did she want them to experience the embarrassment to do that in front of other people. It would take them time to ever get used to it.

Randall must have gotten the clothes out of Maverick's truck for everyone.

Then Patterson reached the Jeep, and half-dressed Bromley threw the door open for him. Before Patterson could jump in as a wolf, he was standing naked in the snow, then hurrying to climb aboard.

Since tomorrow was Christmas Eve, Gina couldn't help worrying how her parents would fare once they were turned.

CHAPTER 19

THE NEXT DAY, GINA PLANNED TO WRAP PRESENTS IN THE morning, and Maverick told her he had to go out and work with the final tour group that morning until they left. Some of the items Gina had ordered were wrapped, and she'd already wrapped her parents' and Weston's presents. But she still needed to wrap Maverick's, Brooke's, and Josh's presents. Plus, she'd gotten some gifts for the ranch hands.

She'd wanted to give Weston a special water wolf dish for when he turned wolf, just for kicks, but her parents wouldn't understand it and would probably think he'd gotten a dog and want to see it.

Playing Christmas music while she wrapped presents, she also had started the fire and then carried all the presents into the living room and set them under the tree. Maverick had placed all his gifts under there sometime last night, she guessed. And she smiled.

Weston wasn't coming to the house until later, just before their parents arrived. She suspected he wanted to give her and Maverick, the newly mated couple, more privacy before he and their parents landed in on them and stayed for the night, knowing that they'd actually be staying longer than they planned once they were turned.

Which also meant Maverick and some others who didn't have trouble with shifting would have to move her parents' things that they needed for longer term to the reindeer ranch too. Josh and Brooke had offered for them and Weston to stay at their place after Christmas since they had the house in town and that would give Gina and Maverick more time alone together.

Gina figured she'd make a light lunch for her and Maverick, and then saw him headed for the house. Perfect timing.

He came inside and pulled off his parka and gloves, kissed her, then washed up, and gave her a hug. His body was cold, so were his lips, and he was chilling her. "You are so frosty."

"That's why I'm warming myself up."

She laughed. "I was going to make something light to eat for lunch since we're having prime rib at Brooke and Josh's place tonight."

"How about grilled cheese sandwiches? After Cassie mentioned having them yesterday, they really appeal."

Gina smiled. "Grilled cheese sandwiches it is."

"I'm making hot cocoa to go with them."

She loved how he was always making them special drinks. This time, he added peppermint candy canes and bits of peppermint candy sprinkled on top of the cocoa.

"Randall texted me with good news. The Calypso Reindeer Ranch staff was a no-show at the event this morning."

"Oh, that's wonderful. Hopefully it will continue to be like that next year."

"And Andy, the radio talk show host, said they talked about the issue with them running off our reindeer. That might have pushed the Calypso management into not taking the reindeer to compete with us this morning. I think we have a good chance at them doing their own schedule away from us next year. Getting all that bad publicity in the news couldn't help but hurt their ranch's efforts to push their agenda." Maverick glanced at the Christmas tree and smiled at the presents. "Looks like Santa's elves were busy."

"You'd think we had a ton of kids."

He chuckled. "We're kids at heart."

"I have to agree with you there."

After eating the melted-cheesy sandwiches and drinking their peppermint hot cocoa, they cleaned up.

"What do you want to do now?" he asked, pulling the dish towel from her hand and enfolding her in a hug.

"You don't have any more work to do outside?"

"Nope. Not for a while. Do you have anything you need to do?"

"Yeah, before all the relatives arrive, I sure do." She took him down the hall to their bedroom for some more Christmas cheer.

———

That night for Christmas Eve, Josh and Brooke had a prime rib dinner at their place for Maverick, Weston, Gina, and their parents, Reggie and Faye. Gina felt so nervous, though they didn't plan to change them until after all their activities on Christmas Day. Still, just thinking about it made her anxious regarding the change to her parents' lives that was coming up and how they would feel concerning it.

"So did you ever see any signs of Bigfoot on your last hunt?" Reggie asked.

"Or werewolves?" Faye asked.

Both her parents were smiling, but Gina's sip of water from her water glass went down wrong, and she coughed. Maverick rubbed her back. Weston cleared his throat. Josh and Brooke smiled.

"Uh, no Bigfoot," Weston said. "We're sure the wolf we saved from the lake was a werewolf though."

Gina gave her brother a caustic look. They weren't supposed to change their parents until *after* they had the Christmas meal tomorrow. She didn't want her parents shifting and having to eat their meal on plates on the floor. She was really sure their mother and father would *not* be happy about that. And she wanted the experience to be as pleasant as it could be for them under the circumstances.

Her parents looked at Maverick and smiled jokingly. "Well, he's one of the best-looking werewolves I've ever seen. We want to thank you for inviting us to your family gathering for both Christmas Eve and Christmas Day," Faye said to Brooke and Josh.

"You're family now," Brooke said, and everyone stopped eating and drinking. She knew she'd made a mistake mentioning it before Gina had told her parents they were getting married, the problem with being mated wolves and not being able to tell humans. But Brooke couldn't take it back now.

"Okay, we didn't get the ring yet, but Maverick asked

me to marry him. He wanted to wait to announce it after Christmas," Gina said.

"So sorry," Brooke said, looking truly repentant and really embarrassed to have made the mistake.

Josh smiled at Brooke, leaned over and kissed her cheek, and rubbed her back with the palm of his hand with reassurance.

"No, it's okay, really. We were planning to announce it tomorrow. Tonight is fine." Gina smiled, trying to appear as though she really felt that way.

"Well, this is great news. We couldn't be happier for the two of you," her dad said, but he didn't sound like he really meant it, more that he worried about it.

Gina knew he was shocked to the core, and she suspected he wondered if this wasn't a little too sudden. If he knew what she did about wolves mating, he would know it wasn't too soon for them.

"Me too," her mom said, recovering from her shocked expression. "So when do you plan to have the wedding?"

"Next summer, and I want you and Brooke to help me with all of it."

"Absolutely," Brooke said.

Gina's mother agreed. "I can't wait to help," her mom said, and she sounded relieved the actual wedding wouldn't happen for several months, giving Gina and Maverick more time to get to know each other.

What they didn't know was that it was already a done deal.

Gina took a deep breath and let it out. Well, that was a surprise reveal Gina hadn't planned for.

Maverick was smiling, quiet, but then he said, "I can't wait to marry your daughter."

"Yeah, and we're like brothers already." Weston sounded proud to be part of the whole wolf family and didn't have any qualms about it.

"Me too," Josh agreed.

"What about your parents?" Faye asked. "How do they feel about it?"

"Uh, we're all orphans." Josh ran his hand over Brooke's back again.

"Oh, I'm so sorry to hear it," her mom said, appearing to wish she hadn't brought it up.

"That means you're going to have to adopt all of them," Gina cheerfully said.

"That's a given," her mom said. Reggie agreed.

Gina loved her parents, and both of them seemed to relax, and they all enjoyed the meal together as one big, happy family.

Thankfully, neither Weston nor Gina had any issues with shifting during the Christmas Eve dinner. She did worry about them shifting in the middle of the night and running into their parents in the house. They had wanted to have their parents stay somewhere else because of the shifting issue, but they couldn't very well suggest it without making their parents wonder why when they had plenty of room for them at Maverick's house. Weston had even suggested earlier in private to Gina that he could stay at Josh and Brooke's home tonight just in case *he* shifted, but they agreed it would seem strange if they split up the family like that for no good reason. If they had gone with the plan, Gina would still have to be careful. Especially with her sleepwalking issues, though she hadn't sleepwalked since that last time.

After dinner, they had Christmas cocktails, and then they all wished each other a merry Christmas Eve. Faye, Reggie, their son and daughter, and Maverick all walked to his home for the night, crunching across the snow.

"Remember to wear red shirts or sweaters and blue jeans for pictures tomorrow while we're opening Christmas presents," Gina said.

"Yeah, we've got them," her mom said.

"If there's anything you need, don't hesitate to ask," Maverick said as he showed them to their guest rooms before they all called it a night.

"Congratulations again to the two of you," her dad said, giving Gina a hug and shaking Maverick's hand.

Gina's mom gave both Gina and Maverick a hug and told them goodnight.

Weston wished everyone a merry Christmas Eve and headed off to his guest room. At least he had never sleep-walked, so Gina wasn't worried about him as long as he didn't leave his bedroom or howl or bark in there.

"Did you tell Brooke and Josh to wear red shirts and blue jeans for the pictures?" Maverick asked, kissing her in the master bedroom.

"I did. And Weston too. How are we going to turn my parents?" Gina asked, helping Maverick get undressed as he worked on her clothes too.

Then when they were naked, they climbed under the covers and cuddled together in the bed for the night.

"I don't want them to think of me as the big bad wolf," he said.

She wrapped her arms around him and kissed his mouth. "You are the biggest baddest wolf I know. And the sweetest and kindest too."

"We normally don't tell people what we're going to do first if they don't know what we are, but in your parents' case, like with Bromley and Patterson, I want to give them a choice."

"Okay." She could just imagine worrying about it all night long.

"Come here," he said, kissing her soundly. "It will turn out fine. Somehow."

But worrying about this and not sleeping wasn't a good thing for Gina and her sleepwalking business. With the moon still mostly full, she thought she would have to shift, and really, she hoped she would get it out of her system tonight before all the festivities tomorrow.

CHAPTER 20

MAVERICK WAS HAVING A DIFFICULT TIME GETTING TO sleep tonight, as if he was excited about opening Christmas presents in the morning. Instead, he was more concerned about both Gina and her brother shifting tonight or sometime during the activities tomorrow and being caught by their parents.

He got out of bed, pulled on a pair of boxer briefs and a robe and cinched the tie, then left the bedroom and walked down the hall to check and make sure everyone was in bed in their kerchiefs and caps. Everything was quiet, and no one was running around in wolf coats or otherwise. He got a glass of milk, finished it off, and put the glass in the dishwasher, thankful that Gina was his mate and that her brother and friends were already turned and were glad for it.

He just hoped that everything would work out fine with Gina and Weston's parents tomorrow.

That's when he heard scratching at Weston's door. *Oh, great.*

Maverick walked down the hall and opened the guest room door. Weston raced out of the guest room past him as a red wolf and down the hall to the wolf door.

Damn. Maverick ran after him. "You have to wait until I can—" Weston barged through the wolf door. *Damn it.* They hadn't locked the wolf door.

Maverick turned to run back to his room and grab his phone to call Randall, but then he saw Gina loping down the hall in *her* wolf coat. "Wait until I get some clothes for you and your brother." He ran down the hall to the room and grabbed a bag of her things and his phone and then came back out, but Gina was gone. He should have locked the wolf door!

He raced to Weston's room and went inside to hastily grab his clothes and then got on his phone and called Randall. "They're running as wolves."

"Now?" Randall asked.

"Yeah, I'm off to chase them down."

"I'm headed out that way. One of us has to join them as a wolf to make sure they don't stray into the woods," Randall said.

"Yeah." Maverick tossed their bag of clothes into the truck, jumped into it, and tore off, his high beams catching Gina and Weston's wolf forms off in the distance, racing through the snow.

Maverick just hoped none of their actions had woken their parents and they were up now, wondering what had happened to all of them. The bedroom doors had been left ajar. Everyone had disappeared into the night. And who knew what Maverick would be coming back with. Wolves or humans?

Then Randall was driving the Jeep behind him, and Maverick parked, stripped out of his clothes, and shifted. He needed to take care of his mate and her brother, and that was easier when running as a wolf so that he could get close and steer them the right way. He wondered then why Gina had run off like that. Weston was more reckless, but he didn't think Gina would have done so. Why not stay in the bedroom and wait for him? He understood the need to run as a wolf, but he also knew she was worried about her parents seeing her and her brother as wolves, so it didn't make sense that she would race off. Unless she was worried about her brother and trying to keep him out of trouble.

Maverick howled at them, and Weston turned and stopped and looked at him and then howled back. But Gina kept running. What the hell?

Sleep-running? *Not again!* She wasn't taking care of her brother. He was trying to watch out for her now.

Maverick joined Weston and raced after Gina. It was his fault. He should have closed the door to the bedroom when he left it to get a glass of milk and heard Weston scratching at the guest room door to get out.

Next time, he was making sure he shut the master bedroom door. He suspected she wouldn't have scratched or barked or howled to get out but would have curled up and gone back to sleep. Hopefully.

Then he was thinking about what it would be like when their parents were turned. What a nightmare. He'd have to have them all padlocked in their rooms at night, or he and Randall would never get any sleep—at least not during the fullest phases of the moon.

Still, any chance he had at running with his mate was good. He was going to have to make sure that Gina got enough sleep from now on, but giving up making love to her wasn't something he was ready for. Rather, he needed to make sure she got an afternoon nap instead.

Twice, he had to steer her away from the river and three times from the woods. Then, as if his stopping her was frustrating her or wearing her out, she turned and trotted back to the ranch homes and Maverick and Weston joined her, running on either side of her.

As soon as they reached Randall's Jeep, Maverick naturally thought that both Weston and Gina would get into his vehicle as he opened the doors for them, but Gina didn't, so Weston didn't either, protecting her all the way.

Maverick appreciated that her brother would. Maverick kept bumping into her to keep her on track toward his truck then, just in case she turned and needed her clothes. But as soon as he reached his truck, she ran on past. *Damn!*

There was no reasoning with a sleepwalking wolf.

Her brother got in Maverick's truck though. Maverick suspected he was shifting, and he would follow them in the truck since Maverick had left the keys in it, but Weston didn't.

Maverick sighed. The house was getting closer, and he hoped her parents were fast asleep. He'd have to take her to bed and then return to pick up Weston if he hadn't shifted back.

Maverick continued to run with her and was glad she at least wasn't veering off to go anywhere else. Maybe she was ready to return to her warm, comfy bed and snuggle with him.

When she reached the house, she barged through the wolf door, and he went in after her.

Her mother was in the kitchen getting some milk, and she shrieked and dropped her glass when she saw Gina and him racing down the hall as wolves to the master bedroom.

"What's wrong?" Reggie asked, coming out of the guest bedroom wearing plaid pajamas and a robe.

"The...the wolves ran into Maverick and Gina's room. You know, the ones that Gina said were red wolves on the newscast." Faye sounded shaken up.

Then Maverick shifted and shut the door. He paused. Okay, so he'd dress, leave the room, reassure Gina's parents, and take off outside to get his truck and Weston.

Gina jumped up on the bed with her snow-covered paws. He'd have to clean them and the comforter, but after he returned with Weston.

He got dressed, took a deep breath, shut Gina in the room, and then headed down the hallway to the kitchen where Reggie and Faye were cleaning up the broken glass. "Hey, is everyone okay?"

He wanted to get Weston, but he couldn't just leave now when their parents had to be still shocked over the wolf situation. He was surprised they hadn't brought up the fact they knew about the wolves at the reindeer ranch during the Christmas Eve dinner.

"So sorry about this," Faye said.

"Don't worry about it. I can handle it in a minute. Listen, I've got to take care of something. I'll be right back." Maverick headed for the front door and heard his truck park at the house, figuring Weston had finally shifted. But then Weston dashed through the wolf door as a wolf, and his mother screamed. Weston ran down the hall and into his guest room and the door shut closed.

A knock sounded on his front door, and Maverick opened it. One of his ranch hands was standing there with Maverick's truck keys. Randall parked next to Maverick's truck, got out, and handed him the sack of clothes. Then both Randall and the ranch hand smiled and got into Randall's Jeep, and they drove off.

Maverick knew they'd be chuckling about tonight's activities. But he still had to deal with Gina and Weston's parents. He headed for the kitchen. "Did you need anything else?"

"Uh, no," Reggie said, the floor all cleaned up, and he had his arm around Faye's shoulders. "We're on our way back to bed."

"Merry Christmas Eve." Maverick grabbed some paper towels, wetted them, and returned to his bedroom after Reggie and Faye had gone back to bed.

Maverick entered the bedroom, set the bag of clothes on a chair, and shut the bedroom door. He would have to return Weston's clothes to him sometime tomorrow. With the damp paper towels, he cleaned Gina's paws and the comforter. Then he removed his clothes, climbed into bed, and pulled his she-wolf under the sheets and comforter. With her back to him, he wrapped his arms around her.

He was glad he hadn't had to try to explain what was going on with the wolves and all the rest that had happened tonight.

Not much longer after he was cuddling the wolf, he was snuggling with his naked mate. Now this was perfect. And then he managed to finally fall asleep, waking later to her kisses, and he smiled and kissed her back.

"You sleepwalked as a wolf again," he said.

Gina's jaw dropped. "No."

"Yeah."

She ran her hands through her hair. "I'm so sorry."

"Nothing to be sorry about. It was my fault you ran off as a wolf."

"What? Oh, no way. Not again. With my parents in the house?"

He explained what had happened, and her face was flushed. "Do you think they suspect anything?" she whispered.

Then they smelled coffee brewing in the kitchen.

"No. They probably figured it was just our rambunctious red wolves. Anyway, are you ready to get up?"

"Yeah. Hopefully, Weston and I got this out of our system last night then, and we won't have any problems today."

"I agree." They got up and dressed. But after they turned her parents? Tonight was bound to be chaotic.

"What about the reindeer and llama?" she asked.

"The ranch hands will take care of them this morning. I'll take care of them after we eat our late-afternoon meal," Maverick said.

"What are we going to say to my parents about the wolves?" She pulled on a red sweater over her red-lace bra and blue jeans over her red-lace panties.

He was searching through his things.

"Get a red sweater or shirt if you have one. And blue jeans."

"Oh, right, for family pictures. We'll say the wolves were boisterous last night, and I went out to make sure they were okay." He pulled out a red shirt and put it on, and she buttoned it for him, kissing his chest on the way up.

"And where are the wolves today?" she asked.

"Out with the ranch hands and the reindeer." He figured that was a good cover for the wolves for now.

"Okay. And then later, we'll take care of things so we can tell them the whole truth. I guess it's about that time to get some breakfast with your brother and sister-in-law and my family."

He pulled her into a hug and kissed her. "Man, I would give anything to just return to bed with you and stay there with you the rest of the day."

She laughed. "If we didn't have so much company, I would agree with you."

——— ═══════════

Gina and Maverick left the bedroom and heard her parents talking low in the kitchen, probably not wanting to disturb them if they had been asleep. Weston appeared to still be in his room, maybe in bed asleep after their wild wolf run last night.

Then Brooke and Josh arrived to have breakfast with them.

Everyone was in a cheery mood, wishing everyone else a merry Christmas, and then Weston came out wearing a blue shirt and jeans while everyone else was color coordinated.

Gina motioned for him to return to his room. "Red shirt or red sweater. You better have brought one."

Weston groaned. "I did, but I needed more sleep last night to remember to wear it."

"We heard the wolves howling last night," Faye said while they all started to help make breakfast or set the table.

"Yeah, we have run into coyotes before, so the wolves go out and chase them off," Maverick said.

Gina kept quiet because she figured it was better if Maverick made up the story and got it right.

Weston returned wearing a red shirt and got a cup of coffee.

"You slept with one of the wolves?" Faye asked Weston.

He glanced at Maverick as if looking for an explanation. But Maverick only raised his cup of coffee to him.

"Uh, yeah, for a while, and then he left early this morning." Weston sipped some of his coffee.

"And the other two joined you and Maverick?" her mother said. "It sure shocked me to see them racing through the house like that. I'm sorry for dropping my glass of milk. Sometimes it helps me to sleep when I'm having trouble with insomnia."

"We have a wolf door for them so they can come and go as they please," Maverick said. "We should have mentioned they run through the house when they want so they wouldn't startle you. No problem about the glass. I could have cleaned it up."

"You seemed to have had your hands full last night," Reggie said.

Then Gina and Brooke slipped into the kitchen and were making omelets for everyone, filled with cheese, ham, bell peppers, onions, mushrooms, whatever their hearts desired, while Maverick made mimosas for everyone.

Josh was making the toast, and Faye stepped in to cook up some sausages.

"We thought they were wolf dogs," Reggie said, starting to take the plates filled with made-to-order omelets and sausages to the table. "Then we saw the news and Gina saying they were red wolves. So we worried when we heard that."

"They're perfectly safe to be around," Josh said.

"They never hurt the reindeer?" Faye asked.

"No, they're raised with them, so they know them from birth," Maverick said.

Gina wanted desperately to change the subject. Brooke smiled at her and brought over the teapot and teacups and teabags for anyone who wanted tea instead of coffee. Gina wondered if Randall had told Josh and Brooke what had happened last night as a heads-up.

"But they're still wild animals." Reggie didn't sound convinced that the wolves could be safe to be around. "And someday, you'll want to have kids, right? I'd really worry about having the wolves around them."

At least her parents didn't sound like they believed they were werewolves, not that she was surprised in the least. Her brother and his friends had been the only believers.

With mimosas in hand, they all cheered each other, wishing each other a merry Christmas.

She sure hoped that the great morning would be just as successful after turning her parents. But she realized she and her brother were already wearing Maverick and Randall ragged with all their unscheduled nightly wolf runs, and her parents would too once they were turned. Maybe they'd all do it together though, but they still had the issue that they needed to have someone come with a rescue vehicle in case any of them suddenly shifted back to their human forms during a run. Particularly tonight because a snowstorm was coming in. She could even smell it in the air.

After they had a lovely time at breakfast, they moved into the living room to begin opening Christmas presents, her mom video-recording the morning, though they passed around the phone to capture her unwrapping presents too. It was a free-for-all, everyone having a blast as they opened fun gifts of colorful-toed socks and funny T-shirts, a really cool, colorful Bigfoot artistically created T-shirt for Weston, a pair of reindeer pajamas for Gina—because she was now part of the reindeer family, aka wolf family, a cowboy hat for Maverick because his had seen better days, and belt buckles with reindeer on them for Maverick, Josh, and even Randall, though Gina would give him his later. Her brother had gotten her a headlamp for camping trips and an ultra-cool lantern, all before he knew they wouldn't need them now with their wolf vision. But if they were with others who were only human, she could use them then.

Brooke had given Gina a collection of gnomes for Christmas after she'd shown an interest in them at the antiques shop.

At one point, Maverick got a text on his phone and said amid all the wrapping paper and opened boxes, "I've got to go feed the reindeer. Randall was going to, but something came up."

"I'll go with you and get it done quicker," Josh said.

"Me too," Gina said, enjoying the time she spent with the reindeer.

"We all will," Faye said, getting up from the couch and wading through the wrapping paper to get her coat, phone in hand. "I love the reindeer."

Everyone echoed the same sentiments.

Gina was glad everyone was willing to help out so they could get back to the party. After starting the turkey, they all headed outside wearing their parkas and gloves. A light flurry of snow was falling, the moon still visible between the snowy clouds.

Her mom got ahead of everyone with her phone to record them heading to the stables, and then she hurried off and went inside.

When they went inside, Gina expected it to be like any other day with the special Christmas lights on in the stables, the reindeer waiting for food, but this time the calves' stall had a huge red bow on top and even more lights around it.

She peeked into the stall and gasped. "Ohmigod, a white reindeer calf!" She turned to look at everyone watching her; even the ranch hands had come to join in on the reindeer fun.

"That's Sugarkin, our newest addition to the reindeer ranch, but she's all yours to raise and study," Maverick said, giving Gina a hug before opening the stall door for her.

She gave him a hug and a Christmas kiss. "Thank you. She's beautiful."

"You're welcome. She had to be special for my special... uh, fiancée."

Wolf mate? She figured that was what he was going for until he remembered her parents were there.

Then she went into the stall and greeted the calves. She couldn't just give all her loving to Sugarkin. All the calves were adorable. So was her mate. She hugged on Sugarkin too, loving her soft white fur, her dark eyes, and her pink nose.

Even though the ranch hands were there, everyone pitched in to help with the reindeer as one big happy family, visiting with each other, visiting with the reindeer and llama. Brooke and Gina finally returned to the house to make hot cocoa for everyone and then brought it out for everyone to drink. This had been the best Christmas ever, though Gina still worried about ruining it when they turned her parents.

CHAPTER 21

LATER THAT DAY, GINA AND HER FAMILY AND MAVERICK and his had a late lunch of turkey and all the fixings. They were having a great time talking about the new year and the party coming up. But the whole time they were visiting, Gina was feeling apprehensive. Maybe they could wait to turn her parents during the New Year's Eve party. It would be the time of the new moon, and they couldn't shift.

"So you want to have the wedding on the twenty-eighth of June?" her mother asked.

"Yes, we figured Maverick doesn't have as much business during the summer and we could have a wedding here." And also Gina had looked up the phases of the moon, something she didn't think she'd ever be concerned with when she got married.

Maverick got a call from someone and said, "Merry Christmas, Leidolf."

Gina's heart skipped a beat, and Weston was watching him to see what he had to say.

Maverick glanced at Gina. "Right, making choices."

She raised her brows at him.

"We're almost finished eating. Thanks, okay." Maverick ended the call. "Would anyone like some more champagne?" He got up to get another bottle.

"Would anyone like anything else? I'll get everyone a refill on their water too," Gina said, joining Maverick in the kitchen. It was open to the dining room and living room, so they couldn't really talk in private there, except to kiss and whisper sweet nothings in each other's ear.

"Sure on the water and champagne," Brooke said.

"Leidolf is bringing an injection of wolf saliva for your mom and dad if we choose to tell them and turn them that way."

She sighed. "I thought of even waiting until New Year's Eve."

He smiled. "You would put it off forever if you could."

"Yeah, I would. Okay, so we wait to tell them after Leidolf gets here?"

"He'll be here with us to talk to them soon."

"Okay." She took the pitcher of ice water to the dining room while he opened another bottle of champagne and brought it in.

"No more champagne for me," her dad said, covering the top of his champagne glass. "I'll be driving home and am the designated driver."

"We want you to stay another night." Gina hadn't talked to them about it earlier because she was certain they would have bowed out. But now with the snowstorm coming, they could convince them it was the right thing to do.

"Yeah, Dad," Weston said. "We have so much to eat, and we want to play board games tonight like we did in the past."

"It's going to snow heavily tonight," Maverick said. "We'd feel better if you stayed another night at least."

"Right, and you know how you don't like to drive in snow or rainstorms," Gina said.

"We don't want to be an imposition," their dad said.

Gina knew he'd say that, which was why she hadn't mentioned it before. She smiled, refilled everyone's water glasses, and then began clearing away the dishes. "It isn't. Besides, we're going to have three different desserts later, and so you have to stay for that."

"More champagne?" Maverick held up the bottle.

Everyone took refills then.

They took their seats in the living room, the lights sparkling on the Christmas tree, the fire glowing, and soft Christmas music playing in the background.

"Okay, so we have some news to share," Maverick started.

He was going to do it, spill the beans, and Leidolf wasn't even here yet?

"Not a baby this soon," Faye said, looking shocked.

Maverick smiled. "No. Though that could be a real possibility in a few months. But you know how your son and his friends, well, Gina too, search for Bigfoot—"

"And werewolves," Gina said.

"Yeah, they found some. Not Bigfoot, but werewolves," Maverick said, his arm wrapped around Gina, and he squeezed.

Faye smiled. "Weston told us *you* are a werewolf, and your brother too."

"Right. And we want you to join the pack."

A knock sounded at the door.

"I'll get it," Josh said and hurried to get the door.

Leidolf, Gina figured. And then she let out her breath.

"Yeah, so Weston wanted to be one of us in the worst way," Maverick said.

Josh said, "Merry Christmas, Leidolf. So this is Leidolf Wildhaven, our pack leader."

Reggie and Faye smiled as Josh introduced them.

"Have you told them all about us?" Leidolf asked.

"Not yet. Maverick was just getting started," Josh said.

"Some of us were born as wolf shifters, *lupus garous*, and some were turned. We have two ways of being turned— breaking the skin or taking an injection, something new we've tried when we need to turn someone," Maverick said.

"Let's say I'm buying into this. Why would you need to turn someone?" Reggie asked.

"Once you know that someone is a wolf shifter, we need to ensure you won't tell anyone else. As a wolf shifter, you have the same stake in this," Leidolf said. "We don't do this without giving it a lot of serious consideration."

"I accidentally turned Gina when I was a wolf as she tried to save me after I fell through the ice on a lake," Maverick said.

"He's right, he turned me accidentally, and we didn't have any other choice. Weston and his friends were doggedly trying to learn the truth about us," Gina said.

"I could understand if this were Halloween or an April Fool's joke," their dad said, "but at Christmas?"

"It's not a joke," Weston said. "I'm glad I'm one of them now too. So are Bromley and Patterson. We know you won't believe us unless we shift. Gina and I went running as wolves last night. Maverick had to come after us and make sure we stayed safe. You were in the kitchen when we ran through the house."

"As wolves," Faye said. "But you're right, Weston, I don't believe any of this. Next, you'll be telling us Bigfoot lives here too."

They all smiled.

"Okay, so you said only you and Gina can shift?" Reggie said. "What about the rest of you?"

"We can shift. We're known as royals, born and raised as wolf shifters, and we can shift at any time," Maverick said. "So I'll give you the choice. We can strip off our clothes and shift into wolves, or one of us will so it's not so overwhelming, or we can go to another room and shift. Your choice. We're used to stripping naked in front of other wolves, but we don't expect you to feel comfortable with it."

"You will never believe it if they don't shift in front of you. It's amazing to see," Weston said.

"Do it," Reggie said.

Faye gripped Reggie's hand.

Gina knew her parents wouldn't believe it.

Maverick kissed Gina, and then he rose from the couch. He began stripping off his shirt and then his boots and socks. When he got down to his boxer briefs, he turned around so he wouldn't embarrass her mother, Gina suspected.

Then he pulled his boxer briefs off and shifted.

Gina's mother and father both gasped. Maverick turned around and sat down as a wolf on the floor.

"See?" Weston said as if he was witnessing the miracle again for the first time. "The shift is so fast, you can barely see it."

"It's impossible to believe," Reggie said.

"It's a trick," Faye said. "Like a magician's trick."

"It isn't, Mom. I think you should go with the saliva injection. Maverick, Josh, and Brooke also want to give you, Dad, and Weston parcels of land so you can build homes on them and live here with us. Weston and the other guys were bitten, their choice, being all macho. Dad, I don't know which way you want to go, but it's up to you," Gina said.

"What's the punch line?" Faye asked.

Leidolf explained all the pros to her parents and then said, "And the con is the shifting issue. You'll need to be with us, with the pack, and believe me, you'll have plenty of friends of all ages. So like Gina said, it's up to you how you're turned."

"If you're bitten, the bite mark is light, just enough to break the skin," Weston said. "The guys wanted to be bitten so that they could tell generations to come. Way cooler than getting a shot. Also, we heal in record time."

"Who bit you, Weston?" Reggie asked, still sounding like he couldn't grasp what they were telling them.

"Maverick bit me. I hadn't expected it, but I would have opted for that the same as the others."

Without warning, Josh started stripping off his clothes and shifted. Her parents had the same reaction as before, jaws dropped, a sharp intake of breath.

"If you want, I can shift too," Brooke said.

"And I can," Leidolf said.

"The wolves at the reindeer exhibit," her mother said, "who were they? Real wolves? Or werewolves?"

"Josh and me," Brooke said.

"And like I said, the wolves you saw last night racing through the house were Gina, Maverick, and me. I went into my guest room, and you asked me if the wolf had slept in my room. It had, but the wolf was me," Weston said.

"I don't believe any of this," Reggie said, shaking his head. Then he shrugged. "But I'll humor you. Since Weston and Gina and their friends went with a wolf bite, I will too. That's saying if I believed in all this."

"Do you want to choose who bites you? We want a royal to do it, not one of your kids because you'll have more royal roots then rather than newly turned wolf genes," Leidolf said.

"It should be family," Reggie said, looking at Maverick.

Josh was family too, but maybe her father felt more comfortable with Maverick doing it because he had already turned his son and Gina and they were both fine with it.

Maverick didn't hesitate to cross the room to join Reggie. Her dad offered his hand. Maverick took a bite.

Reggie cried out and then looked at his hand. Maverick licked it as if he was trying to tell him he was sorry, but Gina figured he was trying to ensure her dad was really turned.

Her mom's eyes were huge, but she didn't run off or anything. Gina had worried about that. Faye just watched Reggie, waiting for something to happen.

Maverick returned to his clothes and turned his back to them, though Faye wasn't watching him now. Her eyes were glued on Reggie.

Gina joined her dad and gave him a hug. "That was the hard part."

Well, the shifting was, but she didn't want to mention that.

"Do you feel any different?" Faye asked Reggie.

"No."

"Everyone handles the changes differently," Leidolf said. "It can happen quickly or take some time for the wolf genes to take effect."

"That's right. I didn't smell that Gina had been turned right away. And then I did. She smelled like a wolf. Humans can't detect the smell," Maverick said.

Faye smiled. "Bite me too. If we're all going to undergo this transformation, someone needs to bite me. That's the way of the werewolf, isn't it?"

Yeah, that was the way of the wolf.

"Josh, you can do it, no sense in you having to get naked on us again, Maverick," Faye said.

Gina took her mother's hand to give her courage. And Josh woofed in a way that made him sound like he was agreeing with her, and then he joined them and bit her mom's free hand, licking it afterward.

"Okay, well, if that's done, you can explain the rest to them about the great things we have planned as a pack and what being one of us entails. I'm going to join my family for the rest of Christmas," Leidolf said.

"Thanks, Leidolf," Maverick said, "and merry Christmas."

Everyone wished him a merry Christmas and thanked him too.

Maverick walked him to the door and let him out, Leidolf smiling and shaking his head. "You have your work cut out for you."

Gina figured poor Maverick did.

Then Maverick shut the door and returned to the living room. Josh trotted back to his clothes, shifted, and got dressed. Then they began playing Christmas charades as if the wolf business hadn't just happened. But she wondered if they could smell all the Christmas feast aromas so much better now that they had been turned and what else they might be feeling. They were playing the game though, and she was glad they hadn't freaked out.

Gina couldn't help watching her parents for any signs they might have been turned, but then she suspected all the royal wolves and her brother were watching for the same thing.

CHAPTER 22

Surreptitiously during the Christmas Day festivities, Maverick and the other wolves were watching Reggie and Faye while they played charades, but then Brooke said, "Does anyone want some pie and coffee, tea, or milk?"

Everyone was eager to have some dessert.

Gina added whipped cream on top of the slices of pies that Brooke had cut for everyone. Maverick made coffee and heated water for the tea. Brooke added some ice cream to anyone's pie who wanted some.

They finally settled in the dining room with their beverages and pie.

"I don't feel any different," Reggie said, cutting into a slice of pecan pie.

"You will be able to smell a lot more scents than you could before," Maverick said.

Reggie took a deep breath. "You're right. I can smell the sweet ice cream and whipped cream and even the pecans in the pie."

"And the pumpkin, cinnamon, ginger, and cloves in the pumpkin pie seems to be even more…fragrant." Faye took a bite of her pumpkin pie.

"You can see in the dark with your night vision, once the wolf genes have taken root," Maverick said.

That gave Gina an idea. "Let's turn out all the lights." Gina left the table to turn off the kitchen lights.

"Good idea," Maverick said.

Josh got the Christmas tree lights, Brooke the dining room light, and Maverick turned off the living room lights.

Maverick smiled. "Can you see us?"

"Yeah. It must be light enough in the room," Faye said. "The fireplace still has a fire going."

"It's nine at night. It's dark in here without the lights on," Gina said. "The fireplace only emits a low, warm light at one end of the living room." She turned off the fireplace. "The same thing happened to me on the campout. I could see as if it were dawn but it was pitch-black out. No campfire. When the guys got up, they were all carrying flashlights and lanterns. I'd made a trip into the woods by myself and then after that was trying to start a fire in the dark and could see just fine."

"Wow. I see what you mean. Even after you turned off the fireplace, I can see you." Faye smiled and turned to listen to something. "What was that sound?"

"Snow falling off the roof, the winds are picking up, the furnace just turned on," Maverick said.

Reggie pulled his hearing aids out. "I can hear without these. With them, everything's way too amplified." He smiled.

Gina said to Maverick in a hushed voice, "I didn't think of that. My dad often turns his hearing aids off because he gets so much 'static.'"

"I heard that." Reggie smiled more broadly this time.

Gina laughed. "Okay, that's a bad thing. Now I can't keep secrets from you when you're around."

Reggie reached over and squeezed Faye's hand. "Why didn't you tell me I could ditch my hearing aids, Maverick? I wouldn't have hesitated to get turned."

"Here I was thinking I'd have to get some hearing aids soon too. Not now." Faye sounded cheered by the notion.

They turned the lights and the fireplace on and sat down to finish their desserts.

Weston was sitting beside his dad and smiled. "Hey, Dad, you smell like a wolf."

"I don't feel any different."

"What about me?" Faye asked.

Gina got out of her seat and hugged her mom and smiled. "You're a wolf too, Mom. Now, if either of you feel like you're having a hot flash and want to rip off your clothes, you're most likely needing to shift into a wolf. Weston and I shifted last night, so it's possible you might. If you want and we can't go with you and you want to run as wolves, Maverick will accompany you." She shouldn't volunteer him, but she knew he would do it too.

"And me," Josh said.

"Me too," Brooke said.

"But you don't have to run. You can shift and just sleep as a wolf in your guest room," Maverick told their parents.

Gina laughed, and he figured she believed he didn't want to go chasing after her parents tonight like he had to for her and her brother last night. Whatever made everyone happy after being turned was fine with him. He just wanted them to know that they didn't have to run as wolves but could sleep through the night instead. Though if Gina and her brother both went out to run as wolves, then it could be fun for all of them to be together as a family, Josh and Brooke included.

"Or we can all go together as wolves," Maverick said.

"As a family," Josh said.

"You said something about a parcel of land?" Weston asked.

"Yeah, so you can build a couple of homes on the acreage. Just think," Maverick said to him, "if you have your own acreage and home, you'd stand a better chance at entertaining a she-wolf at your place and convincing her you are meant to be the one for her."

"I didn't think that's how that worked," Gina said. "That instead the wolf instincts led you to find the right mate."

"True," Maverick said, "but it doesn't hurt for Weston to have a home of his own instead of just having her over to Sarge's place for dates."

"True. Oh and Mom and Dad, Maverick and I are mated wolves. So a wedding is only a formality, but we're mated for life already," Gina said.

"Mated wolves," Faye said. "It sounds like your world has a lot of rules."

"It does." Maverick began to explain more about the *lupus garous*. He figured that they'd remember only a small amount of what he told them after being turned. It was a lot to deal with.

Josh and Brooke filled in all the rest of the details about the wolves that they could think of.

"The new moon? Full moon?" Faye sighed. "I guess it's good that we aren't working any longer and just collect our retirement checks. I like the fact we heal twice as fast as humans. I've always worn my wedding and engagement rings though. Not wearing them except during the new moon phase will take some getting used to."

They ended up talking into the night, though Maverick really wanted to take Gina to bed so she could get some sleep and hopefully wouldn't sleepwalk again tonight. But her parents were so wound up about everything, they just couldn't sleep yet.

He thought of locking the bedroom door, but he had to take care of her parents and Weston too if they took off in the middle of the night.

"Oh, I've got to shift," Gina said. "I'm not ready to get naked in front of everyone like the royals do." She hurried off the chair and ran for the master bedroom.

"I'll be right back." Maverick wasn't going to turn unless she wanted to go running.

But then Faye abruptly left the table and ran down the hall.

"Faye?" Reggie said and hurried after her.

A few minutes later, Maverick returned with Gina in her wolf coat.

Then Weston smiled. "Maybe we'll have a shorter run tonight and you can get some sleep."

"And Gina won't be sleepwalking as a wolf," Maverick said.

"She was doing that again?" Brooke asked.

Gina wagged her tail.

"Yeah, she needs to get more sleep." Maverick began taking plates into the kitchen and started putting them in the dishwasher.

Josh and Brooke helped him. But neither Faye nor Reggie left the bedroom. Weston finally went to check on them.

"Come on, Mom, you're beautiful. Show off your wolf self to the rest of us so we all know you in your wolf form," Weston said in the guest room.

Maverick hadn't considered that their parents, or at least Faye, would be reluctant to show off what she'd become.

"Honey, when I shift, we can go out together, okay?" Reggie said from the bedroom.

But then Gina barged into the guest room and woofed. At her urging, her mother came out of the bedroom with her, and Maverick smiled at the two of them.

Reggie didn't leave the room, and Maverick heard his shoes hit the floor. He must have been stripping in a prelude to shifting.

"I called Randall," Josh said, "so he can follow us in the Jeep with a change of clothes for anyone who might need them. Brooke and I will run with you as wolves."

Maverick was glad for that.

Then Reggie came bounding out of the bedroom as a wolf and howled. Faye looked like she didn't know what to do. Gina howled and rubbed against her mom and dad with reassurance.

"We could all wait for Weston to shift, or—" Maverick said.

"Go ahead. I'll join you when I can. I don't want to hold you up if Mom and Dad and Gina have to shift back earlier because of it and I've delayed everyone," Weston said.

"I'll stay with Weston," Josh said.

"I'll go with Maverick to help keep everyone on track," Brooke said.

"Okay, sounds good. Randall can get the clothes for Gina and Weston out of my truck. I'll grab your clothes too," Maverick said and pulled a cloth grocery bag out of the hall closet. Then he headed into Faye and Reggie's guest room, shoved their clothes into it, and then rejoined them. "If you'll follow our lead, Randall will trail us in the Jeep. We can't cross rivers or go into the woods where he can't easily reach us with the Jeep in case anyone shifts suddenly in the snow. It's also really snowing out there, so we need to stay close to each other so we don't lose anyone." Maverick didn't want to say no to them running as wolves because of the snow, since it was such a new experience for them and being cooped up in the house as a wolf wouldn't be as much fun.

Brooke and Maverick quickly stripped out of their clothes and shifted, and then they led the others outside through the wolf door, all except for Faye. Josh opened the front door, letting her out, since she balked at going out through the wolf door. Then he took the bag of Faye's and Reggie's clothes and gave them to Randall, who was already waiting for them.

"I'm just waiting on Weston to shift, and then we'll be joining you," Josh said.

"Okay, I've got his and Gina's spare clothes from Maverick's truck." Then Randall said to those who had shifted, "Just don't get too far ahead of me. The snow is really causing visibility issues, even with our enhanced night vision."

Maverick and Gina barked in agreement, and then Brooke led the way and Maverick brought up the rear. He hoped Weston would be able to join them soon, and then they could all return home as soon as possible. He loved running in the snow, but he didn't want to lose anyone out here either.

Like wolves would do on a run together in deep snow, they ran single file, which he appreciated, no tangents tonight. Faye was following Brooke, keeping close to her, not wanting to lose sight of her. Reggie was keeping the same distance from his wife, but Gina was giving them a little breathing room. Maverick was right on top of Gina though, not wanting to lose her. Behind them, he could hear Randall's Jeep's engine, the sound muffled by the blowing wind and snow.

And then Maverick thought he heard something approaching from behind and turned to see Josh and Weston racing to catch up to them, running in their snow tracks, Weston following Josh.

Glad to see them, Maverick woofed. The line of wolves all stopped ahead of them and turned. Brooke howled to see them. Then Reggie and Gina howled. Maverick followed up and Josh and Weston joined in on the chorus. Faye looked too timid to try. Maverick loved her and knew they'd make a bona fide wolf out of her yet.

They ran for about a half hour, and then Brooke stopped and turned around. All the wolves stopped, and she barked, letting them know it was time to head back in. Maybe they would have a caramel apple hot toddy cocktail before they called it a night, if anyone wanted one or if they could even shift to have one.

They turned around and headed back in, with Josh moving in front of Weston to lead the way as Randall's Jeep's headlights cut through the veil of snow.

Maverick hoped everyone had enjoyed the run on the wild side, especially Faye since she seemed to be having trouble coming to grips with her wolf half for now.

Josh stopped to howl as he drew nearer to the ranch and howls came from the bunkhouse. Maverick smiled, and the rest of them on the run paused to howl, all except for Faye. Maverick suspected she'd have to practice in private or with her immediate family to begin with.

Then they reached the Jeep, and everyone seemed okay to run home as wolves. They hadn't been out that long, but there was no telling when the newly turned would shift, so they had to be vigilant.

Randall followed them all the way home, and once they were there, he got out of his Jeep to open the front door for Faye. Maverick was giving him an increased bonus this year for all his help with the newly turned wolves, though he knew his ranch manager was happy to help out any way that he could.

Then they went inside, and Randall left their bags of clothes in the house. "Merry Christmas, folks," he said, and they all woofed at him, all but Faye, and then he closed the door, and the Jeep drove off.

They rubbed their paws on the mat at the front door, and then Gina's family headed for their bedrooms. Maverick, Brooke, and Josh shifted by their discarded clothing and began getting dressed. "Did you all want a caramel apple hot toddy before you go home tonight?" Maverick asked his brother and sister-in-law.

"Oh, yes, that would be great," Brooke said. "That was so much fun. I'm glad we were all able to run as a family. Our new family." She glanced at the bedrooms down the hall.

Maverick realized the same thing as she did. No one was dressing that he could make out. And definitely no one was coming down the hallway as a human or otherwise.

Josh smiled. "Let's make the drinks." He hoped everyone would shift back soon.

"Yeah, I'm all for it. And as everyone emerges, they can have their drinks," Brooke said, already getting out the ingredients for the cocktails.

Hot apple cider, apple brandy, whipped cream, and caramel drizzled on top made for a fun Christmas cocktail for the finale of Christmas Day.

And then, as if everyone had smelled the delightful drinks and wanted them, they began to come out of the bedrooms, one by one. Faye was the last to get herself dressed and come out to join them.

Everyone was looking at her hair. Instead of being blonde, she now had dark brown hair with a few strands of gray. He wondered if she'd seen her hair had lost its dye.

"Well, how was it?" Maverick asked everyone as he and Brooke passed out the drinks.

"It was great," Reggie said. "I felt more alive and younger than I've felt in years."

"I loved it," Weston said, giving his mom a hug.

"It was an experience and a half," Faye finally said,

running her hand over her hair. "I never felt warmer on a walk through a blizzard. The wolf coat is amazingly warm, but it's still so unreal. I...I wasn't sure how to howl. I felt if I tried I'd make some kind of pitiful sound."

"You can do it, Mom," Gina said. "You did great. It was a lot to experience all at once, but I'm so proud of you. You know, I've never seen your hair that color."

Her mom sighed. "Don't tell me that's one of the changes to expect with shifting."

"Uh, yes, no hair dye or nail polish will remain when you shift," Brooke said.

"At least I took my rings off before I shifted," Faye said.

"I love your hair color, Mom," Gina said, coming back to the topic of her hair. "It's really pretty. I thought you were hiding the gray."

"No, I just always thought blondes had more fun."

Everyone laughed.

"These are delicious, by the way." Faye took another sip of hers.

"Thanks." Brooke finished off her drink. "A nice way to end a wolf run on Christmas Day. Well, I think we're about ready to head home. Right, Josh?"

"Yeah. We're so glad you all are family." Josh rose from his seat, and everyone else did too.

Then they began to hug each other, and Josh and Brooke left the house to walk home.

Gina and Maverick cleaned up the glasses, and they hugged her parents and Weston, and then they said their good-nights, and everyone headed for their bedrooms.

"It all turned out well after all," Gina said after they stripped out of their clothes and climbed into bed, snuggling together in the master bedroom.

"It sure did. Your mom needs a little more time to adjust, but I think they're both happy with the change," Maverick said.

She chuckled. "I think my mom can even live with her hair color now."

He laughed. "I love you and your family."

"I love you too, and so do they."

And after making love and falling asleep in each other's arms, they were startled awake when they heard a howl coming from her parents' guest room—a new howl they hadn't heard before.

And they laughed. "Your mom is officially one of us now," Maverick said.

"We all are. Merry Christmas, honey."

"Merry Christmas, my beautiful she-wolf."

EPILOGUE

IT WAS NEW YEAR'S EVE, AND GINA'S PARENTS WERE THE happiest she'd ever seen them, fireworks lighting the black sky in a display of brilliant colors, everyone snacking on treats, drinking wine, cocktails, or champagne and dressed to the nines.

"I haven't been to a New Year's Eve party in years," her mom told her. "This is so much fun."

They were all dressed up in shimmering silver sparkly dresses and feeling like a million bucks. And Gina's dad was wearing a tux, the first time in forever and looking just as dapper.

"We'd gotten sedentary in our lives. Now we have so many friends, lunches and dinners out with them when we can't shift. And then movie nights, lunch and dinners in with friends when we have trouble shifting. If we shift, we all just go for a run as wolves. We have so much fun stuff to do that we've never been busier. But it's all been great—horseback riding, running as wolves, even helping out with the reindeer. Your dad can't wait to fish in the spring. I'm working with a group of quilters on projects for cancer patients even. Here we thought our retirement years would be totally boring. We couldn't be happier. And do you know what?"

"What, Mom?" Gina was so thrilled her mom and dad had taken to this way of life so easily.

"Your dad and I decided that we were still meant to be together."

Gina frowned at her mom. That was supposed to have been a given.

"Oh, Leidolf probably didn't tell you, but sometimes when a human couple are turned, they realize they weren't meant to be a mated pair of wolves. But we always knew we were meant for each other."

Gina looked around at all the couples dancing or visiting and saw Leidolf. He raised a glass of champagne to her and smiled. She growled under her breath. No way would she have wanted to see her parents split up once they were *lupus garous*. Though she guessed she had to see it from their viewpoint. Mated wolves lived long lives, and if they hadn't been right for each other, that wouldn't have been good either.

Then she saw Maverick juggling three glasses of champagne and headed their way. She was glad she and Maverick had what it took to be mated wolves.

"You didn't tell me sometimes a couple who were turned might not be wolf mate compatible, Maverick." Gina took hold of two of the glasses of champagne and gave one to her mother.

"I've got to join your dad. See you in a bit," her mother said and headed off to join her dad with her champagne glass in hand.

"Who told you that?" Maverick was frowning, looking surprised.

"Mom. She said Leidolf told her that. Did you know?"

"No. Really, I didn't. I've only known single people who

have been turned. I'd never even considered the possibility that a married couple wouldn't make compatible wolf mates, though I could see now how that might happen."

"Well, Leidolf's just lucky they are."

"And I'm just lucky you and I are."

She kissed him on the lips and then drank some of her champagne. "I want to run as a wolf."

"It's the new moon phase. You can't."

"I know. I still want to run as a wolf."

He smiled. "I'm glad, but right now, it's about time for the countdown. Have you made your New Year's goals?"

"Hmm, to take you on your first Bigfoot hunting excursion."

He laughed. "The last time you went on one of those—"

"I met you, became a wolf, mated a wolf, and became a proud part owner of a magical, year-round, Christmas reindeer ranch, one beautiful, rare white reindeer calf, and a llama."

"How could you beat that experience?"

"If we found Bigfoot?"

He smiled.

Then Weston and Dorinda joined them. "Are you going with us on a Bigfoot hunt?" Dorinda asked.

"Not you too," Maverick said.

Bromley, Sarge, and Patterson headed their way.

"Did Gina convince you to come on the hunt with us? The last time we did—" Patterson said.

"We ended up finding half of what we were looking for," Bromley said.

A Bigfoot hunt. "Only if we do it strictly during the new moon," Maverick said, not sure what he was getting himself into by agreeing to this. But there was no way he was going with a whole bunch of newly turned wolves during any time that they could shift. Even Dorinda could have trouble with it during the full moon phase.

"Mom and Dad said they want to come too," Gina said. "If we could find werewolves, Mom said there was no telling what other mythical creatures we might discover. She's hoping to see a unicorn."

Maverick raised a brow.

"Not really. They've heard us talking about our hiking adventures for years, and after we got ourselves into so much trouble this last time, they want to make sure we don't do that again," Gina said.

Maverick and the others laughed. "All right. My New Year's resolution is to go on a hunt for Bigfoot during the phase of the new moon with all of you."

And then the countdown started. "Ten, nine, eight, seven, six, five, four, three, two, one, happy New Year!" everyone shouted, and the last blast of spectacular fireworks was set off in one final, dizzying display.

Now, Maverick's New Year's resolution was to take Gina home and show her just how much he wanted to start the new year right—with a big bang!

They were kissing though, a prelude to bringing in the new year all the way.

"Let's finish this at home," he said.

"My very thought," she said, and they slipped into his pickup and hurried on home, where they would be a pair of wolves living among a herd of reindeer and one llama, an expanded family of wolves, and with more fireworks to come.

ACKNOWLEDGMENTS

Thanks so much to Darla Taylor and Donna Fournier, who are so much fun. I love that both garden like I do, and they are a great help in finding all my goofs in the books! Thanks, ladies! And thanks so much to Deb Werksman for continuing to believe in my wolf adventures and the cover artists who wow my readers with their artwork and make them just that much more real.

ABOUT THE AUTHOR

USA Today bestselling author Terry Spear has written over eighty paranormal and medieval Highland romances. In 2008, *Heart of the Wolf* was named a *Publishers Weekly* Best Book of the Year. She has received a PNR Top Pick, a Best Book of the Month nomination by *Long and Short Reviews*, numerous *Night Owl Romance* Top Picks, and two Paranormal Excellence Awards for Romantic Literature (Finalist & Honorable Mention). In 2016, *Billionaire in Wolf's Clothing* was an *RT Book Reviews* Top Pick. A retired officer of the U.S. Army Reserves, Terry also creates award-winning teddy bears that have found homes all over the world, helps out with her granddaughter and grandson, and is raising two Havanese puppies. She lives in Spring, Texas.

Need more swoony Red Wolf action?

Keep reading for a look at Terry Spear's

THE BEST OF BOTH WOLVES

Now available from
Sourcebooks Casablanca

CHAPTER 1

EVERYTHING HAD BEEN LOOKING UP FOR SIERRA Redding, a retired army finance officer, since she'd moved to the Portland, Oregon, area before Christmas. At least she thought that. After a day working in a mixed-media-collage intensive workshop for teachers, she was excited and looking forward to setting up "official" art assignments for wolf kids of all ages in the red wolf pack, starting on Monday. The job was just a part-time one, but she had her army retirement pay, and that was all she really needed.

She wasn't sure if she could do this since she'd never taught kids before, but she'd had so much fun at the workshops that she knew this was just what she wanted to do. Initially, she hadn't really thought of what she wanted to do once she retired, but her pack leaders, Leidolf and Cassie Wildhaven, had hired her immediately to teach art classes to the pack-schooled kids. Cassie was eager to find someone trained in art already and who had a talent for it since a couple of the students showed real promise and needed someone who could teach them more skills.

After the long day of art-teacher-training workshops, Sierra entered her Portland hotel room, ready to order some seafood from room service and chill while watching a movie on TV. As soon as she shut the door, she got a call from Cassie. She hurried to answer it while dumping her bag of notes and art supplies on the extra queen-size bed. "Hi, Cassie."

"Hey, how's it going?" Cassie was a wolf biologist, the perfect occupation for a wolf who already knew all about wolf biology on a personal basis. She was often on tours educating people about wolves, when she wasn't home helping her mate lead the pack.

"It's going great. I'm having a blast. I'll be all set for starting classes on Monday, and I already have some adults lined up for art classes at night." Sierra appreciated that Cassie had called to see how she was doing. She hadn't expected to hear from anyone.

"I'm so glad to hear it. I'm thrilled you're all settled in. We couldn't be more pleased that you've joined the pack."

Sierra knew part of the reason was that there were fewer females than males in the pack, and they were always on the lookout to entice new females to join them. It helped when the wolf had a skill the pack needed. They'd even paid for her workshops and her hotel, which was really nice of them.

"I am too." Though Sierra wasn't really settled in—yet. She wouldn't be until she began working and felt she had a mission and purpose in life. She'd loved creating sketches and paintings when she was a kid, and through the years while she was in the army, she'd won a few contests with her wolf portraits. She loved that she'd had such cooperative wolf models. She was always learning new things, and her next great adventure was creating digital paintings from photographs and sharing how to do that with the kids.

"I'm so glad that you haven't changed your mind."

Sierra laughed. She was sure Cassie and Leidolf worried she might still return to Texas to be with her boyfriend. "Yeah, we're good." For now. She had to see how teaching went, how she got along with the pack members, and decide about Lieutenant Colonel Richard Wentworth, the army officer she was still dating back at Fort Hood, Texas.

"Okay, well, I'll let you go now. Leidolf is fixing dinner, and I need to help him with the kids."

"Thanks for calling. I'll talk to you later." Afterward, Sierra called in an order for shrimp scampi at the hotel restaurant and was watching an espionage thriller on TV when her twin brother called. She paused her movie.

"Hey, how are you doing at your workshop?" Brad asked.

Loving her brother, she smiled. He had retired as a Navy SEAL and had mated one of the Portland pack members, which was one of the big reasons she had come here. When they had kids—and often wolves had more than one at a time—she wanted to be here to help out. While she and her brother had both been in the military, they hadn't had a lot of time to see each other, though they'd always been close, so it was time to bond again.

"Great. I love it. Why aren't you busy making little Redding wolves?"

He chuckled.

She teased him about that all the time, though she knew he wasn't waiting to have kids with Janice. She also knew had called because he wanted her to love what she was doing and stay in the area. Her parents were waiting for her to say if she was going to remain in Portland before they made any move from Texas to join them.

"Okay, well, I just wanted to check on you, and I'm glad you're enjoying it. See you soon."

"Thanks, Brad. Sounds good." They ended the call.

She started the movie and then her phone jingled again. *Now* who was calling?

She paused the movie and grabbed her phone. Her boyfriend. She sighed and answered the phone.

"Hey, Sierra. I hope you're getting tired of the rain there."

Not "Hey, honey, I missed you"? Something was seriously wrong with their relationship.

She was starting to get used to the rain as she listened to it softly hitting the window. "I'm glad to be here." She'd met so many wolves in the pack who were friendly and welcoming, something she had certainly been hoping for.

"I miss you."

"I miss you too. I'll be seeing you." She'd told herself she had to give herself time to learn how much she liked it here before she made any decision to return to Texas. Sure, she felt somewhat conflicted about leaving him, but he was doing what he wanted to do, and this was what she wanted to do. Not only that, but she hadn't missed him as much as she'd thought she would.

"All right. I hope that means you're coming back for good."

"We'll see." She was beginning to think that for him, absence made the heart grow fonder. Though she also suspected he was afraid she might find a new wolf to interest her and Richard would be history. He was doing a lot more checking up on her than when she lived in Killeen, Texas. She was really trying to be objective about this and not let any bachelor wolves sway her from her mission: settle in, work with the kids, and see if this was what she really wanted to do.

But she had to admit there were some real bachelor male hotties in the Portland-area wolf pack that she was interested in seeing more of if things were going to work out for her here. Police Detective Adam Holmes with the Portland Police Bureau was on top of the list. He had been all smiles, welcoming her to the pack as if she were staying for good, and had made her feel really great about being here. She supposed another reason he was on her good list was he'd been the first one to sign up for her adult art class for Monday night, though—according to him—he couldn't even draw a stick figure.

Someone knocked at the door, and she figured her shrimp scampi dinner had arrived. "I have to go. My meal is here."

"Home delivery?"

"I'm in Portland at the art workshops this weekend, staying at a hotel. I've got to go. 'Night, Richard." She'd told him last week and reminded him again a few days ago where she was going to be for the weekend. He especially worried about where she was and what she was doing during the weekends, but he never remembered after she told him.

"Later," he said.

He could be controlling, used to being in charge in his position as a commander. And she was tired of him never having time for her when she was actually living in Killeen. Now, he continued to call, email, and text her, hoping she would get her "visit" to Oregon out of her system and would move back to Texas.

Yet she just couldn't give up their relationship. As much as she hated to admit it, she loathed the idea of getting to know someone new as a potential mate.

They ended the call and she answered the door to get her meal delivery. "Thanks," she told the delivery guy, then shut her door.

She knew Richard was miffed at her for not staying in Killeen. No matter how much she had told him she wanted to be with a pack, he just didn't get it. He was more career-minded, wanted to make more rank, and joining a pack was definitely low on his list of priorities.

She settled down to eat a meal that was the best shrimp scampi she'd ever had while finally finishing the movie. Then it was time to shower. She pulled off her clothes and laid them on the bed, then went into the bathroom and brushed her teeth.

The problem was that Richard lived for promotions, which was fine and good—for him. But she was done with the military and wanted more. Once she'd retired, she knew she needed to do something important with her life again. Sure, she enjoyed being with him, when he made the time. But there wasn't a wolf pack in Killeen, and now that she didn't have to transfer to a new location all the time, she wanted and needed the socialization that went along with a pack. Once she had children of her own, she would really need that. Plus, she wanted her kids to live close to Brad's so they could get to know their cousins.

Richard wasn't about to change his mind about moving anywhere else, and certainly he wouldn't leave the military.

She'd had to make so many changes in her life while in the army, and he had been her one constant. One boyfriend for three years. Of course there had been no other wolves available for either of them to date at Fort Hood either. So naturally, from the first time they'd met, the attraction was there between them. But now that she didn't have a full-time job to keep her busy, she wanted more. She wanted...something different. Her parents were happy with each other, and though her dad had made general in the army, he had always had time for her mother, who had been in the air force, both retired now. Richard wasn't like that with Sierra.

She removed her makeup, then started the water for her shower. Soon she was in the bathtub soaping her hair when she thought she heard her hotel-room door shut. She listened. She didn't hear any sounds other than the shower water pelting her and running down the drain. She must have heard a door close for another room close by. That was the trouble with her enhanced wolf hearing. Everything could sound much closer than it was.

She was in the middle of washing her hair and face, soap all over her body, the hot water sluicing down her back, and she was feeling dreamy when she heard a drawer in the chest of drawers squeak open. Her heart began to race and her skin chilled despite the hot water. The bathroom door was wide open because she wasn't sharing a room with anyone else, or she would have at least closed it and could have jumped out of the shower and locked it.

No one should have been in her room, and now she suspected the key-card noise she'd heard just minutes earlier had been the real deal. Who the hell had a key to her room? Whoever it was didn't say a word. The scary part was that even though he had to hear her showering, he ignored it, like he knew he was safe, that she couldn't harm him. And that made her angry. And even more worried.

Another drawer opened in the bureau, and then another. She hadn't unpacked her bags, except for hanging her rain jacket, a shirt, and a pair of pants in the closet. The rest of her things were still in her bags. Her purse and her laptop were also in the closet, where she always put them when she wasn't using them. She knew she should be careful, not worry about her personal possessions and only think about living through this, if it came to that, but she was instinctively a territorial wolf. Allowing him to steal from her without a fight wasn't in her blood.

She quickly washed the soap out of her hair and off her face and body and left the water running. Her phone was sitting on the bedside table, so she couldn't reach it to call the police. She didn't have a weapon... Well, maybe not a gun or knife, but she did have a different kind of weapon. One she was born with. It would have to do.

She called on her wolf, heat rushing through every bone and through every muscle. Confronting a human like this wasn't something wolves would normally do when they were taught to hide their identity at all costs from humans. But the intruder couldn't see her shift and she was afraid—since he was bold enough to remain there when she was taking a shower—she could be in a world of hurt if she didn't do something to protect herself.

As soon as she had turned into a big red wolf with big ears, big teeth, and big wolf paws, she pushed the shower curtain aside with her nose, leaped out of the tub, slid on the bath mat, and tore out of the bathroom and into the room. As soon as the man saw movement, turned, and noticed her coming at him, the would-be thief jumped straight into the air. He cried out with a strangled sound and made a dash for the door.

That was what she liked to see. Him scared to pieces and running for his life. Though her own heart was beating triple time, the adrenaline surging through her blood preparing her to flee or fight. Fighting was more what she had in mind.

But his leaving the room pronto wasn't good enough for her. She had to get a better look at his face so she could identify him in a sketch and the police would have something to go on to catch him. Not to mention she wanted to scare the crap out of him so he wouldn't pull this again with some other unsuspecting guest. No telling how many robberies he'd already committed and gotten away with.

Imagine him thinking he was robbing a defenseless human but suddenly was faced with a snarling wolf!

He had to assume the only occupant was a woman, since her bra, panties, jeans, and sweater were piled on the bed and a pair of size seven women's boots were sitting on the floor next to the bed. There were no men's clothes anywhere in the room.

His back was to her while he was in fleeing mode, and she lunged and tackled him, her large paws slamming into his back and knocking him flat on his chest on the carpeted floor. She wanted to bite him! But she couldn't or chance turning him into one of their kind. They couldn't have that happen no matter what. It was bad enough if they did it to someone accidentally, but doing it on purpose to someone who exhibited criminal behavior? No way.

She was growling, snapping her teeth next to his neck, letting him know just how dangerous she could be. And how stupid he'd been for breaking into her room with the intent of stealing from her.

She smelled urine and growled again. She would have to switch rooms or smell his pee in her room for the rest of the time she was staying here.

On his belly, he struggled to get free of her, terrified, crying out, his body pressed against the floor, trying to unsettle her. She had her front paws firmly on his back, pinning him down, her hind feet on the floor, giving her traction as she spread her large wolf paws out. He was trying to twist away, and then she realized he was reaching with his right hand for something in his pocket or at his waistband under his hoodie. A gun? A knife?

Don't bite him, she warned herself. She desperately wanted to. To show him he wasn't in charge here. In the beginning, she should have let him go, she figured in retrospect, just scared him and forced him to run out of the room, shifted, then locked and bolted the door and called the police. And hurried to get dressed. Now, she assumed he was armed and could be more dangerous than her—only because she couldn't take a bite out of him.

She wasn't sure what to do. Keep him pinned to the floor so he couldn't hurt her and howl to get help? Uh, yeah, that would go over well.

He smelled of beer and pot and pee, and she would remember his scent anywhere now. If she didn't have to turn back into her human form, she could have tracked him down once he left the room. He finally managed to roll over so that she lost her grip on him, and then she studied him, growling.

His face was filled with fear as he sat up and scooted away from her like someone doing a fast crab scuttle. She was glad she could get a good look at his long chin, the bristly dark hair covering it, pale thin lips, and wide hazel eyes. His hair was cut short, and he had a rattlesnake tattoo around his neck.

He quickly scrambled to his feet and continued to back away toward the door and, at the same time, pulled a gun out of his pocket. She remained in her spot, ready to dodge if he fired a shot, but she suspected he didn't want to use the gun if he didn't have to and alert everyone within hearing distance that someone was firing a gun in a hotel room.

Still, her heart was hammering triple time. What if he shot her accidentally, if not on purpose? She wanted to sit down, to show him she was letting him go, but she was afraid to make any kind of move at this point.

He backed up all the way to the door, probably having heard that you never want to turn your back on an angry dog. And she was an angry *wolf*.

He bumped against the door and fumbled behind with his free hand to reach for the handle. She should have locked the safety bar across it after the man delivered her meal. And especially before she stripped out of her clothes and took her shower. *Damn it.*

Then the would-be robber pulled the door open and maneuvered around it, his eyes on her the whole time. Yeah, she had a real good idea of what he looked like and *smelled* like.

As soon as he made his way out of the room, he pulled the door shut as fast as he could. She raced to the door, shifted, and shoved the security latch in place. Then she ran and got her phone and called Police Detective Adam Holmes, a red wolf like her. If she couldn't get him, she would call Josh Wilding, also a red wolf with the pack and Adam's former police detective partner, recently retired. She knew they would take this threat seriously.

Thankfully, she got ahold of Adam right away. "I've had a break-in at my hotel room." She gave the name of the hotel and found an address on a notepad. "Hurry. You might catch him! I'm in room 308."

"Are you all right?" Adam asked, his voice deeply concerned.

She heard Adam's Hummer door slam shut and his engine roar to life. "Yes. He ran out of the room, but I've got to get dressed." Still naked, she hurried into the bathroom and turned off the shower, but she was glad Adam was coming to aid her and that it wasn't someone she didn't know.

"You were showering?"

Astute wolf's hearing.

"Yes, but I'll be dressed before you get here." She put the phone on speaker and grabbed a towel to dry herself off. Then she seized her phone, returned to the bedroom, and dug in her suitcase to find a pair of panties and pulled them on.

"Hell, Sierra. I'm on my way. What did he look like?"

She slid her bra straps over her arms and fastened it. "I'll draw you a sketch, but if you see him race out of the hotel or anywhere in the vicinity when you get here, he's wearing a black hoodie, blue jeans, tears in several places on the thighs and knees, black sneakers, white male, approximately mid- to late twenties. He was scrawny, had short, brown hair and bristly chin whiskers, and a rattlesnake tattoo around his neck. He smells of pee and pot and beers, oh, and he has a diamond or fake diamond earring in both ears."

"And he has *your* description," Adam said, sounding worried that she was an eyewitness and the guy could retaliate against her.

"As a red wolf. Yep." She fumbled through her suitcase for a flannel shirt to wear.

Adam didn't say anything for a moment. "You shifted?"

"That's the only way he would have my description as a red wolf. Got to go, Adam. I need to get dressed." She could envision the police at her door while she was still trying to dress!

"Be there soon. Calling it in now."

She finished dressing and then started drawing the sketch of the man on her sketch pad at the little table for two in the room before she forgot anything.

It wasn't but about ten minutes later that Adam was knocking at Sierra's door. "It's me, Adam Holmes."

She hurried to let him in. He looked so spiffy in his suit, like an FBI agent, his green eyes narrowed as he considered her appearance, and she knew he was making sure she was okay. She was surprised that no one else was with him.

"I have men downstairs talking to the clerks and trying to learn how he got a key to your room. I wanted to talk to you privately first. Are you okay?"

She folded her arms. "Yes. And I know I should have secured the safety bar on the door." She figured he would lecture her about that and about shifting.

"Correct. Did he see you shift?" He was still frowning at her.

"Of course not! I was in the shower, and he was rummaging through the empty bureau drawers." As if she would do something so foolish. If he'd come into the bathroom, well, she would have shifted, but behind the shower curtain, not in front of him.

"But he heard the shower going and that didn't deter him from staying in your room?"

"No, which was why I was really worried. The bathroom door was wide open, and I couldn't jump out and lock it without him catching me at it. Oh, and he had a 9mm gun."

"Sierra." Adam sounded totally exasperated with her.

"What? I had to chase him off the only way I knew how. I didn't bite him, but I would have if I'd known it wouldn't turn him. I didn't know he had a gun."

Adam let out his breath. "We're certain this guy is part

of a team of thieves who have hit numerous hotels. We still don't know how they're breaking into the rooms using the hotel keys, but you're the first one who has actually witnessed a break-in." He looked over the sketch and glanced at her. "Hell, this is really good."

"Thank you."

"You're hired."

"What?"

"We need an additional sketch artist at the Portland Police Bureau. It would be part-time so you can still teach your art classes. I'll talk to the boss when I get back, if it's something you would consider doing for us."

She opened her mouth to speak, and Adam said, "The kids need you for your art expertise, but we need you to help us catch criminals. You're hired."

She smiled. Adam had such a way with words. And the more she got to know him, the more she really liked him.